DANCE WITH ME

ROBINSON

Elegance Press

Copyright © 2022 by Shea Robinson

All rights reserved. No part of this publication may be reproduced, distributed, or transmitted in any form or by any means, including photocopying, recording, or other electronic or mechanical methods, without the prior written permission of the publisher, except where permitted by law.

This is a work of fiction. The characters and events portrayed in this book are fictitious or are used fictitiously. Apart from well-known authors, any similarity to real persons, living or dead, is purely coincidental. "Camouflage" and "Don Quixote" written by Mark Robinson, reprinted in full with his permission. The *Dance With Me* playlist is for suggestive purposes only. Producers and artists retain all rights to the recordings.

Elegance Press
PO Box 5814
Sacramento CA, 95817
www.ElegancePress.com
Printed in the United States of America.
First edition.

Cover copyright © 2022 Shea Robinson. Cover design by Talharehmn
Map copyright © 2022 Shea Robinson. Map design by Hannah Silva. Find more of their work @citrusroe
Chapter sketches copyright © 2022 Shea Robinson. Chapter sketches by Nazeerhunzai
The Space Between Breaths copyright © 2022 Shea Robinson. *The Space Between Breaths* written by Breanna Hardy. Find more of her work @bhardypoetry
Copyediting by Lydia McNabb and Leo Burke.

Library of Congress Control Number: 2022901136
ISBN: 9798985529937

Dedication ~ To the boy in the Farmer's Marketplace dressed in fresh corn tamales and sunshine ~ To the aunt who planted the seed to dream bigger than the short story ~ To my English teachers—Mrs. Barnes, Mrs. Henley, Mrs. Owens, Mrs. Combes, Mr. Wexler, Ms. Creasy, Mrs. Coombs, and Professor Dolan—who saw the light in my eyes and never let it dim ~ To my brother, Conor, who taught me to think critically about the false narratives we tell ourselves about the world ~ To the boy who gave me my first writing journal with a cover as sensory and illusory as the story I hoped to tell ~ To the hassle of falling in love ~ To the old friends who didn't see this through to the end but were a cornerstone of support in the beginning ~ To my high school best friends, Marlaina and Dominique, and my high school librarian, Mrs. Abarbanel, who read the first draft ~ To the girls who snickered behind my back but fell silent when I passed ~ To the libraries and used bookstores that afforded safe haven ~ To Los Angeles whose tree-lined medians taught me to breathe ~ To Lydia who nurtured my self-esteem and reignited my passion for writing ~ To Solano Writers Society for offering me a dedicated space to cultivate my craft ~ To my dad, Mark, who taught me how to hear the music ~ To all my beta readers who kept saying, "Shea, this is really good" ~ To my A+ extended family including Peters Anne, Amy, Allen, and Anne who never let me doubt how much I was loved and that my thoughts mattered ~ To my editors: Jenna, who gave me the confidence to believe in the rewrite, and Leo and Jennifer who gave me the advice I wasn't ready to hear yet ~ To UC Davis whose shady bike paths felt like freedom ~ To Alex who has been in my corner cheering me on since the first time he saw me play rugby ~ To Amanda who reads my stories in one sitting and believes in me more than I believe in myself ~ To my sister, Leah, who has listened to me read this story aloud twice and gushed with me afterward about the details ~ To my mom, Randi, who is the buoy to my swell ~ To those of you who rooted for me in the beginning ~ To those of you who don't remember my name ~ To those of you who have read all thirteen drafts ~ To those of you *who became characters so I could make peace with how we failed ~ To those of you whose characters were relegated to earlier drafts so I could better tell Charlie's story ~ To the scared little girl whose parents divorced at nine ~ To the fat teenager who believed she was unworthy of love ~ To the sophomore aching for someone to see her as she truly was ~ To the readers and writers and empaths and silent observers who are learning to claim space for their voices to be heard ~ To my home in Sacramento, the City of Trees ~* **I dedicate this to you**

DANCE WITH ME

CONTENTS

TWO STEP	4
LOCK AND POP	13
WINDMILL	24
PIROUETTE	34
FAÇADE	51
JETÉ	62
MIME	77
ARABESQUE	85
ASSEMBLE	97
PIVOT TURN	112
RUNNING MAN	124
FREEZE	139
STEP TOUCH	149
GRAPEVINE	162
JAZZ SQUARE	171
DENOUEMENT	188
Appendix	194

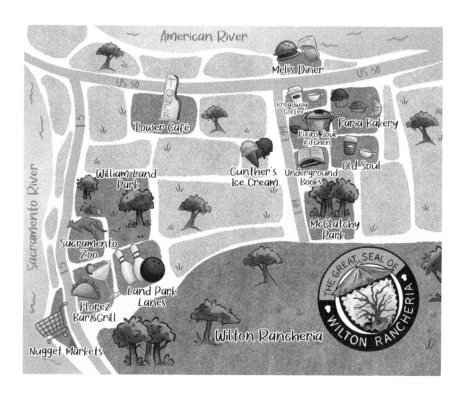

Come Dance With Me
by listening to the playlist on Spotify
shorturl.at/cerK4
Love,
Charlie

Dear Reader,

I don't like diaries. There's something unnerving about giving voice to my thoughts, about making them more real than they already feel. Better to leave them alone in my head.

But if I did keep a diary, I'd wonder why my life existed behind a shadow. I'd wonder why mine couldn't be a love story, something simple where the girl gets the guy. I'd wonder why my parents left me. I'd wonder why friends don't stay forever. In trying to explain it to myself, maybe I'd better understand why things happened the way they did. Maybe my story is pretty typical. Maybe it's a one-of-a-kind experience. I'll let you come to your own decision.

Love,
~~Charlotte Locke~~
Charlie

TWO STEP

He found me upstairs reading *The Book Thief*. I was so engrossed in becoming Liesel, stealing books from the fire under the caretaking eye of Death, that I didn't even know he was there. I felt something hit my face and block my view of the lines, and that's when I woke up to the world. I was sitting on his bed and he was standing in the doorway looking at me expectantly.

"Scott! Gross." I pulled the shirt from my face and tried to go back to reading. Sure, I'd spent all afternoon setting up the party happening downstairs, but it wasn't about me. I wouldn't be missed.

Scott took a running leap onto his bed, crashing into me and grabbing my book. We wrestled as I tried to steal back my dearest treasure and he tried to keep it out of reach. He got up laughing, book still in hand.

I gave him the famous lockedown stare and threw his pillow at him. "You are so annoying!"

He caught it easily. "You can try the lockedown on me all you want, but you can finish your book tomorrow. We need you downstairs!"

I unclenched my jaw, relaxed my eyes, and started laughing. "What, did we run out of beer?"

"I'm not that big of dick. Is it so bad that I want my best friend to party with me on our last day of summer vacation?"

Scott's voice had a careless aspect to it, like he wasn't invested in what happened when he spoke or who was affected by it. Or how it made me feel totally helpless.

"Fine but give me back my book!"

"Charlie, c'mon." He set my book on his desk, grabbed my hand, and pulled us out of his room.

We ran into Fran on the stairs. She gave his shoulders a squeeze and folded me into a hug that smelled like cookies and Nag Champa incense. I took in all the love and self-worth that a grandma's hug bestows and then stepped away.

"You be good now." She winked at me.

"Pinky swear."

Scott and I grew up as neighbors, which meant that Scott's grandma, Fran, was basically my grandma too. Fran was the type of grandma who moved in when Scott's parents were deployed to Syria and was the type of caretaker that would rather have Scott being stupid at home than getting into trouble elsewhere. The parties were a secret between grandmother and grandson.

As I headed down the stairs, I shook my head thinking about how ballistic Scott's parents would be at the thought of him partying after "everything he put them through." Never mind that the only way to get them to come home was for him to get in trouble.

I brushed those thoughts away and fell into the mayhem of the party. Though I loved my books, I actually didn't mind getting pulled into Scott's world of parties. For me, a party was all about the noise. The rhythmic bass of the sound system vibrating my thoughts. My center of focus shifting from my dad to feeling like I belonged here in this moment. The loud laughter, screams of exhilaration, and living like tonight was the only moment that mattered. It was like a Jumanji stampede of joy, and I couldn't help but get swept along.

In the living room: a vigorous Super Smash Bros. battle with players roasting each other and spectators cheering. I laughed and cheered with them. In the kitchen: a group of girls making margaritas. My eyes fell on the Queen Bee. She looked up and our eyes met briefly, but I broke eye contact first. She could have the floor tonight. Out on the patio: the end of a very close beer pong game.

I watched Scott's white shirt disappearing through the sliding glass door. I checked my watch and followed him outside.

I grabbed a beer from the ice chest and noticed Scott stepping in for a celebrity shot. He brushed his perpetually messy blonde hair out of his eyes. He had a line of freckles across his nose that rose like a wave when he snickered. The scar above his left eyebrow dipped like a checkmark as he narrowed his eyes in determination and he threw the ball.

Scott's shot was spot on. We all erupted in cheers and I turned to share a knowing smile with my best friend but found him looking at someone else. He high-fived a girl at the table, keeping his hand intertwined with hers and pulling her in for a kiss.

I looked away and started gulping my beer, grasping for some other means of distraction. My eyes landed on a guy who kind of took my breath away.

He was handsome and he knew it. As I watched him mill about the party, I felt a flash of insight that he didn't let his attractiveness go to his head. This only heightened my attraction to him, whether or not I was right. His skin was sepia-toned and beautiful, brilliantly contrasting with the brightness of his smile. He wore a simple black t-shirt and jeans, and I couldn't help noticing the way his biceps filled out his sleeves. *It must be nice to be held by those arms.*

To my surprise, he made his way to me. "Hey, you're Charlie, right?"

I tucked a piece of hair behind my ear and nodded in a way I hoped was flirtatious.

He gave me his hand to shake. "I'm Jared."

I liked that he shook my hand, instead of doing that demure thing where boys didn't actually shake my hand because I was a girl.

He smiled at me and took a sip of his beer. "So, I hear you're the champ to beat when it comes to the Slip 'N Slide." He nodded his head towards the people sliding down the slide, running to the lanes of water supplied by Fran's gardening hose, and doing their best not to spill their beers.

I laughed. "Something like that."

"Okay, good, because Scott has his money on Phoebe, but I'm betting on you."

I looked over at the girl that Scott had his hands around and swallowed uncomfortably. Before I could doubt myself, I flashed him a grin. "I won't let you down."

"That's my girl!" Jared punched me lightly on the arm.

Minutes later Phoebe and I were gearing up for our match. I tried not to think about how perfect she seemed compared to me. My long, dark brown hair was forever slipping out of my ponytail; I was fit from dancing, but my body would never know a thigh gap or crop top; my laugh was kind of embarrassing.

I smoothed the hair out of my face and tightened my ponytail. *Time to focus.*

We each were handed a red Solo cup, filled to the brim with beer. The goal was to slip down the Slip 'N Slide and make it to the end with the most beer. You then swapped cups with your opponent, downed their cup of beer, and sprinted back to the group. You wanted to keep as much beer in your cup while you slid, otherwise you'd be giving your opponent an advantage. If you fell while sliding, you had to go back to the beginning and start over.

Since I've been a dancer my whole life, I easily beat my opponents on stability alone. But now that I had to go up against Scott's boo thing, I was feeling nervous. I took off my shoes and socks and rolled up my jeans.

"Let's go, Charlie!" Jared yelled. I flashed him a quick thumbs up and then tried to focus on the task before me. I needed to drown out the crowd of people gathering and get my eye on the prize: winning Scott's affection. *Oops, I mean winning the Slip 'N Slide.*

"Let's goooooo!" Scott hollered, leading Phoebe over to me and placing his arm around both of us. "Are my ladies ready?"

I bit my lip to keep from blushing.

"Will the competitors please clink their glasses?"

Phoebe and I obeyed his command.

"On your marks, get set...go!" Scott screamed.

Phoebe and I took off running towards our respective Slip 'N Slide lanes. I didn't hesitate and immediately jumped onto the slide, raising my cup to balance out the movement and reduce any potential sloshing. I noticed that Phoebe had immediately gone down, pouring out half her beer. She laughed on her way down and then shakily got back up. I started laughing too, which made me slip and slosh some of my beer.

I finished my slide with a couple of running steps off the mat. Then I turned to wait.

Phoebe was entering the slide again, sliding down the tarp the way someone who's never ridden a skateboard might hop on a board for the first time. I started to feel kind of bad for her.

Finally, she made it to me, and we swapped cups.

"Oh my god, there's so much in here!" She laughed and started chugging.

I downed hers in two gulps and raced back to the start, finishing off the competition with an easy win.

The crowd started chanting my name and Jared grabbed me around the shoulders in a happy embrace. I laughed and cheered with the rest of the party as Phoebe made it back to the group.

We shook hands as worthy adversaries.

"Oh my gosh, you were so good!" Phoebe said.

I knew I had won easily, but I still blushed when she said so. We shared a nice smile. I could see why Scott liked her so much.

Scott ran over. "Baby, you did great! Charlie had so much more beer than you, otherwise you probably would have won!"

The smile fell from my face. *Of course I had more beer. That's why I won.* I opened my mouth to tell him that, but when I saw the way they were looking at each other, I realized this was an A and B conversation that I needed to see my way out of.

Jared winked at me and gave me a soft tap with his elbow. "Thanks for being my champ."

"You're welcome," I said, heart fluttering. I thought maybe he could serve as a worthy distraction, but he had turned away from me and was already talking to someone else.

And we're back to square one, I sighed. I glanced around the party for something else to pay attention to and saw some commotion happening on the stairs inside. Rebecca was rushing out the front door, followed closely by Colton, and then a minute later by some other girl. Colton glistened with sweat, the top buttons of his shirt were open, and he was barefoot.

I made my judgment: Colton had cheated on Rebecca. With her friend. Again.

We all stopped what we were doing and rushed to the front yard to witness the fight. It was kind of like watching a car crash: everyone knew what was going to happen, but we were still excited to see the wreck. I hopped on one foot as I put my shoes and socks back on, running with the rest of the group out the side gate.

We spilled out onto the street, swarmed around cars, and settled on hoods.

"What are you mad about? Nothing happened." Colton put his hands on his hips.

Rebecca took dainty steps, pacing back and forth in front of him. Even in her anger she was lithe. This could be the scene from *The Great Gatsby* where Gatsby falls for Daisy yet again or the scene from *Pride and Prejudice* where Elizabeth accuses Mr. Darcy of acting inappropriately. Only time would tell which one it would be.

"What? So, you're going to give me the silent treatment? That is so like you, Becks."

We all knew Colton was in for it. Colton should have stopped talking when Rebecca stopped pacing and turned to look at him. Instead, he launched back in.

"Typical girl being so fucking emotional."

When she smacked him, we all went "Oh!" She might have looked petite, but he had underestimated the strength of a prima ballerina.

We leaned forward to see what would happen next. None of us were huge fans of her, but we disliked him even more.

The color in Colton's cheek took up the space left by his dwindling pride.

"God damnit, Colton." Rebecca looked away, slumping forward as if she were falling into herself. I wanted to catch her, but this wasn't my fight and we weren't friends anymore.

"You're not worth this." Colton huffed to his car, starting it up and revving the engine to show us his male prowess before roaring off.

Anger and resentment swelled in Colton's wake, and it was too easy for Rebecca to be pulled into the torrent. She turned to the girl who had followed Colton out of the bedroom and punched her in the face, using the momentum to tackle her to the ground and land blows until her friends pulled her back.

Rebecca looked at the girl on the ground. "You're dead to me. And don't even think about trying to be friends with anyone else at Haynes High." With a final look of disgust, the Queen Bee clucked to the rest of her drones, and they all disappeared in her car.

I walked over to the girl and lent her a hand up from the ground. Scott handed her an ice pack, then turned to the group of us waiting for our cue.

"The party isn't over!" Music suddenly jumped out of the open front door of the house. The crowd moved reluctantly back inside. What could possibly top that for excitement?

I decided this was my time to bow out, and as the partygoers milled their way up the front steps, I headed for my house next door. *My book!* I turned to face Scott's. *Ah well, I'll just have to get it tomorrow.* I continued for home and lightly ran up my porch steps, moving quickly inside, and shutting the door softly behind me.

I listened for my mom and little brother upstairs. The only sound was the music from Scott's.

My house was dark, save for the three lights shining down on the wall of photos to my right. I walked over and caught my reflection in the glass of the first photograph. I kind of liked what I saw—a girl flushed from the excitement, hair pushed back from her face, eyes filled with sadness but searching.

I moved past my reflection and zeroed in on the photo. It was from one of my dance showcases when I was younger. Must have been when I first started because I looked about six years old, maybe seven. I was in the spotlight caught in the middle of a cartwheel. The picture was a blur, but you could just make out the look on my face—total bliss.

The next picture was my parents and me a couple of years before my dad died. We were on a bench; I can't remember where. I was sitting on my dad's lap poking him in the nose. My mom was laughing, one arm around my back, one arm resting on my dad's shoulders. I closed my eyes and willed myself to feel that moment—what it was like to have a living, breathing dad, rather than the shade of his memory. What it was like to have my mom's laughter fill the house rather than her silence. I felt nothing and it made it worse that I didn't know if this picture jogged a real memory or if I had looked at it so many times that I had filled in the holes.

The last picture was my first day of kindergarten. I was running towards the camera with a big grin on my face, my hair streaked with paint. I could still remember the anguish of this day, my mom leaving me for the first time. I had been a wreck, gripping her hand as she walked me into the classroom, begging her not to go. I think the teacher had to escort her out with encouraging smiles that this was all totally normal and that I would be okay. Within minutes, I had completely forgotten about her and had become best friends with the finger-painting group.

I scanned my little face, reaching out for the joy encapsulated in the photo. I rubbed my tired eyes. It seemed foreign that I had ever been dependent on Aimee. She didn't even deserve the title of "mom" anymore.

There were no pictures of my little brother, Danny. Time stopped when my dad died.

I continued down the hall and into the dark kitchen. Something about the dark made me feel closer to my dad. Like the lack of being able to see *anything* made it less painful that I couldn't see him. Like I could pretend he was actually here, just out of reach. Like the darkness was a hug from the afterlife letting me know I wasn't so alone.

I walked blindly into the pantry, grabbing the Oreos. I walked to the fridge and grabbed the milk, shielding my eyes from the light. I ate my way through the rest of the package, dunking every Oreo into the glass of milk, placing the entire cookie into my mouth, and crunching down to enjoy the full sensation.

I noticed the stack of folders my mom had left on the counter. Dusting my fingers free of crumbs, I reached across the counter to grab the one on top. I flipped it open and scanned the case notes, straining my eyes to see. Another asylum case from Afghanistan. This whole family's life would change because of her. *If only she'd remember us too.*

I closed the folder and laid it gently back on top.

I thought back to Phoebe laughing as she slipped on the Slip 'N Slide. Why were pretty girls pretty even while doing silly things? I thought of the way Scott's eyes undressed her and my heart ached, wishing that were me. *What would it feel like to be desired like that? To have someone think about me as much as I do about him?*

I sighed again and cleaned up my mess. I wasn't cold, but now I had a shiver I couldn't shake.

I tried to pretend like everything was fine. That the darkness was my friend. *Ha, as if the grim reaper were my ally.* But I could never forget, no matter how much distance there was, the shadow that covered every moment of joy. I crept into the living room and walked over to the piano. I padded the tops of the keys with my fingertips as I slowly brought my eyes up to meet the photo of my dad. I opened my mouth and closed it. I wrapped my arms around myself and my teeth began to chatter. A warm shower would be just the thing. I headed upstairs.

The rest of the weekend slipped by like sand through my fingers. There was nothing left to protest; summer break was over, and my sophomore year had begun.

LOCK AND POP

Getting ready for the first day of school, I took a deep breath and tried to be rational: *I know what I'm doing, right? This can't be that much harder than last year.*

I double-checked that my backpack had everything I needed and headed downstairs. As I flicked on the lights in the kitchen, I tried to quell the wave of sadness, but the room was empty and the hurt came rushing in anyway. My mom had already left for the day without even a note of "Good luck on your first day!" *No time to dwell.*

"Danny! Leaving in one minute!" I called up the stairs.

I made our lunches, filled up our water bottles, and organized his backpack so it would all fit inside. He walked into the kitchen as I was pushing his lunch pail into his backpack. He didn't want his jacket so I looped his arms through his backpack straps, and we headed out the door for the bus stop at the end of the street.

"Have a great day, okay? Kiss, please." I knelt and gave him a hug and kiss. I watched him run towards the line of kids and board the bus before I headed back to my car.

My car.

It was my dad's car. His 2015 black Toyota Corolla with the picture of a pregnant Aimee and a baby me hanging from his rear-view mirror.

Sometimes I forgot it was his, too stressed by dance or school to notice, and the smell would knock the wind out of me. No matter how many times Lela, Malcolm, and I piled into this car after the Academy, it still smelled like him. Like when I would bury my face in his chest during a hug.

I closed my eyes, pictured him smiling at me, opened my eyes to nod to myself, and let out the breath I was holding. I put on my seat belt, shifted my rearview a mirror a tad to the left, and headed to Haynes Charter High School.

Living in a city like Sacramento meant there was never enough parking, so I had to find a spot on the street and hoof it to campus. I jogged slowly under the trees, slowly so as not to get too sweaty and or accidentally slip on an acorn.

At my locker, I pulled everything out of my bag and double-checked my schedule for which binders I would need.

Haynes Charter High School			
Name Charlotte Locke	**Grade** Sophomore	**Locker No.** 112	
Period	**Subject**	**Teacher**	**Room No.**
1 M-F	English	Mr. Cours	302
2 M-F	Algebra II	Dr. Wudel	146
3 M-F	Chemistry	Dr. Crisp	135
4a MWF	World History	Mx. Owens	307
4b TR	French III	Mme. Allemand	200

My school had rotating periods, so on Mondays, Wednesdays, and Fridays I started with English class and dropped French; on Tuesdays and Thursdays, I started with French class and dropped World History. I never played water polo, but everyone knew Coach Wudel was the kind of coach who cared and the kind of teacher who got you excited about math. Everyone knew about Mr. Cours's dry, sarcastic humor that could quickly cut you down if he was displeased. I hadn't heard anything about the rest of my teachers, but I felt good about French since I'd been in French classes since junior high.

With the first bell, I grabbed the binders I would need for the next two classes, closed my locker, and headed to class. We had a second bell, but I never liked to chance it. Besides, then I made my own destiny. If I showed up early enough, I got to choose the chair that would be mine for the rest of the year. It was one of the unspoken laws of high school.

I was the third to arrive. I waved at Felicity who had taken the middle seat, front row. We had Biology and Geometry together last year. Sitting in the back looking like he still hadn't woken up yet was Ryan. *Typical.* We had English together last year too, and I'm not sure how he passed.

I weaved my way through the seats, settling on second row, third to the right. It was a spontaneous decision, but as soon as I had my notebook and mechanical pencil out, I knew it was the right choice. I clasped my hands in front of me and waited.

Students continued to file in as the second hand marched closer and closer to the twelve. When the minute hand hit the eight, we heard the bell ring for the final time, bringing Mr. Cours walking briskly through the door, leading the way in with his Old Soul coffee cup.

Without so much as a hello, Mr. Cours set down his things on his desk and began writing on the white board. He turned to face us, gingerly touching his fingertips together. We looked from him to the white board in silence. He had written *"Define humanity."*

He assessed the room, nodding at a few familiar faces. He and I made an uncomfortable amount of eye contact before he continued his perusal of the room. I swallowed the lump in my throat, determined to be the student who annoyed him less than anyone else.

Finally, he said, "Welcome back. Over the summer, I asked you to read *Do Androids Dream of Electric Sheep?* and watch Ridley Scott's 1982 debut of *Blade Runner.* Now," he paused for dramatic effect, "how many of you read the book and watched the movie?"

Not wanting to be a disappointment on the first day of school, everyone raised their hands.

Mr. Cours looked nonplussed. "That's better than I thought. I'm sure you won't mind if we start off with a pop quiz, then?"

A stressed murmur filled the room. *This was going to be harder than freshman year.*

"Let's try this again. How many of you actually did the assignment?" This time, about half of us raised our hands. I was proud that I raised my hand confidently. "That's more like it. How about instead of starting with a pop quiz, we will start with a discussion to aid you in your essay due by the end of class. Seem fair?" Dead silence. *Was he asking a rhetorical question?* "If it's not fair, we can just take the quiz now."

"Nah, man, I mean, sir," Treyvon called out. "We need to talk about this more."

I turned to look. I recognized him as one of Malcolm's friends.

"So, what do you think?" Mr. Cours pointed at the board.

"About defining humanity? Man, I don't know. It's just like Mr. Tyrell needed to chill. Like, robots are cool and shit, ah, my bad, I mean they're cool, but I don't know about all that other stuff."

Felicity raised her hand. "Well, like, humans have blood and androids have wires. So, we could define humanity as those that are, like, organic."

"Isn't organic that expensive shit from the store?" someone behind me said.

I looked over my shoulder as Ryan snickered, and he and Treyvon did a quick handshake. Mr. Cours ignored Ryan's comment.

I raised my hand. "You could define humanity based on our fight-or-flight instincts. Humans respond to danger, whereas the androids aren't worried about their survival."

Mr. Cours nodded like he was mulling it over.

When no more hands were raised, Mr. Cours turned back to the board and started writing down the points that had been offered so far. I always liked how teachers could take our incoherent statements and make them smarter, more dignified. He turned back to face us, waiting for more. We stared at each other in silence. Many painstaking seconds later, another hand was raised.

"Calli," Mr. Cours called.

"Well, humans have emotions and androids don't."

"So humanity is based on emotions?" Mr. Cours asked.

Calli weighed the options in her head. "I guess not, because even animals have emotions."

Shiva snickered behind her, causing Calli to turn around and glare.

"Now, Calli has a point," Mr. Cours said. "Does having emotions mean we are human?"

Calli smirked triumphantly back at Shiva.

Shiva spoke without raising her hand. "So, if you don't have emotions, then you're not human? Like what about sociopaths and stuff?"

That last comment got a lot more students talking and for the next twenty minutes, the debate was alive with what constituted humanity.

"I think these are great points," Mr. Cours said, picking back up his coffee mug and taking a sip, "for you to continue thinking about in your essay. I want a thesis and two topic sentences with two arguments in each paragraph—one from the book and one from the movie."

There were more groans from the class, but I was ready. I double-clicked my mechanical pencil, flipped open my notebook to the first page, and started writing. I had enjoyed the book and was disappointed by the movie. *No surprise there.* Comparing the book and movie in my head, I decided to make the argument that the androids had the same level of humanity, since both group's emotions were artificially regulated: the androids by artificial intelligence as seen in the movie and the humans by the empathy box as written in the book.

Mr. Cours let us go as we finished. I stepped out of the classroom and breathed in and out with a smile; my first sophomore class was complete. Looking at my watch, I realized I had some extra time before my next class, and I knew exactly where I wanted to be.

I walked across the quad, keeping my head down as I passed a couple of seniors. *They must have a free period.* I tried not to blush as I passed them, tried to look like I knew what I was doing. Seniors were always so cool. I hoped I would feel like that when I was a senior.

I opened the double doors of the library with a sigh of relief. I was home.

"Good morning, Mr. DeVault!" I said, using my library voice.

"Charlie! Good morning. How was your summer break?" Mr. DeVault was carrying a stack of books in his hands as he made his way to the front desk. He was a youthful forty-year-old, the wrinkles around his eyes and lips the only give-away. His kind eyes sat in perfect symmetry on his face, his lips forever curled into a smile. He was the kind of person I imagined my dad would be if he were still alive. This gave me both a warm feeling in my stomach and made it hard to breathe. I hoped one day my dad's death would be less of a trigger.

We dove into chatting about books. He handed me *All the Light We Cannot See* and I told him about just finishing *The Book Thief*. It would definitely be one of my favorites and would have been exactly what I needed when my dad died five years ago. Sometimes when I closed my eyes at night, I liked to pretend that Death from the book was a shade watching over me like he watched over Liesel. It always made me feel a little better.

I perused the cover of my new book as I said, "I loved the narrator! And that bit on understanding life and humans through colors, so good."

"Yeah, I loved Zusak's take on death during World War II. There are a number of authors doing some interesting things in that time period. Let me know what you think of Doerr. If you like him, I can get you on the pre-order list for his work set to come out next year."

I thanked him and then disappeared to the other end of the library, wanting nothing more than to plop in my favorite armchair and lose myself in the story, as I soon found out, told in alternating chapters between a blind French girl and a young German solider.

Too soon, the next bell rang. I took a bookmark out from a stash I kept inside an old cigar box and placed it in the book. I checked out the book at the front desk and then headed to World History.

Turns out Mx. Owens had a family emergency, and so the sub was showing us a documentary on the development of human civilization instead.

At the end-of-class bell, I left class and walked to my locker. On the second try of the combination lock, I swung open the door and swapped my binders from the morning for the notebooks I needed for the afternoon. I grabbed what I needed for lunch and then took a deep breath as I headed for the sophomore section of the outdoor lunch area.

Seniors had the prime spot in the Main Commons, juniors had the area near the lockers, sophomores had the quad near the gym, and freshmen had the quad nearest the front gate. Basically, each grade claimed a space farther and farther away from watchful eyes.

I made purposeful steps towards my friends and kept my chin up high until I found them sitting on a brick wall around a tree on the edge of the quad. They waved as I walked up.

I surveyed where they had staked out our territory and was quite impressed: close enough to other sophomores to be in on the action, but also separated so we could do our own thing.

I sat down between them—my short stature highlighted by the height of my friends. Malcolm patted his afro and continued eating, his elbows sitting squarely on his knees as he took small, graceful bites. Today he was wearing an extra-large black t-shirt with Biggie in his crown and fresh-out-of-the-box white Jays. I felt like he could eat for days and still not gain a pound. Lela spun her long black hair up into a messy bun to keep it out of her face as she ate. Even though she was tall, she and I shared the same struggles in that jeans never fit our curves. She had gotten hot food lunch that didn't look half bad. Can't go wrong with burritos.

I opened my avocado lunch pail and pulled out my peanut butter and jelly sandwich. Having a lunch pail that made a statement was kind of my thing. Last year, I had one that looked like a stuffed animal hedgehog. This year, my lunch pail had a white background with a bunch of avocados and sayings like, "Holy guacamole, Batman!" with an avocado wearing a black mask and cape. It made me crack up.

"Locket, can you believe I already have homework in Spanish?" Malcolm asked. "Man." He finished the last bite of his sandwich and crumpled up the plastic packaging.

Malcolm was the only one who was allowed to call me that. When I was in eighth grade, Rebecca got everyone to call me "locket" after one particularly difficult French class. I was the only one who just could not get the pronunciation right. I got more and more frustrated as I butchered everything I said, until I had worked myself into tears. Rebecca knew I was embarrassed, I'm sure of it, and jumped at the opportunity. In front of the whole class, she said, "Locket up and stop being such a baby," and then everyone started calling me "locket."

Malcolm had my back, though, and reclaimed the name so that whenever he said it, it made me laugh, and it took the power away whenever the Queen Bee said it.

I nodded. "I had an essay this morning in English."

"You got Mr. Cours, huh?" Lela said. "Yeah, I got homework too. Fifty calculus problems due by Wednesday."

I nudged her. "Yeah, but you'd do homework all day long for Mr. Palmer."

"Oh yeah, I'm hot for teacher." Lela laughed, licking some beans off her thumb. Lela was super gifted in math and had Mr. Palmer for math last year too.

Malcolm and I cracked up.

"So, I think I figured out my music for the showcase," I jumped in.

"You mean the showcase that is four months away?" Lela gave me a pointed look.

"Damn, locket, you are crazy," Malcolm laughed.

"I just want to be ready." I took a bite of my sandwich.

"Girl, I love dance just as much as the rest of you, but you are the only one I know who is this intense about the Winter Showcase. Especially one that Jules lets us work on at the Academy."

Malcolm said nothing and continued to laugh at me.

I shrugged and Lela gave me a playful push.

Malcolm, Lela, and I had been friends since we were six, all attending Sacramento Dance Academy. Malcolm and I also went to the same schools our whole lives, whereas Lela was homeschooled on her reservation until joining us at Haynes High. They could laugh at me all they wanted, but dance was the closest thing I had to remembering my dad. They didn't have to understand.

When the bell rang for the end of lunch, we said our goodbyes and headed to class. Coach Wudell was everything I thought she'd be, and I actually had high hopes about enjoying math this year. Dr. Crisp was educated in China, and the labs on the syllabus all seemed really cool. After Algebra II and Chemistry, I was free. It was a great first day.

I met up with my friends at the lockers, before we carpooled to dance. The 50 was never pretty at 3:15 in the afternoon, so by the time we finally arrived at the studio, we were ready to dance off the awful stop-and-go traffic that had us feeling like worn-out yoyos.

"Hello, hello, welcome back, welcome." Jules, our dance instructor, high-fived us as we entered the room. We filled the cubbies with our things at the back and found a seat on the ground facing her.

"I trust you had a great summer break. Nice to see so many familiar faces returning to the room, though I've seen a few of you every open dance period."

Jules and I made eye contact for a touch longer than needed, and I sensed some sadness in her. During the summer, Academy dropped from five-days-a-week practices to three, and I hadn't missed a single one. *Excuse me, but I don't have a mom that's going to whisk me away on some vacation.* Jules had moved on to asking about our vacations and encouraging us to share. I zoned out and tuned back in when it seemed pertinent.

"Thank you, Julian and everyone else for sharing. Up and at 'em, y'all. Let's get to work," Jules said.

We got up from the floor and moved some distance from each other to start stretching. I leaned into the stretches, breathing into the discomfort and making it my friend. Then we moved to group warm-up, each of us in a corner of the room. Jules started us off with some De La Soul, calling out an eight-count and a core-move for us to do across the floor. Our rolls and flips moved me into that familiar space of contentment.

Contentment.

I rolled that word around in my head as I rolled around the dance floor. The Academy was the only place I felt content. Free from responsibility for Danny, from upset with my mom, from heartache about my dad, from whatever feelings I had towards Scott. It let me be me: happy, empty, and, by the end of class, too exhausted to feel anything at all. I couldn't always feel happy, so I was content to let emptiness and exhaustion fill that space.

After I dropped my friends off—Malcolm lived in Curtis Park closer to me, but since Lela lived in way off in Wilton, I always dropped her off at her cousin's place, Faria Bakery, in Oak Park—I took a detour to my favorite place besides the school library: Underground Books.

As I parked, I looked at my car clock: 5:47. I was cutting it close, but I figured Violet wouldn't mind. Underground Books, with its bright lights shining out against the dark street, lured me like a siren. It was a clue to a mystery and I was Nancy Drew on the hunt.

I headed to the building and was happy to find the door still open.

"Violet?" I called out. Nothing. Maybe she was in the back.

I walked forward and began perusing the new arrivals, taking meditated steps like I was walking on a curb. I scanned the titles eagerly for the next book to add to my stack.

I passed two bookshelves before one book jumped out at me. It had a mysterious brown cover wrapped in yellow and orange lines and was titled *I Am the Messenger*. I recognized the author, Markus Zusak, from the book I had been discussing with Mr. DeVault. Plus, someone had tucked a little bookmark inside the front cover with their recommendation.

"Imagine the softest, toughest, most beautiful song you know, and you've got it."

It was the weirdest book recommendation I'd ever read. I dove in.

Whoever this person was, they were right: I was hooked from the first sentence. It didn't take me long to start laughing. Where *The Book Thief* was enthrallingly morbid, *I Am the Messenger* was mysteriously funny. Now instead of Death, I had Ed standing in the dark, waiting for the moment to step into my life and tell me which way to go.

I read for pages. I read until I remembered I was reading.

I looked around. Violet still hadn't come back. I went behind the counter and looked for some paper to leave a note. I scribbled, "Violet, found another keeper. I owe you $13. 11 bucks plus interest." I signed it with a heart, my name, and my phone number. With a final look around, I left, already forgetting the mysteriously quiet bookstore as I prepared myself for a shower and a night of reading.

WINDMILL

It wasn't until weeks later that I finally remembered the money I owed Violet. School picked up, I was diving deep into my dance routines for the Winter Showcase, and every time I reminded myself to swing by, I would forget again. By the time I remembered, I was too full of shame to follow-through.

I had Wednesdays and Sundays free from dance, so one Wednesday after school, I headed to Old Soul to get a chai latte and do some homework. Danny had karate on Wednesdays with friends who took him home, so this was the one day of the week I didn't have to worry about picking him up from school. Old Soul had the perfect homework vibe: comfy couches for working on my laptop, plenty of tables for working on math, the delicious smell of coffee wafting through the air, and the ample background noise that was both pleasing and stimulating.

I'm embarrassed to say that even as I passed by Underground Books, it still didn't jog my memory. Instead, what caught my eye was a guy my age working the register inside. I'd never seen him before, but he smiled like he knew me. I tucked my thumbs underneath the straps of my backpack and ducked my head down as I kept walking, smiling to myself. I thought about him the whole way to Old Soul. His half-turned smile. His long hands gently holding a soft, blue paperback.

I ordered my latte and tried to focus on my work, but my heart rate wasn't cooperating. I checked my phone for notifications and was rewarded with a text message from an unknown number.

> "When I walked into the bookstore and saw you reading, even though you were in my space, I could not disturb you. You seemed like a work of art, like a still life, and I wanted to delight in your beauty, a beauty borne away by something we need not want, may cherish something we need not desire."

I sat back in my seat and reread the text. At first, I was totally confused. Then, I got nervous and weirded out that a rando would send me a text that was so poetic and vulnerable. I thought about deleting the message and blocking the number, but instead, I sat there and reread it. Something tickled at the back of my mind.

Was that a reference to the last time I was at Underground Books? Was someone else there?

Then I had another thought. *Could it be the boy from the register at Underground Books? So then is he quoting a book? But how would he have my number?*

The note I left Violet! Oh shit, I never paid her back.

I got up from my seat to march back to the bookstore and drop off a twenty-dollar bill, but then I stopped, suddenly nervous about seeing my potential suitor.

I took a deep breath and went back to his message. *Should I have stopped to talk to him?* Apparently, he had the chance but didn't take it. Instead, he sent me this text.

He said I was beautiful. My arms lit up in goosebumps and my heart was loud in my ears. Not knowing what to do or how to react, I read his message again. I tried to start my homework and then thought about just going back to Underground Books to get this over with.

I shook off the nerves and tried to think straight. *So he sent me a text with a line from a book...like a book riddle that he wants me to figure out.*

I scanned the memory of his face, but already it was in shadow. I tried to dive deeper into the shadows, but instead I saw myself swimming in darkness with no shade to guide me.

My heart whimpered in my chest, somehow delighted and afraid at the same time.

I decided I would text him a couple of lines to show him I recognized the book, and then I would finish my text with a couple of lines from a new book that he had to guess. *I just need to figure out what book he's quoting...and what he means by that quote.*

I reread his message and decided that I would take him at face value. My beauty had taken his breath away. *I'm a work of art.* I giggled to myself and tried to recall some of my favorite books from memory. But there were too many and it had to be perfect. *Should I Google his quote? No...I want to figure this out on my own.*

So I set that aside, tucked my twenty in my pocket for later, and started my homework.

When I got home, I was met with a surprise: my mom was home early. I looked at my watch. *5:42.* It was rare she was home before seven. I was also surprised to find she was cooking dinner. And it smelled delicious.

"Hi, mom."

"Hey, darling," my mom said, not looking up from her cooking.

Danny ran to me to say hello. *And she picked him up from karate? Wow, it's a big day.* I opened my arms but realized my mistake too late.

"Ew, you're all sweaty!" I laughed. He just nuzzled closer. "How was school, bud? Show me what you learned at karate."

Danny bounded away from me and started showing me his moves.

"Nice job! You're doing great." I high-fived him. "C'mon, bud, let's get you clean. Do you want a bath or shower today?"

Hand in hand, I walked with Danny up to his room. He decided on a shower, so I sat on the toilet and talked to him through the shower curtain about his day. When he was done, I wrapped him in a towel and got him in his pajamas.

Since my mom was handling dinner for once, I sent Danny downstairs to help and went to my room. I stared at my bookshelf, willing the Underground Poet's book forward, visualizing the book hopping off the shelf to alert me which one it was.

I laughed at myself at the sudden nickname of the boy from the bookstore. *The Underground Poet...the name could work.* I got nowhere before I was called down to dinner.

My mom was sitting at the head of the table, Danny in his seat to her right. I sat to her left in what was my dad's seat, to see what she would do. She started but quickly recovered and forced a smile.

She scooped rice onto my plate and ladled chicken tikka masala on top. I resisted the urge to remind her I wasn't a child and could fill my plate myself. Instead, I helped myself to some broccoli. There were only the sounds of forks clinking on plates as I wondered what to say and my mom did the same.

"So, how was school today?" she finally asked.

I was shoveling bites of chicken and broccoli in my mouth and not thinking of anything until I realized Danny wasn't answering. I looked up.

"Oh," I said out of the side of my mouth. I chewed, swallowed, and washed it down with some water. "School's fine." *What was I, seven?* I thought of what else I could tell her. *Didn't adults only ask this when they knew nothing about me?* "I got an A on my *Blade Runner* essay."

"Charlie, well done! Go grab it. I want to see."

At first, I didn't think she was serious. I furrowed by eyebrows. *I don't need her fucking gold star.*

"I got a gold star on my writing assignment!" Danny said, hopping down from his seat and running to his backpack to show my mom, no provocation needed.

I put my fork down and walked begrudgingly to my backpack upstairs. Part of me prayed that I had left it in my locker at school, but I found it tucked in the flap of my English binder. I sighed and surveyed the bright red A at the top of the page with one of Mr. Cours's notoriously short comments, "Well done."

I headed back to the table and put the paper in my mom's face.

I thought she would just glance at it and say more uncharacteristically mushy stuff, but instead she put down her glass of wine and started reading the essay.

My cheeks burned as I pushed the food around on my plate.

"That's right, the book was called *Do Androids Dream of Electric Sheep?*," she murmured to herself. She fell silent, eyes scanning the page in slow, deliberate reading. She chuckled to herself and took another sip of wine. I almost choked on a broccoli floret, reddening at the inherent praise meant in a chuckle from my mom. I swallowed uneasily. *Is it good? Does she like it?*

She flipped the page over and looked to see if there was more, then laid the paper to the side. She flashed me a smile with wide eyes and went back to her chicken.

I waited impatiently for her approval. "So?" *Damnit, why do I care so much?*

My mom looked up from her plate. "It was good, Charlie. Obviously, since you got a good grade."

That's it? Then why did she have me go all the way upstairs to get it?

"You're a lovely writer," she added.

But it was too late for that. I gave her a half smile, pursing my lips to stop the bile that wanted to erupt. *So she never wants to be in my life, but then the one time she does, she doesn't even do it right.*

She moved on to my brother's work, patting him on the head and exclaiming to him what a good boy he was. I looked at this woman in confusion. *Did she think she had dogs instead of kids? What was her deal?*

I found myself giving her the lockdown, so I relaxed my face and went back to eating. I finished my meal, dumped my plate in the sink, and stormed up to my room. I was aflame with a strange mixture of emotions that I didn't want to deal with. I would just do homework the rest of the night, get ready for school the next day, and hopefully avoid my mom until this storm of yearning and resentment had passed.

Even as early as it was in the school year, Tuesdays and Thursdays were going to be hard for me. Every day now, I had the Underground Poet on the brain, so every second was like, *Will I see him? What will I say when I do?* I was constantly tucking my hair behind my ears and taking deep, steadying breaths. Tuesdays also meant my schedule rotated, so I was starting my day with Rebecca.

Why was Rebecca in French III with me? Great question, except I seemed to be the only one who cared. She pretended like she was fluent in French, walking through our halls like she was better than everyone because she was French. But if she was so fluent, why would she need to be in a class studying French?

To be fair, I knew why. She was born in France but moved to the States when she was three. Rebecca grew up with her mom speaking to her in French, but the Queen Bee still needed help with the grammar, or so she told me at her birthday slumber party when we were eight. Every girl in our grade got invited, but I was the only one who didn't fall asleep. Rebecca and I sneaked into her dad's office and swiveled in chairs while eating popcorn and whispering excitedly about her life as the mayor's daughter.

That was eight years ago. *Was it eight years ago?* Losing my best friend in middle school was brutal. And since we were no longer friends, it was like the cardinal high school rule that she had to make my life miserable. Coining me the nickname "locket" and getting everyone to snicker behind my back. Speaking to me in fast French and then rolling her eyes when I didn't understand. Making me second-guess whether my friends actually liked me or if I was so lame that they just felt stuck with me.

All that said, Tuesday became unnecessarily difficult when Madame Allemand glided into class and rattled off my name with Rebecca's for the video project we would be working on for the rest of the year. Not going to lie, I sat in shock for a couple of seconds before glancing over at Rebecca. She sat in her seat scowling.

I couldn't let her know I felt the same way. To show I was better, I went over to her and sat down with a smile.

Before I could open my mouth, the Queen Bee said, "Well, locket, I'm busy every evening until nine, so I'm not sure how much help I'm going to be on this project."

Classic Rebecca. I knew that she danced in a premier ballet troupe, but I also knew that she knew I danced in a competitive hip-hop team and so I was also tied up most nights. I decided not to argue the point and turned my attention to the directions, reading them in my head. *"Research the history of French immigration. Choose a country to study and then record a five-minute video describing the hardships, the successes, and the reasons behind the move."*

"Have any fabulous ideas?" Rebecca asked, reaching into her bag to grab a nail file.

"We could do Mexico."

Rebecca laughed and stopped moving to stare at me. "Oh, you're serious. We're not doing Mexico."

"So then what do you want to do?"

"I don't know! But I feel like we should do somewhere in Europe."

I gave her the lockedown. "Europe is so overdone. Let's do somewhere in North or South America. Like Mexico."

"Um, no. People from Mexico come here; people don't go to Mexico, locket." She really amped up the derision with which she said my nickname.

I laughed meanly. "Well, that's racist. French people account for like a quarter of the population on this continent."

Heat rose in Rebecca's cheeks at getting called out. "No, they don't."

I sighed. "Rebecca, just because your family was able to come here so easily doesn't mean it's the same for everybody else."

"Like you would know."

"I would actually. My dad's book won the Pulitzer Prize and it's set in Mexico." I crossed my arms.

I'm not sure how long we glared at each other, but it was long enough to make Madame Allemand come over.

"Ladies, do we have a problem?" she asked in French.

"Pardon," we said in unison, dropping our heads and pretending to be writing.

I glanced over at Rebecca and for the smallest fraction of a second, we shared a knowing smile at getting caught by the teacher. Just like old times. *Well, almost.*

Rebecca's smile slipped back into a scowl. She grabbed her bag and slammed it down on her desk.

I pushed her bag to the side and grabbed my crumpled papers. *Guess I am doing this on my own. Fine. It will be easier that way anyway.* I thought back to her racist comment and felt my stomach roll. That wasn't the Rebecca I remembered. *But people can change a lot in four years. She is the Queen Bee after all.*

By the time lunch came around, I was in a royally bad mood. It was just Lela sitting alone at the base of our tree today.

"What's up with you?" she asked out the side of her mouth—I had caught her mid-bite. When I said nothing, she sighed. "Girl, you cannot let Rebecca get to you like that."

I stabbed my salad angrily with a fork. "Where's Malcolm?"

"Spanish help."

I nodded. I should do that for my classes too. *But not today.*

"Remember when my cousin used to let us help make the croissants?" Lela was trying hard to cheer me up, and it worked.

I broke into a smile. "And they'd be totally terrible, but he'd still put them out to sell. Oh my god, those croissants were everything."

"Like there's no way he actually sold them, but we totally thought he did," Lela laughed.

"I would pretty much give up my whole life for a Faria baked good right now."

"You know you're always welcome."

I smiled and took a less angry bite. "I know. I just, I wish there was time now. I miss that. Just the hanging out with no worries."

"Yeah, I feel you, girl."

Lela didn't say anything else about the fact that I hadn't hung out at her cousin's in forever, for which I was grateful. I'd only eaten half my salad when I gave up and told Lela I needed to go to the library. She knew the drill and told me to text her later. I thought maybe Mr. DeVault would be able to help me figure out which book the Underground Poet was quoting.

Mr. DeVault wasn't at the reference desk when I walked in, so I wandered around until I found him. He was restacking books in the history section.

"Hi, Mr. DeVault!" I whispered.

"Charlie!" He pushed in the two books he was holding. "How are you? What can I help you find today?"

"I don't know. It's a book maybe about still life, like, you know, art?"

"Are you looking for a book on art or art history?"

I shook my head. "I'm pretty sure it's fiction. Nothing like that is ringing a bell?"

"Who's the author?"

I shook my head, getting embarrassed. "I'm sorry, I don't know. I just know a quote." I recalled my Underground Poet's last message. I'd read it so many times that I knew it by heart.

"A beauty borne away by something we need not want, may cherish something we need not desire." I decided to leave out the part where I was the beauty.

Mr. DeVault's eyes twinkled; this was a mystery he wanted to help me solve. He tapped his finger on his chin. "I have a couple of ideas. Follow me." He led us out of the history section and to fiction, in the aisle labeled "B–C."

I followed him like Alice follows the Cheshire Cat, unclear what path I was on but sure it was the right one.

He found the first book he was looking for and handed it to me over his shoulder, *The Elegance of the Hedgehog* by Muriel Barbery. He walked briskly away and stopped at aisle "P–Rs." Telling another student that he would be right with them, he pulled out two more books, *Ishmael* by Daniel Quinn and then with a shrug, *The Golden Compass* by Philip Pullman.

"That's the best I can do, Charlie, though I get the feeling you won't be *that* disappointed in having been assigned three more books." He winked at me.

"Thanks, Mr. DeVault! You're the best." I headed to the reference desk and a library aid checked out the books for me.

On my way to Algebra II, I caught the Underground Poet just as he was entering the classroom across from mine. *He goes to Haynes High?* was my first thought. *Oh man, he is cute,* was my second. We shared a smile that I thought about for the rest of class.

I ended the day with Chemistry and then I was free to dance out my nerves at the Academy. I never had a hard time focusing, but for some reason today it took all my willpower to actually watch myself in the mirror, perfect my form, and hear the eight-counts Jules was calling out. Every other second, it seemed like, my brain was falling back into the Underground Poet's smile and wondering where he was or what he was thinking or if he was texting me. I tried to shake it off and use my friends as mental reminders that there wasn't time for games—I needed to focus, because the Winter Showcase would be here before I knew it.

PIROUETTE

Scott was waiting for me when I got home, as we had planned. We grabbed our bikes and headed to the park in our neighborhood, Land Park. The clouds were growing by the minute, thick and dark, so I waved to the gods and goddesses at Mt. Olympus hosting a parade in Zeus' honor.

"You are such a dork," Scott laughed. I stuck my tongue out at him and looked back at the sky, hoping it would rain.

We found a spot near the pond and laid out a blanket. Per the usual, I had my book—the first one I'd picked up from the library, *All the Light We Cannot See*—Scott had his guitar, and we were sharing two Cherry Blade Lemonade Bang Energy Drinks.

I didn't know why I always insisted on bringing my book when it was too hard to focus on anything besides Scott. At least this park brought me a sense of peace. Like attaining contentment only while dancing, it was only here I could breathe a little easier. I loved watching the ducks, hearing the kids scream with excitement, and feeling the breeze whisper through the grass at our feet.

Scott took a sip of his Bang and started strumming. He asked me over the notes, "How's your showcase coming?"

I laid my book to the side and picked at the grass in front of me. "It's all right."

"Now, I know that's not true. It's always way better than you think it is."

"I mean, maybe. Like, my individual routines are coming along for sure. But you know how we always have this big Summer Showcase? Well, this year it's called, 'A Change is Gonna Come,' and everyone has to choreograph a set of routines based on how we respond to change. There's 'Running Away,' 'Blissful Ignorance,' and 'Stuck in Limbo.' How cool are those? But no, Jules gave us 'Acceptance' and I just don't know what to do with that. Like, how blah is acceptance?"

Scott started singing.

"Charlie says, 'I don't like your acceptance,'
Charlie says take back your stupid theme,
Charlie doesn't like your acceptance,
take it back or you'll get locked down."

I pushed him on the shoulder laughing. "Exactly."

He put down his guitar and picked up his Bang, lying down on his stomach with me. "So, you'll be at the Homecoming pre-game at Jared's, right?" He reached into his bag and grabbed his vape.

I turned to look at him in confusion about the party but looked away as he blew out a stream of vapor. My stomach flip-flopped. I picked at the grass.

"I hate that, you know," I said, quietly.

He looked over at me and took another hit. "Charlie, it's fine. I'm not selling anymore. Weed's legal in California."

I gave him the lockdown. "You know we're still minors, right? It's just stupid given everything it's put you through." I sighed. "So, what about this party?"

Scott opened his mouth like he was going to say something else about smoking, but instead followed my change of subject. "A bunch of kids from your school are going to be at this party. I figured you would have heard about it by now."

I pretended like I knew what he was talking about, like the popular kids from school would have invited me. "I don't know if I want to go yet."

"I knew it. I knew you weren't going to go. But now I know, so now you have to go."

"Oh, I do, do I?"

"Uh, yeah, and to make sure you don't run out on me, I'll pick you up."

With that offer, I couldn't say no. I blushed to myself and started picking at the grass again. Even if Scott had broken up with the girl from the last party, he'd probably have a replacement by now. *But still.*

Scott sat up and began strumming again.

I fell into the notes, losing myself in the pauses of the melody. That was the part I loved most about music. That delay. That fermata. That pause before everything changes. Before you know how it will conclude.

That Friday afternoon, after twelve outfit changes, I ended up with something simple: a green blouse, jeans, and matching green flats. I pulled my long brown hair into a messy French braid—like I was trying, but not trying too hard. I tried to do the same with my makeup, but I knew nothing about contours and eye shadow and ended up feeling like the Wicked Witch of the West. Half an hour later, my lips and cheeks were rubbed raw from the failures. Natural blush and mascara would have to do.

I closed my eyes and let out a slow breath, trying to keep all the shades at bay. *I'm going to a party!*

I wanted to be happy and in the light tonight. I was tired of that constant pull to disappear into the darkness. I didn't want to look at myself and hate what I saw, outlining all the parts of my body I wished were different. I did not want to see the green eyes or sharp chin that made me look like my mom and that made me feel nothing like my dad's daughter.

I would have given anything to look in the mirror and find my dad. He had these eyes that melted like the horizon during sunset, completely disappearing into the rosy hues of his cheeks when he laughed. I laughed and squinted my eyes. He had these thick, wondrous cheeks with a dimple only on the left side. His "good side," he used to call it. Those same cheeks smiled at me from the picture hanging from my rearview mirror. I pushed my left cheek in to create a dimple.

Despite my best efforts, his image faded a little more each day. I closed my eyes and reached out to him in the darkness. I saw myself reaching out my hand, but no one was there.

I took another deep breath and considered calling the whole thing off.

My concentration was broken by a loud thump in Danny's room. I ran to his room. "Bud, you okay?"

I found Danny hopping around his room with a big smile on his face.

"Yeah! Oreo is showing me how to land with both feet."

I wasn't sure who Oreo was, but I jumped in the room with him. "Like this?"

Danny giggled. "No, you have to make sure your heels land too. Right, Oreo?" He said, confirming the instruction with his invisible friend, or so I surmised.

We hopped around his room, Danny's laughter building as I didn't hop right.

"Did you know humans jump and land mainly on one foot?" My brother looked up at me with his big brown eyes and long eyelashes. "But Oreo says it's much more practical to land with both feet."

Of course, but who would say it like that?

I followed Danny's pattern and tried to do what he said.

"Yeah, like that!" he cheered me on. On my last jump, I landed wrong and fell down, laughing. "Dog pile!" Danny cried, jumping on me and tickling me.

"No, Danny!" I laughed.

We paused mid-tickle fight when the doorbell rang. "Scottie!" Danny said, getting up and racing down to open the door. I got up and straightened my shirt, then took a deep breath and headed downstairs. My heart skipped a beat when I saw Scott. *Oh man, he looks good.*

Danny had jumped into Scott's arms and my mom was talking to Scott about when she went to her Homecoming game.

"Okay, great, well, good night!" I said, trying to get us out of there before my mom could be any more embarrassing.

We were soon speeding down South Land Park Drive and all I could think was, *I'm going to a pre-game! With Scott!*

"I like that shirt," he said, breaking me out of my reverie.

Despite myself, I blushed. "Oh, yeah? Thanks. I wasn't sure what to wear."

Scott didn't respond, drumming his hands on the steering wheel and humming along to the beat of the music inside his head. I thought I recognized it as one of the new melodies he was working on.

"I'm glad you came out tonight, Charlie." He looked away from the road to smile at me. "I think—" he shook his head and laughed, "I think you're going to have a great time."

I tucked a piece of hair behind my ear and looked out the window so he wouldn't see me blush again. "Well, you'd better be right."

"Oh, I'm right."

In another couple of minutes, we pulled up to an apartment complex just a few streets over from my house.

I took it in. *So this is Jared's place? And so close too.*

Scott entered without knocking. The door opened into a living room full of Jared's family, which I only knew because Scott was pulled into hugs by a man he called Tío, before he was dogpiled by a group of kids Scott called niños. Even though he'd only been at his new high school for a couple of months, he seemed intimately connected to the family of his new friend, Jared. If I were Scott, I'd look for a new family wherever I could get it too.

There were three guys smoking on the couch, but the patio was the place to be. Jared's papa, maybe, was at the grill, a hand towel over his shoulder, and the smell of carnitas and asada drifted its way through the house. Someone stood at the sound system bumping very loud merengue.

Scott took my hand and guided me past the living room and into the kitchen where two women talked while they flipped tortillas over a gas burner. I took in the whole scene while also trying to absorb every spot that my hand momentarily entwined Scott's. It was something about this party and the warmth of Jared's family that made me feel like this hand-holding was something special.

He let go and grabbed one of the many handles of alcohol on the counter.

Once free, I didn't know what to do with my hands. I started moving my hips to the beat, taking small steps left and right, allowing my hands to follow the rhythms.

Scott chuckled to himself and started setting up our shots.

"Okay, so here's what you do," he said, grabbing us shot glasses. All the shot glasses were mini red Solo cups. *Cute.*

"Hey, grab me one!" Jared yelled behind us, giving brief hellos to his cousins, as he made his way to us. He put one hand on Scott's shoulder and another on the counter beside me so that I was enclosed between them. I stopped dancing, and immediately felt a rush of heat through my hands and face.

"Knock back this shot of vodka and chase it with this shot of Coke. It's called a chaser," Scott instructed me.

"Why are you explaining it like she's never done shots before?" Jared said, looking from Scott to me in confusion.

I tried to show him I was still cool. "I can't believe your parents are okay with you doing shots." I bumped him with my elbow.

He smiled down at me. "What? I basically grew up on tequila."

"Three, two, one, go!" Scott said. We clinked our glasses of vodka and I took my first shot.

Oh god. I tried to keep my face neutral, but I must have done it wrong because all I could taste was rubbing alcohol and I wanted to puke. I wrinkled my nose and stuck out my tongue involuntarily. Jared burst out laughing.

"Drink the Coke, drink the Coke!"

Oh, right. I knocked back the soda. *Ah, that's better.*

"Yeah, the first one's always the hardest," Scott said as he set up three more shots.

I tried to be ready. It must have showed because Jared mouthed a silent "you okay?" I smiled eagerly to show him I could do this.

"Rum is a milder liquor. Should go down easier."

I watched his lips move and wondered how many people he had kissed. I looked at Scott and wished I knew what it felt like to kiss him. He winked at me, my heart squeezed, and we knocked back a shot of rum, followed by another shot of Coke. That was way better. I'd stick to rum from now on.

"What do you think? One more?" Scott asked as he poured another set of shots. I missed which liquor Scott went for next, but when the liquid went down, I couldn't keep my hands and feet from moving to the beat. I felt the rhythms of the music in my bones.

I grabbed Jared's hand and we all tumbled outside to dance. Jared took both my hands in his and started showing me how to dance merengue. I laughed, looking down at my feet so I could match him.

Halfway through the second song, a cousin of Jared's grabbed my hands while Jared was passed someone else to dance with. The cousin brought me close to his body so I could follow his lead.

"Chica, eyes on me," he said. There was no time to be nervous at the proximity of our bodies. I looked up and stepped up to the challenge of matching his pace to the fast tempo. The harmonies of the drums, trumpet, and guitar were incredible. But there was one instrument I couldn't place.

"What's that one instrument called?" I said to my partner.

He leaned in close to my ear. "The tambora or the guira?" He spun me in a circle and brought me back.

"Both!" I laughed, and we fell back into the multi-step rhythms. I caught the eye of the girl Jared was currently dancing with and we shared a grin. I tried to follow the way her hips moved in a figure-eight at the same time as my feet stepped to the beat.

"Ey, okay, I see you!" my partner cried out. "What you're hearing is the guira, a metal instrument crucial to the sound of merengue, and the tambora, which is a drum you can hit from either side."

"I'm in love," I closed my eyes, letting my partner guide me and allowing the music to make me totally happy.

After several songs, I needed to sit down. I thanked my dance partner and he let me go with a wave.

I found a couch at the back of the outdoor patio and plopped onto it. The world rushed up at me and my vision went blurry. I leaned my head back against the couch, eyes closed. I saw my dad motioning at me to rejoin the party. *Go have fun! You deserve it.*

Scott sat down next to me. "Charlie, you are drunk!" he said and laughed. "Well, that's enough for you tonight."

I opened my eyes and watched him disappear. He was replaced by Jared. "You okay? Should we have gone a little slower on the shots?"

I tried to shake my head but remembered that was a bad idea. "It's okay. I'm fine." I smiled at him, which got another laugh from Jared.

"How is it you can chug beer all night, but three shots and you're done?"

In the silence that was created as I attempted to respond, someone dropped into Jared's lap. She gave Jared a huge kiss on the cheek and then swung drunkenly to me.

"You are so cute!" She looked back at Jared. "Jared, tell her she's cute."

Jared snaked his hands around her waist and looked his girl in the eyes. "Carmella, she's cute." The way he said her name with so much love made me know how little this conversation had to do with me even though it was about me. I had no time to feel sad about this thought before Carmella was looking back at me with a big grin.

"I told you. So where are you from?" she said.

Jared spoke for me. "She's with Scott."

My heart fluttered. *I'm with Scott.*

"You snagged that bad boy, huh? Good for you!" She poked me in the nose, which instead of bothering me, made me smile. She stood up, pulling Jared up from the couch with her, somehow maintaining her balance in her ridiculously high heels.

I was impressed and forlorn at how much I paled in comparison. The way she was dressed, the way she moved, the way she seemed so comfortable with herself. I envied it all. I waved as they walked away, wishing I really was with Scott, instead of alone.

"Charlie, you coming?" Jared called over his shoulder. My heart soared. I got up from the couch and followed them through the front door and into Jared's mom's car. I found myself suddenly surrounded by several people from the party.

When we got to campus, we all piled out of the car and headed to the long line waiting to get into the football game. I tried to walk normally, a sense of foreboding descending on me as I realized just how much trouble I would be in if one of my teachers realized I was drunk.

I swallowed nervously, pulling the ticket from my pocket and fingering it anxiously until a woman—it was a parent I didn't know, thank god—scanned me in. We stepped into the stadium.

We were late; the game was already in the second quarter. We entered the stands to the right and found a spot in the middle. The crowd erupted in cheers and I started clapping and hollering along with them. I tried to see the scoreboard to see what happened, but it was too hard to see in my drunken state.

I had entered the stands first and was on the outside edge of the group. The person next to me was someone I didn't know who was talking over the person next to her and laughing with Jared and Carmella.

I looked away and tried to watch the game. The other team had us on our fifteen-yard line. It wasn't looking good, but we didn't allow them to make another first down and forced them to kick a field goal.

"At least it's just three points," I said. I turned to look next to me, but I was talking to myself.

The wind started to pick up and I crossed my arms, really wishing I had worn a jacket. The referee called pass interference, and we all started booing.

As the cheerleaders came out onto the field for halftime, Jared stood up and started taking the group's orders for food from the snack bar.

I popped up from my seat. "I'll help."

"Oh, you don't have to. Don't you want to stay and watch the halftime show?"

I gave a brief glance to the shaking pom poms. "I'm good."

Jared gave me a wicked handsome smile. "Then I accept."

We walked in silence down to the snack bar and got in line. *Why can't I think of anything to say?*

"The flats didn't work, huh?"

I looked down at my feet and realized I had been stepping back and forth from my left foot to my right foot to release the pressure from my pinky toes.

"Carmella always tells me that shoes make or break the night."

I laughed. "I guess she's right."

"So, what shoe would have been better?"

He looked like he was being serious, but I couldn't understand why. Guys didn't normally ask that sort of question, nor did they even seem to notice shoes in general. *Why was he talking to me? Where was Carmella?* "Probably my Converse. They're more...me."

"I feel it. There's a lot of pressure for girls to look a certain way. I wouldn't want to trade places."

We took a step forward in line. Some of my nervousness fell away and I began to get a little indignant. I crinkled my brow. "Yeah, but all the pressure comes from guys..." *like you.*

"Like me, huh?" He gave me a smirk.

I blushed, not wanting to offend him. So I said what I was trying to say. "Well, Carmella is beautiful."

"I agree. I'm a very lucky guy." He looked at me like he was sizing me up. We took another step forward in line. "But you say that like you're not also attractive."

As attractive as Carmella? No way. I swallowed nervously. *Was he hitting on me or just being nice?* I tried to shrug casually. *Girls like me didn't get the guy.*

He kept going. "Looks are important, don't get me wrong, but that's not what it's about. I love the way she makes me laugh and makes me feel good about myself." He reached in his pocket. He took out his wallet and started counting his cash. Without looking at me, he said, "You have a lot to offer too, I'm betting."

I felt my cheeks go red and looked down at the ground, hands in my pockets. "Maybe."

He looked over at me. "No maybes. The kind of girl who goes to a football game and actually cares about the game. I think that's pretty cool. And I think you'd think so too, if you weren't you."

I blushed again. *He saw that?* Part of me felt embarrassed, but the other part had me feeling like maybe I should start believing I was pretty cool. Jared seemed to have that effect on people.

"Just make out already!" Scott said right before he barreled into us from behind.

"Scott!" I was simultaneously embarrassed that he would think that I would flirt with someone else's boyfriend and flummoxed that he would think I liked someone else.

"Whoa there, buddy," Jared said, as we sank under Scott's weight.

"I am so hungry! I can't wait to eat."

The three of us inched up to the window together. Jared placed the order with Scott cutting in every other word with something else he wanted to eat. Then we stood to the side with our drinks and waited.

Now that Scott was here, the two friends switched to other subjects like who was traded from the Clippers and who was injured on the Warriors. After a few minutes, I realized they had switched to baseball and were now discussing the World Series. They moved onto talking about going to a River Cats game.

"Is that something you're into, Charlie?" Jared asked me, inviting me back into the conversation.

I stopped biting my straw. "Uh, yeah, I'm always down for some baseball." I wanted him to know I knew what I was talking about. "My dad used to take me to River Cats games at Raley's Field, uh, I mean, Sutter Health Park, when I was little."

"Me too! Those were the best."

"Yeah, parking and walking over the Tower Bridge felt like escaping into a new world." I smiled at him and wondered if we had ever attended the same game. I also let myself remember being there with my dad. It was like my dad watching me from the shadows. He would be proud.

"Order 53!"

When Scott tried to help, Jared and I gave him a gentle "no" and instead manhandled the food ourselves back up the stairs. We were welcomed like gods bearing gifts and I almost felt like part of the group.

But as the liquor wore off, so did the happy feelings. I seemed to recognize for the first time how outside the group I was and how little anyone cared. The nachos felt heavy in my stomach, the chips scraping my throat and making me parched. I was long out of soda, so I sucked on the ice cubes instead, making my way to the bottom of the cup like it was my mission in life.

There wasn't another glance in my direction from Jared or Scott. I checked my phone for notifications. Nothing. I even glanced again at the last message from the Underground Poet, but there was nothing to say yet. I watched the rest of the game go by in slow agony.

As soon as the last second ran out on the clock, I was ready to jump up and run away. But looking like a loner was worse than waiting on the group. So I waited, and pretended the stars were beautiful and that I had notifications to look at on my phone, and then waited some more as everyone started calling their parents to come pick them up. Jared and I convinced Scott that he shouldn't be driving, so Scott was coming home with me.

After what seemed like an hour, my mom finally showed up and we climbed into the back seat. I prayed Scott would behave himself. Scott being a total wreck was nothing new, but I didn't really want that tied to the drinking I had done tonight.

"Good to see you, Scott! How's Francine?" my mom welcomed Scott more warmly than she ever did me. She barely glanced in my direction.

After the normal pleasantries, they fell silent.

Finally, my mom turned to me. "How was the game?"

"It was good," I mumbled.

More silence. *Why couldn't my mom just be normal?* I sighed quietly and looked out the window at the long line of cars trying to leave the game.

Unfortunately the silence was broken by Scott. "Hey Mrs. Locke, can we please go to McDonald's?"

"Mom, it's fine," I quickly interjected, trying not to upset her. I gave Scott the lockedown. *How could he be hungry after everything we just ate? And why is he still drunk?* I looked a little closer. Maybe it wasn't just that he was drunk.

My mom ignored him and kept driving.

"No, c'mon, Mickey D's!" He gripped her seat and leaned in closer. "Fine, In-N-Out! C'mon, I'm so hungry." He started to say something else, but what came out instead was all the liquor he had downed that evening.

My mom's hands went up reflexively and she started screaming as the hot, chunky liquid streamed down on her head. Her hands went back to the wheel and she swerved out of the lane next to her, to the furious horn of the car we almost side swiped. She pulled to the side of Freeport and slammed to a stop, stepping out of the car, leaving the engine idling.

My heart leapt into my throat and I almost wanted to puke at how angry this would make my mom.

"Mrs. Locke, I'm so sorry!" Scott stumbled out of the car after her.

"Stay away," my mom put up her hand as she crumpled to the ground and started puking herself.

I got out of the car too, to escape the noxious smell emanating from the driver's seat and to do something with my anxiety. *This is not good, not good.*

"Oh god, oh shit, ah, I'm so sorry." Scott looked helpless as he decided whether to keep trying to help my mom or stay away as she demanded.

I started scavenging in the car to see if my mom kept any kind of napkins or towels. Unfortunately, my mom kept a pretty clean vehicle and I came up empty. My heart hammered in my chest at what my mom would do or say next. I couldn't just stand and wait.

"Scott, c'mon," I grabbed his hand and marched him to the stop light. "Mom, I'll be right back!" I told her.

We crossed the streets to Chipotle, stole a bunch of paper towels from the bathroom, and then ran back to my mom.

She took them without a word and began patting herself dry.

I danced on my feet side to side, waiting for my mom's cue, swallowing nervously, hands clammy.

Once all the paper towels were used up, she turned to me. "Charlie, grab my jacket from the trunk."

I grabbed it for her.

"Scott, turn around." He dutifully obliged and she stripped off her shirt and put on the jacket, zipping it all the way up. "Back in the car," she snapped. She threw her vomit-soaked shirt in the trunk and then returned to the driver's seat.

The car ride home was painfully silent. When we dropped Scott off at his house, he turned around to apologize again, but my mom held up her hand.

"Scott, do me a favor and clean up your act. You're smarter than this."

Scott nodded and shut the car door with care.

Once parked in our driveway, my mom and I escaped to our respective rooms and showers. The tears started once I was in the water and steam, but I couldn't get them to stop. What's more, I felt dumb because I didn't know what I was feeling. I let the water fall around me like a waterfall, hoping the warmth and steam would warm my soul. It was no use. The shiver remained. I shut off the shower with a grumble.

I stepped out and dried off quickly, trying to slip into bed unnoticed, but my mom knocked on my door and came in anyway.

"Can we talk…" she paused when she saw the tears. "Oh honey, what's wrong?"

I shrugged, not sure what to say or if the fact that I had been drinking was going to get me in more trouble. I just wanted to do or say whatever I needed to so she wouldn't take this out on me.

She looked at me in silence, apparently debating whether or not to give me a hug. I would have given anything to be wrapped in my mom's arms right now. She decided against it, which made me cry more.

She sighed. "I keep wanting Scott to make smart decisions, but I would have expected better from you."

My fear of her turned to anger at the injustice.

"Are you serious? I called you, didn't I?"

"Do not use that tone with me. I am your mother."

She's seriously using the mother card right now? Like right now? But all I said was, "Perfect, just perfect."

"What is that supposed to mean?"

It all came tumbling out. "Why can't you be a real mom?" It was meaner than I meant it to be.

My mom's face grew taut, her lip beginning to tremble. She wiped at her lip to get it to stop and cleared her throat. "I'm not having this conversation with you when you're being like this. You're grounded."

But I was going to get the last word tonight. "You know you have to be home to ground me, right?"

She left my room without another word.

I cried until my pillow was wet and my nose was so stuffy that I couldn't breathe. I turned on my bedside light and tried to read. At first the words floated in front of my eyes, and I got a headache trying to force comprehension through the fog of post-drunkenness and tears. But I didn't care. I'd rather be in pain reading than in pain thinking about how miserable I was.

When I checked out the books on Tuesday, I had made myself finish *All the Light We Cannot See* and then read the first chapter of all three books Mr. DeVault had given me, before continuing with the one that intrigued me the most.

I opened to the fourth chapter of *The Golden Compass* and snuggled down into the covers. This book was fascinating. I had read similar books, of course: set in early England and with magic. But I loved the idea of a daemon, a piece of your soul in animal form, and loved imagining myself as the brave Lyra, tackling evil and willing to do anything for a friend.

My eyes started drooping around three in the morning, too heavy to keep reading even though I had less than one hundred pages left. But I still wasn't ready to face my dreams. I tried journaling, but only got a few sentences down before I was disgusted with myself.

I got out of bed and put on some sweats to dance. I headed to my back patio. I left the lights off and breathed in and out to calm my racing heart. The darkness was good. The darkness was my friend. Let the shades dance.

I put my earbuds in, put my dance playlist on shuffle, and stretched to the opening song. After I warmed up, I began pacing left and right. I walked the length of the patio, sometimes shooting out an arm, sometimes stopping abruptly and moving my torso side to side, whatever the beat called for, whatever would let me stifle these emotions. Push the unwanted emotion out. Leave the pain behind. Focus on the music. The beat of the songs was the beat of my heart and I let them take me until I didn't have space left to feel.

When my mom's light shone through the upstairs window letting me know she was waking up for the day, I crept back to my room, finished my journal entry, and fell asleep.

Dear Diary,

~~No one loves me and I hate it.~~

Is there something about teenage girls that makes us unlovable or is it just me? I can't be the only one who feels like life is hard. All I want is my mommy to tuck me into bed. I know I'm too old for lullabies now, but that's not even what I'm trying to say. I just miss her, you know? I miss her so much. My mom hasn't really been my mom since my dad's funeral. She barely looks at me. She rarely hugs me. It seems like all her attention is on Danny. Cuz she doesn't care. I guess I'm just supposed to be silent and keep doing her job, take care of Danny, get good grades, be perfect in my dancing, stay out of trouble, be happy, be thankful for my life, understand what she does for me, for us. But I can't keep doing all of this alone. I need her. I'm right here, standing in front of her, and she keeps pushing me away. And so does Scott. I mean, how much more obvious could Scott be? It's just like the harder I try, the more I don't get what I want. The only person who ever seems to notice is Jared and he's taken. And in those moments, I haven't been trying very hard; I've just been me. I wonder what that's about.

I'm sick of thinking about it.

Love,
Charlie

FAÇADE

In dance that evening, my group struggled to put our routines together. Even though Jules had given us the theme weeks ago, accepting change was hard for us to accept. We decided that rather than waiting for inspiration to strike, we were going to have to sit down and draw the inspiration from our well of nothing. So, we sat in a triangle and bounced around ideas.

"I mean," Malcolm said, "we could do the change from year to year. You know, ninth to tenth, tenth to eleventh, right? Each of those is a big change and you can either accept it or complain about it."

Lela nodded and wrote it down on the notepad before her. She bit her pencil. "I was thinking something about fitting in. Like, we all come from different backgrounds, and our cultures aren't exactly appreciated here in the U.S. of A. Accepting that change is a big one."

Malcolm sighed. "Yeah, I feel you on that. I feel like I will always be Black before I'm American."

Lela said, "Yeah, and I will never be Miwok. It's always like, 'What are you? Chicana? Indian?' They're always trying to figure it out, but it's never American, either."

I didn't think my dad ever had to deal with that coming from Ireland. I tried to see it through their eyes and understand their pain. "So then the only question is if you're up for that emotional challenge of accepting that change," I said.

Lela took a deep breath, letting it out like a dragon through her nostrils. Then she smirked at me. "How about this: we'll do a piece on our cultures if you do a piece on your dad's death and accepting that?"

Even though I should have known it was coming, her comment still felt like a slap in the face. I closed my eyes and saw nothing but darkness. I was alone.

It's time and she's right. Five years is long enough. I nodded, and the pact was made.

The good thing about brainstorming was that once we started, the ideas burst forth. Malcolm and Lela were creating pieces on self-identity and finding their place in American culture, solidifying two of our nine routines. Malcolm's family included two separate stepfamilies with multiple children, so he was also going to create a piece about joining families. Lela's ancestors had been here since before Columbus, so she was going to create a piece about the interface of her family with the artificial boundaries of U.S. state lines. Plus, the change from year to year and my dad's death. Now that we had the big ideas, we could get going on some choreography.

We started with Malcolm's family piece. He envisioned that each of us could act out his family members. There would be a lot of groundwork for his younger siblings and some high jumps and multi-person moves for his ancestors. He pressed play on his playlist, and we spent the next hour creating his vision with Jay-Z's voice as our backdrop.

We came together in beautiful harmony, and I felt the dance high our whole drive home—even through dropping off my friends and picking up Danny from his afterschool program. But feeling happy was too good to be true. My heart sank a little when Danny and I arrived home to a dark house.

I resisted falling further into sadness and brightened at my little brother. "Danny, guess what's for dinner? Pizza!"

He spun in a circle of excitement. I ordered a medium pepperoni pizza with mushrooms and olives for delivery and dug in the fridge for the ingredients to make a salad. I threw together some romaine lettuce, sprinkled some Parmesan, tossed in some croutons, and called it good.

We read on the couch until the pizza arrived. I dished out the salad in two bowls and grabbed us some water before sitting down at the table with Danny.

"But Oreo needs water!" he demanded.

I clasped my fingers together, elbows on the table, and gave my brother the lockdown. Oreo was cute and all, but not if Danny was going to personify him like this.

Danny looked down at his lap and then looked back up at me. "Charlie, can you get Oreo a glass of water too?"

I waited. He took the hint. "Please," he said eventually.

"I'd be happy to, Danny." I got up and grabbed a glass, then handed it to him.

He skipped to the fridge. When the glass was a third of the way filled, he brought it back to the table. He made sure his friend was satisfied and then smiled and started eating his salad. I watched this exchange in silence, not sure what to make of it all.

Danny said, "Did you know that kangaroos only have to drink water every couple of months?" When I shook my head, he continued. "Yeah, so when they finally do drink water, they are very thirsty. Do you know why I only filled it up to here?" He touched the glass. Again, I shook my head. "For his snout," he said matter-of-factly.

"Of course." I dug into my salad. *So, Danny's imaginary friend is a kangaroo named Oreo. As long as he's happy, I guess. I wonder if I ever had an imaginary friend?*

After dinner, Danny helped me load the dishwasher before I scooted him up to bed.

"Do you think mom will be home in time to read with me?" he asked as we climbed the stairs.

I halted on the step. *Why does she always make me cover for her? I don't know if she even cares but here I am pretending that her work is just really important and that there's no place she'd rather be than home with us.* I ran up the rest of the stairs and caught up with him in his room. "I think she's still working, bud, but I know she really wants to."

I grabbed him some pajamas and he changed into his clothes.

"I get five stories tonight because I'm five!"

Maybe I felt my mom's absence harder than he did.

I gave him a smile. "You can have five short stories or a couple of chapters from a long story, okay? Otherwise, we'll be up all night!"

Danny conked out before the end of the second chapter in the twentieth book of the *Magic Tree House* series. I kissed him goodnight and then went to my room and tucked myself in with my book. I had finished *The Golden Compass* with no luck on finding the lines my Underground Poet had referenced and was only a couple of chapters into *The Elegance of the Hedgehog*.

At first, I was concerned where the story was headed given the twelve-year-old girl's preoccupation with committing suicide; her grief about the world hitting a little too close to home. But I didn't have to worry about the story overwhelming me with reminders about my dad's death. In fact, it reminded me more of his joy for life. In Paloma's journey to find out what makes life worth living, she meets her neighbors, Renée and Monsieur Ozu, who are enthralled with books, music, art, and companionship. That felt so akin to my dad that it made me want to cry. It was like he was here.

As I read and the time went from very late to early morning the next day, I realized how screwed I was going to be for school. I was going to be exhausted. But I kept reading because I liked how I felt when I was lost in a book, especially one as beautiful as Muriel Barbery's. This book was like walking into a painting. I felt like the real world was a touch more beautiful simply by seeing the world through Paloma and René's eyes.

The whole chapter was a work of art, but I nearly lost it when I realized I was in it. I had found my Underground Poet's quote.

> "When we gaze at a still life, when—even though we did not pursue it—we delight in its beauty, a beauty borne away by something we need not want, may cherish something we need not desire."

I read the chapter from the beginning and then reread my Underground Poet's text message to glean every ounce of meaning I could. Normally, being attracted to someone, to even the idea of someone, made my heart flutter like a butterfly's wings. But the idea of talking with this boy from the bookstore made my heart flutter like a leaf floating on the wind or like fingers on a piano playing an arpeggio. Carefree, hopeful, flying.

I closed the book and texted him back with a few lines from *The Elegance of the Hedgehog* and then grabbed *The Giver* and read until I had the perfect lines to combine into my response. Because the scene I wanted was a piece of dialogue, I worried that it might not be clear enough for him to recognize. So I gave him some help.

> "If this is life, constantly poised between beauty and death, then I'll gladly accept a partner in helping me track down those moments that are dying. I'll accept the Giver's warmth, his offer of family, that feeling of being a little more complete. I like the light it makes, shining bright on where I'm supposed to go."

I was too tired to worry I might wake him up or what he might think about getting a text so late. I just hoped he would be okay that I was sharing that bit of emotion, that I was looking for connection, something that I only seemed to find in books.

Until I met you.

I closed my eyes and fell asleep thinking about him.

It was all I could do to keep my eyes open during my classes the next day. I stayed awake only by the constant fear of being yelled at by a teacher for looking bored. It helped that they shocked us with announcements about midterms the weekend after Halloween. I rubbed my eyes, opened up my calendar, and started penciling in study sessions with Lela and Malcolm. I always took Danny trick-or-treating on Halloween, and Scott usually threw a party the weekend of or prior; since Halloween happened on a Friday this year, studying would need to happen in these two weeks leading up to the 31st.

Dance did a great job keeping me awake as well. Lela figured out another one of her routines—breakups. We could all identify with that piece, so the choreography simmered off of us. This piece was about us working together with abrupt distancing. Like a move where Lela and I swung Malcolm back and forth as he did backflips, but on the fourth flip, we let go. Lela slid stage left, I did a cartwheel stage right. He landed his flip and came center stage looking for us, but we had disappeared.

As exhausted as I was, my friends kept me awake while we were together, but then it was just me, myself, and I as I drove home. I rolled down the windows and blasted the music, promising myself that as soon as I got home, I would sleep. I switched from music to talk radio and scanned until I found something that kept me alert: a station doing a piece on the newest of John Green's books, in the process of becoming a major motion picture. John Green was my favorite brain candy author—you know, the books that feel so good to read that you don't even realize you're learning something about yourself in the process. The interviewer had just asked him to talk about his favorite of his own works.

John Green chuckled. "You know, that's like asking me to name my favorite kid. I will say the one I had an absolute blast working on was *Will Grayson, Will Grayson*. David Levithan was a great partner. We'd stay up late going back and forth about our ideas for the book. No idea was too strange or crazy. If we thought it would be fun, we wrote it. Our characters are teenagers. And, you know, it's a tumultuous, vulnerable time. And it feels so real. It is real. Just because it's happening for the first time doesn't make it less real. We wanted to connect with that. And I think our readers did too."

I love that. I thought back to my Underground Poet. He got it. It was real for him too.

I pulled into the driveway and decided that I wanted sleep more than food. I walked into my house already dreaming of my bed.

"Darling, is that you?" my mom called out as I closed the door behind me.

My weariness faded. I dropped my things at the stairs, kicked off my shoes, and headed cautiously to the kitchen. We hadn't exactly been friendly since the Homecoming game, so I wasn't sure if this was a trick.

My mom was stirring something lovely and aromatic on the stove. She opened one of her arms for a hug. It was so natural that I entered her arms and gave her a real hug. She smelled good and her arms felt safe.

It was over too soon. She was already back to her meal prep, cheeks reddening as if we had done something wrong. Like she had tried to be a mom and couldn't handle it.

I took a step back and tried to rewind the moment like a movie so I could try to figure out what had just happened.

She didn't let the moment dawdle. "Grab us some bowls. I think it's about ready. And then I want to hear all about what you're working on in dance."

I followed her orders without a word, suddenly back to being excited and curious and anxious about sharing my life with her. It was hard to know how to be. *Did she want me? Do I show myself? Or was it safer to hide?*

Danny came lumbering down the stairs and plowed into my arms. I kissed the top of his head and then we all sat down to French onion soup and salmon fillets.

"So, you're still dancing with Malcolm and Lela, right?" my mom asked.

I blew on my spoon full of soup and nodded. "Yeah, the showcase this year is called 'A Change Is Gonna Come' and my group got 'Acceptance of Change' as our theme. We were all broken up into groups and tasked with creating a set portraying how we respond to change."

I counted on my fingers. "There's Avoidance, Ignorance, Limbo, and Acceptance."

"And what does your choreography look like so far?"

I was good with answering questions; it didn't leave me time to wonder why she suddenly cared.

"Like what moves are we doing, or what story are we telling?"

"I guess both, whichever you feel like sharing."

"Well, we have most of our stories set. So we have a breakup, we have getting older, like from ninth to tenth and so on." I paused as I tried to remember them all. When we were dancing, it was different. Everything flowed. But off the top of my head, it all came out scattered. Plus, I was nervous talking to her like this so I wasn't thinking clearly. "Oh, Lela and Malcolm are doing ones on being Black and Miwok and how that mixes with being American. And then I'm doing one on Dad's death."

The part about my dad just came out; I hadn't meant to bring it up. Had I anticipated my mom's reaction, I would have steered clear of it. But we were finally talking and so I had let my guard down.

My mom's face drained of color, and she started fiddling with her fork. I could hear her knee bouncing underneath the table. Then she brightened. "So Danny, how was school today?"

And just like that, I was shut out of the conversation. We were done. I searched my mom's face for a way back in, but her wall was up. I wanted to cry; I wanted to fight; I wanted to scream. But the tiredness hit me like a tidal wave and it was all I could do to put spoon to mouth.

After dinner, I fell into bed with my clothes on.

I was too tired the next day to handle being social, so I begged off my friends and went to the library to read. I said hello to Mr. DeVault, and we chatted about *The Golden Compass* as I checked the book back in. He was excited to hear I found my clue in *The Elegance of the Hedgehog*. I told him I was still totally going to read *Ishmael* just for fun.

I headed to my favorite armchair and sighed with the utter bliss that always came from diving into the pages of fiction, especially ones as lovely as Muriel Barbury's.

Someone dumped their things at the foot of the chair across from me, and it took me a second to register that there was a person expecting me to respond. When I realized that person was Rebecca, I wished I hadn't noticed.

"You're such a nerd, locket, I thought this is where I'd find you." She sat down on the arm of the chair opposite me, back perfectly straight. "So what are we doing for our project?"

I closed the book and resisted the urge to sit up. "I don't know, are you done being racist?"

She opened her mouth and closed it. I could tell she wanted to tell me that I was wrong, but then she would just be proving me right. She changed tactics.

"I don't know, are you done crying over being a complete failure?"

"Nope, I need more time. Looks like this project's all on you." I had long ago learned that the best way to deal with the Queen Bee was to go along with whatever she said. I opened my book and looked back at the pages.

"Nuh uh, you're not getting out of it that easy. Look, just, let's at least figure out what our topic is, and then we can, like, each do separate things, okay?"

I closed my book again and looked at her. "Well, I told you we should do French immigration into Mexico. I know a lot about it, and we'll get creative points because I think everyone else will go with here or the U.K."

"Fine."

"Fine." We looked at each other in silence. "How about you do research on the reasons behind emigration from France, and I'll do research on the response to immigration into Mexico?"

Rebecca looked noncommittal, but I decided that she was resignedly accepting my offer.

When she still didn't make any suggestions, I said, "We probably should meet up at some point to collaborate."

Rebecca stood up. "I know." Her statement seemed definitive, yet we still hadn't made a plan. I sat there waiting, watching her stare down at me in silence. Finally, she said, "Give me your phone." When I didn't respond, she got flustered. "So we can talk about our project."

"I still have your number. Did you delete mine?"

A glimmer of a shadow passed across her face. She snatched her bag and walked away. "I'll text you my availability," she said over her shoulder, leaving me with a swamp of annoyance.

I sighed, wondering for the umpteenth time what I had done to make her hate me. *We used to play Barbies and swing from that rope in my backyard into the pool. We used to run neighborhood 5ks.* Those memories seemed like a movie of someone else's life, but I knew they were mine because the pain was real. I could hear my dad telling me to forgive her, but I was over having to forgive everyone and being left with nothing. I grabbed my things and headed to class early.

When I got home from dance that night, I forced myself to work on the routine about my dad's death. I headed out to the patio, popped my headphones in, and put on my "Dad" playlist that had all the songs I refused to listen to after he died. If I was going to do this, I would have to be ready to spiral.

I took a deep breath and pressed play on the first song, "To Raise the Morning Star." I closed my eyes and let the tears fall, not bothering to wipe them away. I pictured him sitting on the porch watching me, just like when I was little.

The rhythmic piano chords came marching out. My shoulders shot together, tense and awkward. I pushed them back down. Holly Near's voice came in soft, calling out to me. I danced to the beat, slipping through time, landing on the night my dad died. I perched precariously above the memory and came crashing down hard, just like the night his motorcycle slipped off the road.

I opened my eyes and found I was on the ground sobbing so hard I couldn't breathe. I couldn't find my dad; I couldn't see him; I couldn't feel him. I tried to control the noise, but my brain had moved firmly into a panic attack and it was all I could do to keep breathing. I shut off the music and whimpered in the darkness. Eyes closed, night air on my wet cheeks, I found my way back to breath.

After the tears subsided, I laid there with my eyes closed. Slowly, like a shimmering mirage, my dad came back to me. The darkness unnerved me, but it also felt like a friend. It felt like he was whispering across the ether that I would be okay. It was just going to take time.

Eventually, I headed upstairs and showered. I climbed in bed and whispered the lullaby my mom used to sing to me when I was Danny's age. I never knew why she stopped. Maybe broken hearts don't have much of a voice.

JETÉ

I felt the gulf between my mom and me widen in the following weeks. I'd open my mouth to ask her a question but find I didn't know what I wanted to say. There was so much I still didn't understand about this distance between us. *Did she still remember the lullabies? Did she miss them?* I could never get the courage to ask. I knew what my dad would say. He'd tell me that she needed me. But she could apologize first.

It helped that midterms were on the horizon and I could focus on studying in between each of my dance classes. Study sessions with Malcolm and Lela happened late into the night and spilled over into lunches and car rides to the Academy. By the time Halloween arrived, I was ready to forgo it all and read for the entire weekend. I slipped under the covers Friday night and settled in with *The Elegance of the Hedgehog*. I was going to finish it tonight.

Way too early Halloween morning I was awoken by the small blonde head of my little brother tickling my nose as he snuggled up under my covers. I let him curl up into my arm and gave him a kiss on the head. "How'd you sleep?" I yawned.

"I had a dream about dad."

I hadn't dreamed about my dad in forever. I kind of missed that. "Oh yeah? Was it a good dream?"

"Well, we went hopping and I won."

"Hopping? What's hopping?"

"Like with the squares and you throw a rock and you have to hop on one leg to get there. So, you have to have good balance and I won," Danny said all in one breath.

"Oh! Hopscotch. Okay, so the two of you played hopscotch and you won. Then what happened?"

"We were playing and then he..." Danny paused, and I felt his body grow tense.

"Did you have a nightmare, bud?" I asked quietly. I felt him nod. I pulled him into a closer hug.

"Yeah, Dad turned into this monster, and he started roaring and showing me his teeth and I was scared." He pushed away from me and got out of bed. He started walking around my room looking at things. "I ran away because I was so scared. But then I fell, because I tripped, so I fell, and then he was standing over me. I tried to get away, but I couldn't." He trailed off and came to a stop in front of a picture frame sitting on my bookshelf. To my surprise, he took the frame and threw it on the ground.

"Danny!"

Without a word, he ran out of my room.

What the hell was that? I got out of bed, gently picked up the frame, and placed it back on the bookshelf. It was a picture of my dad and me with butterflies painted on our cheeks. I gently touched the frame and saw myself back in the moment giggling as the paint tickled my cheeks.

All I wanted to do was go back to bed, but now I felt too miserable to do so.

I grabbed my phone and scrolled on TikTok for a while. I moved on to Instagram, watching Scott's story in dismay as he sat alone at his pool and took shot after shot with the caption, "So bored." *Why didn't he call me?* Shock gave way to disbelief when I opened Snapchat and saw he was driving. I checked the time stamp; there was no way he was sober. *Why's he so broken?* I thought about what I could do to save him and realized with a sinking heart that I was powerless. And he didn't want me anyway.

The heaviness in my heart from thinking about Scott and Danny started to sink me like a stone in water. As the hours ticked by, I became more and more angry. I was in a royally bad mood by the time I needed to leave for dance.

I bit my tongue so I didn't snap at my mom when I had to remind her that I was heading out to the Academy, meaning she needed to take care of Danny. When we got to the studio, I threw my stuff in the cubby and tore off my sweatshirt. I couldn't meet my friend's eyes. I knew I was being ridiculous and yet I couldn't stop. I could feel them giving each other a look.

I let the top half of my body float into a downward stretch, legs wide, and listened to my friends talk about their pieces.

"Malcolm, how's your family routine coming along?" Lela asked.

I could hear Malcolm take a deep breath and lean into his stretch. "It ain't much, to be honest."

I wanted to be helpful, but I couldn't bring myself to speak. I was lucky that Lela was a good friend.

"What's going on? Where do you feel stuck?"

"I just don't know where I'm going with it. Like, it blends too much into my identity routine."

"For me, it's all the same, you know what I'm saying? Like who I am and my legacy of being in what is now the States isn't separate from how I'm a sister, a daughter, et cetera."

I knew Malcolm was letting this idea settle in his head. He always did this thing when he was thinking where he'd close his eyes and try to visualize it.

"So, you're letting it be more of a blurred line. That makes a lot of sense, all right."

"Try that out and see how it goes, maybe."

"Yeah, I will. That's really helpful. Thanks, sis."

We stretched for a bit longer, then Lela stepped up to lead the first routine, one of the pieces I had decided last week: changes in the weather, thunder and rain to sunny skies. I tried to shake it off and fall into the music. I was so numb, I couldn't connect once the dance started.

We moved on to Malcolm's piece, since he needed the most support. When we took our water break, I couldn't stand still. We moved on to Lela's piece about her people's connection to the land breaking through invisible boundaries. I felt about ready to break something, so this was perfect.

I followed Lela's lead with the choreography, aggressively matching her movements, forcing the tension out of my body, imagining it moving up and out with each drop of sweat that left my pores. When it was time for me to jump into Malcolm's arms, using his legs to spring into a backflip, I did so easily. I felt like the energy was moving through me on its own accord.

"Damn, locket! Nice flip!" Malcolm high-fived me at the end of the song.

Lela nodded as she sipped some water. She wiped a bead of sweat from her face with the back of her hand.

I nodded and smiled my appreciation, but this time his use of my nickname reminded me of how Rebecca used to say it, like I wasn't good enough. Something mean was stirring inside of me that I couldn't stop. I tried an invisible lockedown on myself.

It didn't work. When Lela suggested going over my routine again, I snapped, "I don't have time just because you need the help."

I closed my eyes. "Shit, Lela I'm sorry. That's not what I meant. I'm in a terrible mood."

"Let's just move on," Lela said.

When I got out of dance, I saw a text from my mom saying that she had dropped Danny off at a friend's house and was heading to work. *Why can't Aimee just be a mom for two seconds? She had to spend one day with him, and she couldn't do it. She shoved him off on someone else as soon as I left.*

I simmered the whole way to the friend's house. Luckily, Danny was so excited about trick-or-treating that he seemed over whatever happened between us this morning, especially when he heard Scott would be joining us.

When we got home, I showered before helping him put on his Spider-Man costume. I forgot I would also have to help Oreo in what I could only imagine was a similar costume. *Maybe Spider Pig*. I laughed to myself, momentarily forgetting I was grumpy.

I was going as Iron Man, wearing my dad's old lacrosse helmet and a red long-sleeved shirt, red pants, red gloves, and white heels. I also cut out a white triangle to hang in front of my chest and attached a white circle to each of my gloves. I put on the finishing touch of red lipstick, and gave myself a demure smile in the mirror. Then, I slid the helmet on and pretended I really was my dad. I hopped into a defensive position, pretending I was holding my lacrosse stick and preparing for an oncoming hit. The helmet still smelled like him and I hoped he would bring me a bit of luck tonight.

At the doorbell, I heard Danny run downstairs. I took the helmet off and tried to calm my breathing for Scott's arrival.

I heard Scott's voice first but left my room in confusion when I heard another person's voice. My face fell when I saw their costumes—Ash and Pikachu. Instead of being mad that he had ditched our group costume idea—he was supposed to be Captain America—I suddenly felt so dumb compared to whoever this girl was in her skimpy little yellow dress.

I bit my lip, trying to control the anger that had been welling inside of me all day and was now dangerously close to exploding. Scott and I had barely talked since the last party, and he had never apologized to me for the horrible night he spent puking on my mom.

"Charlie, it's cool that I bring Tisha along, right? I told her so much about Danny, she wanted to meet him."

She's not here to meet me; she's here for my little brother. Of course, why would I matter?

Tisha was leaning over talking to Danny in that baby voice I hated. It took everything in me to put on a fake smile. "Sure. Nice to meet you, Tisha."

"Nice to meet you!" She pulled me into a hug before I could resist. "I've heard *so* much about you!"

"Are you ready, bud?" I took Danny's hand and we headed out the door and down the sidewalk to begin trick-or-treating. But I grabbed the wrong hand, accidentally taking the hand he had been holding with Oreo, so he ripped his hand away from me and grabbed Tisha's instead. Great, even my little brother was intent on making me feel like the odd one out.

I sighed and tried to find some happiness in Danny's excited energy. Halloween was supposed to be fun.

At the first house, we stood back and let Danny run up the pathway with a princess and a pirate. Their chorus of voices called "Trick or treat!" before Danny was running back to us to show us his first treats. We zigzagged through the neighborhood, walking up one side of the street and then down the other so as not to miss a single house. Hours later, we returned home with Danny's plastic orange jack-o' lantern filled to the brim.

While Danny counted and categorized his candy with Oreo, I ordered us dinner. "Hold on one sec," I told the woman at Florez Bar & Grill. "Scott, what kind of tacos do you want?" I called into the living room. He shouted back and I finished the order. "Steak, please."

I joined them in the living room, tossing Scott and Tisha each a can of Bang. "ETA forty-five minutes."

Tisha set her Bang on the coffee table unopened. "I'm trying to avoid added sugar."

"Well, I'm not," Scott said, burping loudly.

I did my best not to roll my eyes and sat next to Danny on the floor. I snagged a fun-size Crunch bar to Danny's cry of "Not fair!" He protested more when Scott stole another, but then we started tickling him and he couldn't stop laughing. We left him to his candy and chatted until the tacos arrived.

"These are actually really good," Tisha said. She took a small bite from her first taco while I was working my way through my third.

"Everything we get from here is good." I tried not to be defensive, but I was failing. This girl wasn't doing anything wrong except being here.

I turned my attention back to Danny. "It's time to start getting ready for bed." I looked at my watch. "Bedtime's in thirty minutes."

I could feel the mean part of me swelling up again, wanting to be petty toward my brother for his being mean to me. I reminded myself that Danny was five, and if I was feeling put off by a five-year-old, I was the one with the issues.

Before he could protest, I continued. "Or, if you promise to go straight to bed afterwards, I'll let you watch *Hocus Pocus* with us."

Full of sugary energy, Danny leapt up to his feet and bounded into me with a hug. If all I needed to do was bribe my little brother to get him to like me again, I'd have to do this more often.

"Oreo and I will go straight to bed! Won't we Oreo?" Danny conferred a bit with his friend and nodded back at me in agreement.

"Okay, you and Oreo go brush your teeth and get in pj's while we get the movie started."

I cleaned up the candy wrappers and dirty dishes and cued up the movie. A couple of minutes later, Danny thundered down the stairs.

"Did you even brush your teeth? Let me smell." Danny leaned forward sheepishly and then ran away giggling. "Brush for a whole minute!" I called after him.

"Well, we gotta go," Scott said. He stood up with Tisha's hand in his.

"Oh, okay," I tried to keep my voice even. "Thanks for coming." I hugged him and then took a deliberate step back from Tisha.

"See you tomorrow, Charlie!" Scott called over his shoulder, wrapping his arm around Tisha's waist. I walked them out and locked the door behind them. They weren't even off my porch before they started making out.

I rolled my eyes and headed back to the TV, grabbing the remote to turn up the volume. I watched the movie until Danny fell asleep, then put him to bed. All my anger was still at the surface. I was not yet ready to sleep so I went out to the patio to dance. I put on some Alexisonfire and let my body slam into the rhythms.

I danced for a few songs but then shut the music off in disgust. *Why isn't dance fixing this? And why am I still so angry?* I tried to rationally sort through my emotions but it wasn't working. Rationality wasn't what I needed. I reached for something, anything to pull myself away.

I checked my phone and saw a text from my Underground Poet. A smile crept into my heart as I read his message.

> "We relinquished color when we relinquished sunshine. I've been delivering myself into rural silences ever more profound. Help me bring back the sunshine."

Silences ever more profound... that's exactly what it felt like. I looked up at the night sky almost expecting to see rain. The sky was clear; the stars shimmering. But I felt it. The darkness felt close enough to touch, the rainstorm just a shudder of a breath away, the shades dancing outside my vision.

I reread his message and saw the sunshine peeking through the clouds, bringing light and hope. He seemed to be validating that life was hard. Maybe he had some rough stuff going on at home too, and maybe adults made it worse by not giving us any answers. I didn't want to just forget about it; I wanted to figure it out. Here he was asking me to join him.

I grabbed my phone and headed to my room, determined to find his source material and join him in bringing back the sunshine. The shades in the dark were comforting, but wasn't it time to be a normal teenager and feel the possibility of some light?

I approached my bookshelf with a focused eye, scanning the titles for one that would unlock his clue. I didn't have my books in alphabetical order—only by genre—so I read each title and waited for the book to jump out at me.

No, not Steinbeck, not Melville. Hm, maybe Vonnegut? The ache of the silence seemed to resonate with Vonnegut the most. I didn't have much Vonnegut, but I crossed my fingers his quote was from one of the works I owned.

I grabbed *Slaughterhouse-Five* and was instantly rewarded. I snuggled into bed and read beyond the first few pages with his quote. At page fifty, I bookmarked the page with one from my stash inside the old cigar case and got back out of bed to grab *The Lacuna* by Barbara Kingsolver. I skimmed a few pages before grabbing my phone again to compose my response.

> "Let me ask about this silence: how wide it is, how deep it is, how much is mine to keep. I'd like to add some sunrise to your pocket and some mercy at your shoes."

I wanted him to know that I knew exactly how he felt. I wanted to learn more about what he was going through. Did his happiness also live under a shadow? Could he be the one to make my dark clouds disappear?

That night, my dreams were rough. Scott laughed maniacally at me but wouldn't tell me why. I turned to run away but tripped on my shoelaces that were suddenly untied. I braced myself for the landing, tucking my face underneath my arm and tightening my body, but I never hit the ground. I opened my eyes and saw nothing but darkness. I thought I heard my dad's voice, but I couldn't find him.

I followed the light below me until I landed in a grassy field. An armed guard came to take me away. The image was fuzzy at first, but as he grew closer, I saw it was the Grim Reaper. Someone screamed "Off with her head!" but I couldn't find the voice.

Suddenly, the guard was upon me. I realized it was my Underground Poet. He gave me a wink, took my hand, and we began to run. We made a break for an exit.

But instead of the guard, my Underground Poet was now the Queen of Hearts. He was pointing at me, giving me away. He sent his demons after me—lions, bobcats, badgers, and crocodiles. I raced and raced and raced. At any moment, I would stumble and be caught. they would strike, and I would be nothing.

I tensed, but nothing came. I stopped running and turned around. I was alone.

Was I safe? In every direction I looked, I saw nothing but white. And not a sea of white. Not white sands. Not white clouds. White like a computer screen, like I was smashed onto a writer's page and I only had seconds before the cursor appeared to delete me. I tried to scream but could make no sound. I began sobbing instead. My body hiccupped noiselessly with the movement, but it didn't matter. I had no voice.

The white faded away and I was in the auditorium where I performed as a kid. A young Charlie was dancing across the stage, my mom and dad sitting in the audience. I sat down next to them and tried to get their attention. But it was as if I was watching the movie of my life; I could no more participate in this scene than I could bring my dad back. I soaked in every feature of my dad's face, wishing fervently that the little girl on the stage would take this moment, run to my dad, and hug him with all her might and ask him to never let her go.

I knew it was a dream and that I was awake before I opened my eyes. I left them closed and hugged my pillow tighter, feeling the tear-stained pillowcase press against my still wet eyes. This world was no better than the dream. I was alone.

Eventually, I blinked open my eyes and cleared away the sleep. I looked at my phone. I had four notifications from Scott: three texts and a phone call. It was late. I had slept until three in the afternoon. I read the messages and saw that Scott needed me twenty minutes ago to help with the party planning.

Part of me wanted to pull the covers back over my head and disappear. But the other part of me, the one screaming loudly to be seen, wanted whatever kind of attention Scott was willing to give. So, I got dressed, brushed my morning breath away, and headed next door.

I was still waking up when I walked in. Scott came out of nowhere. "Yes! Charlie's here. I knew I could count on you to help me! I'm making a total mess."

He grabbed my hand and pulled me into the kitchen. He wasn't kidding. The kitchen was a disaster. There was food half-open on platters mixed with Halloween decorations mixed with open bottles of alcohol. "Don't even ask. Just work your magic. Please."

I tucked a piece of hair behind my ear and got to work, disentangling the food from the non-food. Scott went back to working on whatever it was he was trying to cook. I connected my phone to his Bluetooth speakers and turned up the volume so I could drown out our confusing chemistry.

I nodded my head to the rhythms and started to relax, even smile. By the time I was done, the kitchen was clean and there was something ghoulish to eat and something magic to drink. Scott poured cups for each of us.

"Cheers." We took our first sips, and I was surprised to find I liked the taste. *Maybe I should eat something first?* But that thought was immediately replaced by the thought that I had never drunk on an empty stomach and that this weekend would be a good time to try.

We headed outside to finish our drinks, sitting by the pool with our feet in the water.

I bumped him with my shoulder. "What would you do without me?"

Scott squeezed his eyes closed, laughing. "I think I like drunk Charlie. But honestly, I ask myself that every day. How would I even function?" He downed the rest of his drink and started filling up his cup with water from the pool.

"Don't you dare!" I started to say, but Scott had already thrown the cup in my face. I wiped my eyes clear. "Oh, you are going down!" I downed the rest of my drink and tackled him into the pool. Or at least, that's what I tried to do, but instead, Scott deflected my attack and I fell in alone. I surfaced to find him belly laughing. This made me mad, so I started splashing him with all my might. Now that he was nearly soaked, he was not laughing so hard.

The next thing I knew, Scott had stripped off his shirt and cannonballed into the pool. I was momentarily caught off-guard by my shirtless best friend and therefore was completely unprepared for the hands that gripped my legs and pulled me back under. I opened my eyes underwater to find Scott grinning at me, so I swam at him to try my hand at tackling him again. This time, he couldn't evade me and so it came to be that I was hugging Scott underwater. I forgot what I was doing and when we came up for air, I let him go, cheeks burning.

Scott was still laughing. He effortlessly popped out of the water, which made me fall for him even harder. He shook his hair out like a dog and gave me that classic Scott grin before heading inside to get us towels and more drinks. I hugged the side of the pool as he disappeared inside, wishing I could stay in this moment forever.

But the wind picked up and as the sun set, I realized how cold it was. I ran back to my house for dry clothes and returned in time to get pulled into a game of beer pong with Jared against Scott and some other guy. Beer pong is the great equalizer and soon we were high-fiving and talking all kinds of crap to Scott's team. I'm not sure if Jared carried our team or if I found my new calling, but we owned that round, and I was the proud owner of being overwhelmingly drunk. And needing to pee.

I stumbled into the bathroom and laughed as I sat down too fast.

I'm not sure how long it took me to pee, but I felt like I was on a carousel ride. As I washed my hands, I inspected my hands under the running water in fascination. Why was everything in slow motion? *Go home, Charlie, you're drunk.*

I left the bathroom and headed for the front door. Jared met me on the way out. "You all good, Charlie?" I liked the sound of his voice. I looked him up and down, trying to get my eyes to focus. I reached over and ran my fingers through his hair. I looked back at him, noticing the way his eyes twinkled.

Instead of responding to his question, I felt the need to tell him, "Your eyes are twinkling like Santa Claus." He took my hand out of his hair, tucked it around his arm, and we left Scott's house together.

As we walked, I started to realize that he shouldn't be here. He should be with his girlfriend. She was so pretty. They deserved each other. But when I tried to push away, I pulled him closer instead and leaned my head on his arm. *No, bad Charlie.* But the alcohol pulsing through my head started to lessen and as we faced stairs leading up to my front door, I realized I couldn't climb them alone.

"I got you, Charlie." Jared placed his other hand around my waist and guided me up the stairs. He tried to open the front door, but it was locked. "Do you have a key?"

I nodded before I realized he wasn't just asking. I let go of his arm and reached into my pocket and started to hand him the key. I had a brief moment of panic when I realized my mom and Danny were probably asleep. But then Jared was unlocking the front door and guiding me inside.

"I'm fine." I let go of him and waved as I started crawling up the stairs. It was too hard to walk.

"Here, let me help."

"No, it's okay." I waved him away. I kept crawling. My stomach flipped and I thought maybe I needed to throw up. *Can I make it to the bathroom?* I looked up the stairs. The top was so far away. *I need to sleep. Here seems nice.* I laid my head down. The wooden step felt cool against my flushed cheeks. I felt a hand grip me and I realized Jared was still here.

"C'mon, Charlie. Let's get you some food." He lifted me easily and we walked into my kitchen. He was surprisingly strong. *I wonder what my Underground Poet would do in this situation? His arms probably feel nice.*

I smiled to myself and then it was like I was seeing Jared for the first time. "Why are you still here?" I thought maybe that sounded mean, but that's not what I meant. *Why isn't Scott here? Why isn't Jared with Carmella?*

He smiled at me and sat me down at the table. Instead of answering, he made his way into my kitchen like he knew what he was doing. He brought me a glass of water and then started pulling ingredients out of the fridge. I sipped the water cautiously but found I was parched and chugged the glass dry. Jared appeared magically and filled up my glass. My stomach started rolling, so I sipped this one slower. Something started smelling delicious. My head was so heavy. I placed my glass to the side and laid my head down on the table. It also felt cool and refreshing.

I was walking my dog and Danny was running in front of me. The dog started barking and Danny giggled. "Rai!" He called. "C'mere boy!" I let the leash go and Rai started running towards Danny.

"Charlie." I woke up from my dream and lifted my head. Jared placed a grilled cheese in front of me and one in front of him. "Eat."

I took a big bite. It was the most delicious thing I'd ever eaten. I could feel the butter running down my chin. I wiped it up with my thumb and kept eating. I gulped my water and let out a loud burp. "Sorry, 'scuse me," I said around a mouthful.

"Glad you liked it." Jared smiled and took a bite of his sandwich.

The food seemed to help. My vision got a little less blurry, my stomach a little more settled. I finished my water while gazing at Jared. "Thank you."

He nodded and finished his sandwich. "You're welcome, Charlie."

I liked that he kept using my name. Part of me felt like I should be upset he was here with me, but that thought drifted away like a red balloon.

I brought my water glass to my lips and then remembered that it was empty. I looked at Jared looking at me. *He shouldn't be here. But I can't just leave. This is my house.*

Jared grabbed his plate and mine and put them in the dishwasher. We walked to my front door. I opened it, unsure what to say.

He turned to look at me. "You have a good rest of your night, okay, Charlie?"

"You too," I managed.

He waved and headed back to Scott's, without another look in my direction.

I was so confused, but also too tired and drunk to think. I needed sleep. Maybe this would make sense in the morning.

Dear Diary,

So this weekend was…eventful to say the least. So much happened and I'm not even sure where to start. Scott has a new girlfriend. Of course that's where I'd start. I hate myself for it, but I can't stop liking him. No matter how many times he chooses someone else. No matter how many times I'm sure he's giving me signs that he's not interested. But then there will be a moment like yesterday in the pool. Not only were we kind of wrestling, but I also like hugged him underwater and he let me. I don't know what that means. And it's not like we haven't hugged before but this felt different. Am I reading into it because I like him? But why would he push me into the pool if he didn't like me? Then I got really drunk at the party. I didn't eat and then drank a lot. I know, stupid. Believe me, this is the only thing I've been able to focus on all day and I don't ever want to drink again. But Jared walked me home last night. He made me food and basically put me to bed. Why would he do that? I tried to sleep on it, hoping maybe it would make more sense in the morning. But now I'm even more confused. Who does that? Scott doesn't. My mom doesn't. I do that for Danny. I just don't know.

Love,
Charlie

MIME

Haynes High teachers had total disregard for our weekend activities, piling us up with more homework than usual and scheduling midterms the Monday after Halloween. I'd go so far as to say they forgot they were ever teenagers.

Aside from the midterms in Chemistry and Algebra II, I also dreaded the upcoming midyear check-in for my French project.

I wanted to blame Rebecca for our lack of anything to show, but I knew what our topic was; I could have been doing research all along. There was no one to blame but myself.

I resolved to spend all my hours tonight on the project and I'd just have to cross my fingers that Rebecca did the same.

Halfway through school, I remembered the long grocery list stuck to our refrigerator door and kicked myself that I had to push back my homework plans. After dance, I swung by our local Nugget Markets, glad that I remembered the reusable bags in my trunk.

I started in the produce department and grabbed bananas and a couple of different types of lettuce for salad. I looped around the back to the meat department to grab some bacon and ground beef, then made my way down the toilet paper aisle.

Oh no. My spidey senses went up. Rebecca was nearby.

I stopped midstride, trying to place where the voices were coming from, but it was too late. She rounded the corner and I had nowhere to hide. My fear turned to sadness as I noticed that she was accompanied by her mom, and her mom was furious. For most of the aisle, Rebecca had her head down, arms gripping each other, as her mom whispered something nasty. I looked down at my hands gripping the handle of the cart. Maybe if I didn't make eye contact they wouldn't see me. I breathed a sigh of relief as they moved around me like water flowing around a boulder.

But I couldn't resist. At the last second, I glanced up and Rebecca and I locked eyes.

I froze.

Rebecca wiped the tears from her face. I wasn't supposed to have seen that, I knew, and now I had witnessed a private moment. Her eyes got cold; her lips pressed together in a straight line. The emotion shocked me, and I could almost feel the electricity zipping through my fingertips and toes.

I felt rooted to the spot. I had to physically shake off the feeling of being petrified and finish my groceries in a hurry. I kept looking over my shoulder as if I were in Mystery Inc. and a ghoul was chasing me. I skipped most of the items on the list and finished by grabbing some eggs and milk. I got in line, shoulders hunched as if waiting for an attack.

The checker's cheerful greeting brought my attention back to the groceries and the issue of payment. I paid with my mom's credit card and hightailed it to Danny's school to pick him up.

Danny was quite the chatterbox, so I let him fill the car with his day to distract me from the weirdness of the grocery store incident with Rebecca. I wanted to relax, but Danny was another yoyo in my life, where I needed to be on constant guard to see if he was going to be happy that I was his sister or mad at me for something. He helped me carry the groceries into the house while telling me about how he and Oreo played on the jungle gym.

I realized Danny had kept talking and so I tuned back in when he said he got in trouble at school. "Danny, what?" I stopped and turned to him, leaving the refrigerator door open and putting the milk down on the counter.

He looked away and then back at me. "I got put in time out."

Danny never got in trouble. I closed the fridge and walked over to him, crouching down at eye level. "Bud, what happened?"

"I pushed Kyle." He glanced away.

Thoughts warred inside my head. *Should I be the parent and scold him for his inappropriate behavior, or should I be the big sister and defend his honor?* I went with the former.

"What did Ms. Henderson say?"

Danny kept his chin down against his chest. "She said that I needed to keep my hands to myself and use my words."

I breathed a sigh of relief. So, it was already handled. This was something I didn't have to add to my plate. "That sounds like good advice." I stood back up and finished putting the groceries away.

"Well, I asked him nicely to stop and he didn't!"

Because I hadn't been listening properly on the car ride home, I didn't know what Kyle's deal was, but I didn't want Danny to think I didn't care. So, I did the best I could. "That's true, but if you're having trouble, then you need to get help. You don't push, okay?"

"I did get help, but no one listened!" he yelled at my back.

I sighed, and I could feel my heart breaking. I wasn't handling this right. But instead of softening towards my brother, turning towards him and pulling him into a big hug, I turned around to face him and wound up pushing him away. "Well, you need to use your words, not your hands. Let's get going on homework, okay?"

He eyed me defiantly. "You can't tell me what to do. You're not my mom!"

"Fine, Danny."

I walked away from him and headed upstairs to grab my laptop. I hated myself, but I was already too far in and couldn't stop.

Despite his bluster, Danny followed my lead, grabbing his homework and joining me at the table.

I kept looking over at him, wanting to say something or apologize. Instead, I researched French immigration and ignored him. We worked side by side until our mom got home, and lucky for me, she was handling dinner tonight.

She put Danny to bed, and I moved to my room to continue doing my homework. When my eyes started to glaze over, I put my laptop to sleep and got ready for bed.

As I climbed in, I hesitated, and then stooped under my bed to grab the box of books hidden there. I lifted the flaps and grabbed the one lying on top.

The book was tattered, the lining about to fall out, the bindings creased and oily. I rubbed the cover softly and mouthed the title with the smallest whisper, *Time Enough*. With gentle strokes, I traced the letters of the author's name. *Devin Locke*. I flipped to the back of the dust jacket and stared at the picture of my dad, rereading the bio as I had so many times before.

"Locke grew up in Ireland before becoming a citizen of the United States in 1990. Locke has been a prominent face in nonfiction for the last decade. Despite his many awards, including winning the Pulitzer Prize in General Non-Fiction for his series set in Mexico, Marigolds and Mole, he says his greatest achievement is his daughter, Charlotte. He lives with his wife and daughter in Sacramento, California."

I could transplant myself to the memory of buying this book as if it were yesterday. There it was, eleven years ago, sitting like a beacon of light on the shelves at Capitol Books. I had been so proud as a little five-year-old, so adamant about buying a copy at "the big store." I had a seat of honor in the front row of my dad's first book signing and then he had given me cash so that I could buy my own copy. I walked out of the store holding the book like a delicate flower.

And then it began to rain. The rain was my favorite. Books and rain! What a great day! My dad and I ran hand in hand down the sidewalk, hopping in puddles and genuinely not minding that we were getting soaked. We made it several blocks before I remembered what I was carrying and noticed the book curling in my hands. I burst into tears, and was uncontrollable, positive that I had ruined my dad's big day. He picked me up in his arms and let me burrow in his coat as we ran to the car.

I cried the whole way to Old Sac, only cheering up when presented with a hot chocolate from Steamer's. I looked at my dad's beaming face and realized I hadn't ruined anything at all. We finished the day riding the carousel and as my dad and I looked down from the top of the world, I forgot all about my mistake.

I put *Time Enough* aside and dug around the box until I found *Marigolds and Mole*. Flipping through the pages, I started to smile. This would make a great script for my French project. I closed the book and drummed my fingers on the cover. *Yes, this is perfect.* It was almost like the shadow of my dad's memory was giving me a nod of approval.

The next day, all thoughts of the French project were stripped from my mind as I focused on dance. We were closing in on the final weeks before the Winter Showcase. While the Summer Showcase included individual and group routines, the Winter Showcase was only for individuals. So everything rested on my shoulders. I'd been putting in the hours, but I was nowhere near where I wanted to be. Today, I was going to spend some extra hours on my own at the Academy. Malcolm and Lela never minded driving themselves when I needed the extra time.

Dancing outside on my patio was fine, but things really came alive when I had the studio to myself and the mirrors to correct my form. I always finished feeling more excited about my routines, more confident about the showcase than I had a few hours prior. But all that dissipated when I saw Scott leaning against the car next to mine in the parking lot with one of the other dancers.

I looked at them in dismay and almost considered turning around and staying inside until they were done.

I set my resolve with a lockdown and headed to my car, not looking at them.

"Charlie!" Scott grinned, catching my eye. "I was hoping I would see you. Then you already know Lina."

Lina's eyes furrowed. "How do you two know each other?"

I swallowed my anger. *How is it possible that Scott comes into my space, yet I'm the one to feel like the third wheel?*

"Lina, baby, Charlie's my best friend. We go way back. You're not seriously worried?"

Lina put her arm around Scott's waist and pulled him closer to her. I was too tired for this.

"You guys have a great night!" I said as I climbed in, glad that he stood up for me but angry how final his statement seemed. *Charlie's just a friend! Like a sister!* I drove away in a huff.

When I got home, I decided to dance more. I didn't want to feel. I danced until I was too exhausted to think, so that I could take a shower and fall asleep without worrying about how I felt about Scott.

I walked through my classes the next day like a zombie, paying just enough attention to scrape by unnoticed. After classes, with no dance and with Danny at his afterschool program, I went home and slept.

A few hours later, I woke up feeling only a bit better. I headed downstairs in time to see Danny being dropped off by the parent of a fellow classmate. They had watched *Lady and the Tramp* in his afterschool program, so Danny was all excited about making spaghetti and meatballs for dinner.

"Maybe mom will eat with us tonight!"

"Yeah, bud, she just might." *She's usually home by seven.*

We got excited, thinking about the look on our mom's face when she came home and saw what we had made her. We cooked quickly, racing against the clock for when she would walk in the front door.

At 7:15, I pulled the garlic bread out of the oven and Danny and I arranged everything out on the table.

At 7:45, we decided to eat and save a plate for her.

At 8:15, it was Danny's bedtime, but I thought pushing it back just for tonight would be okay.

By 8:45, Danny was starting to nod off, so we left the table and got him ready for bed. Story-time took longer than normal because he kept bounding up from his bed at every little noise, thinking it was our mom.

At 9:15, I kissed Danny goodnight and walked downstairs to a still quiet house. I sat at the table with growing unease until 10:00, when I grabbed *Ishmael* and headed to the couch to read.

At 10:45, I heard the low hum of a motor stop in front of the house. I tiptoed to the window and, after a minute of staring, realized that she was talking on the phone. I moved to the table and sat down, bouncing my foot in agitation until I heard the door open.

She was making a concerted effort not to let her heels click on the wood floor. The look of surprise on her face when she saw me matched the look on my face when I saw she was still talking on the phone. She ended the call abruptly.

"Charlie, what are you still doing up?"

I waved to the prepared dinner, now congealed from sitting out for so long. "Danny and I made you dinner."

"Oh, Charlie!" she exclaimed, reaching for a hug that I resisted. She set her things on the kitchen island and sat down.

"Please don't," I said when she tried to eat. It was too late for that, and I knew she was just trying to avoid conversation. "Who were you talking to?"

She searched my face like she was assessing what would get her in less trouble. "I was talking to a client."

"It's kind of late."

She laughed. "You don't get to make that call."

"Oh, I don't, huh?" I crossed my arms and sat back in my seat.

"No, you don't. You're a kid and don't understand the stress I'm under."

"So then explain it to me!"

"I don't have to explain myself to you." She got up from her seat.

"Why don't you ever want to talk to me?" I got up from the table and chased after her.

She turned around, eyebrows raised, but saying nothing.

"Did you know Danny asks for you every night when I tuck him in?" Her lip quivered.

"I'm supposed to be the kid, I want to be the kid, but you're not letting me. So, yeah, I think I deserve to ask why you're out so late and talking to someone else instead of your kids."

I started to walk away but turned back around. "And I still need you, you know, even if you're never home to see it."

I left my mom standing in the kitchen and headed up to my room. It was always the same train going off the tracks, and I could never find the right words to say. She always seemed to misconstrue what I meant. It was so frustrating.

I knew I should go to bed, but I grabbed my phone instead and was delighted to find that my Underground Poet had texted me back.

> "Such silence exists because we bury it away and pretend it's just a missing piece, a lacuna. So I'll sing this song until you find me, 'How sweet to be a cloud floating in the blue!'"

He wants me to find him. My heart soared. And despite the dismal evening, a smile stole across my lips. *I'm helping him find his missing piece.* I rubbed the part of my chest above my heart. It did kind of feel like a lacuna. *It's like we walk around with these holes inside of us, but we're supposed to pretend like we're whole. Like Aimee pretending it's fine that my dad's dead.* By not allowing him to be dead, she was also shading his memory from being seen. But my Underground Poet got it.

I let myself feel another moment of levity. *Maybe I can let him help me too.*

ARABESQUE

November swept quickly by and brought to mind the end of the semester and finals. *Already? It's too soon!* So that meant I really needed to stop putting off my World History field trip. It wasn't a big deal; because we were studying the Incan Empire, Mx. Owens asked us to go check out the Incan Empire exhibit at Crocker Art Museum. I was actually looking forward to it—the Crocker Art Museum was so expansive that I felt like I could visit it a thousand times and never see everything—but it just felt like one more thing on my list to do. Plus, their hours of operation were pretty short and I kept just missing the window.

So finally, one Wednesday we had a half day, and I headed there straight from school. I had planned ahead and biked to school, rather than driving.

It ended up being a gorgeous day—blue skies that felt like summer, but cool temperatures that kept the sweat off as I biked. I had a good idea of where I needed to end up, so as I left school, I didn't look up directions on the GPS. Instead, I took whatever street seemed right.

I loved biking through Sacramento. There was something about the trees that made it feel like I was always on a wonderful adventure, like I was looking at the world with new eyes. That no matter where I ended up, the journey would be worth it.

I weaved down Oak Park and into Richmond Grove, before choosing one of the alphabet streets at random. I followed S Street all the way down to 9th Street, stopping to check out the Little Free Libraries in the neighborhood and gaze at murals along the way. I found three more books in the *Magic Tree House* series for Danny and book one of *The Broken Earth* trilogy by N. K. Jemisin, an author I'd been meaning to check out for a while. My favorite mural today had to be the gigantic tiger winking at me in black and white.

I turned on O Street and came to a stop in front of the museum, locking my bike to the bike rack. I walked through the large double doors and headed to the ticket counter.

"Are you a student from Haynes High? Wonderful, so if you just show me your student ID, you will get a student discount, and then I can show you on the map where to find your exhibit."

I thanked the woman at the desk and did as she asked. Then, she took out a pamphlet and showed me the path to the Incan Empire exhibit on the second floor.

I took the stairs two at a time, but stopped on the landing to watch the silent film playing against the wall. It was a video of a little girl jumping in the puddles in a rainstorm. It was a black and white film, but it kept switching the point of view from whoever was behind the camera to hers as you jumped with her into the puddles.

And all of the sudden I was eleven again and at my dad's funeral.

I knew I was too old to be jumping in puddles, but I hated sitting there listening to everyone talk about him as if he were still alive. So, I got up from my seat and found the closest thing that made sense. I wanted to feel as cold and miserable on the outside as I did on the inside.

The sky was overcast, grey like someone had colored it in with a pencil. I hated the clouds and their stupid darkness. I hated the trees that surrounded his burial plot, so full of life, standing so strong against the elements. I hated my mom most of all for sitting there stone-faced and serious while people cried around her. And I hated that I didn't feel anything.

Looking back, the funeral was filled with people who loved my dad. Fellow acclaimed, published authors. Friends from college. Neighbors, including Mr. DeVault and his husband. People had flown in from all over, too, including Ireland and Mexico. But the people I remember most were these two guys, Jesus and Jean. They were the only ones who didn't tell me that they were sorry for my loss. They were the only ones who really seemed to care.

After the ceremony was over, they were kicking around a soccer ball, and Jesus kicked it my way. I watched it roll into the puddle, and then, being the terrible pre-teen that I was, I kicked it as hard as I could away from them. They shared a sad look, before Jean ran after it and kicked it back to me. I stopped the ball with my foot and picked it up. I watched the dirty water run down my hands and stain my dress. I wiped the water off my hands and then threw the ball at Jean. He caught it and then walked over and bent over so he was looking at me at eye level.

I scuffed my shoe in the water and watched the air bubble up to the surface.

"I miss him too, kiddo."

I refused to look at him. He didn't know what I was going through.

"Did you know your dad was my first friend when I was your age?"

I looked up at him in surprise, but then stared at him defiantly, not ready to believe him.

"It's true. I was brand new at school and didn't know anybody. But it was your dad who came over and introduced me to his friends. That's how I meant Jesus." He pointed to the man standing behind him.

"Is he your husband?" I finally asked.

"That guy?" Jean laughed. "Never. But he wishes." He winked at me, and Jesus said something in Spanish behind him. Jean replied to him in Spanish and then looked back at me.

"You keep this okay?" He handed me the ball.

"It saved my life when your dad gave it to me, so maybe it will help you. Any time you feel angry or sad, just give this ball a mighty kick like you did before, okay?"

I took the ball from him cautiously, expecting some kind of trick.

He held out his hand for me to fist bump. I curled my hand into a fist and bumped his gently.

"C'mon, let's go back to your mama." He held out his hand. I ignored it, but walked back with him to where she was waiting for me at my dad's grave.

I never saw them again, but when I first got to high school, I friended them on Facebook and liked their photos of their kids and dogs.

I came out of the reverie and watched the little girl jumping in puddles for another few minutes, before I continued up the stairs and found the exhibit I needed for my history assignment. The exhibit wasn't very big, and so I was able to loop it twice, pausing at each painting and sculpture for several minutes and take notes.

Then, I found a bench in the middle of the exhibit and jotted down some notes on what I witnessed, my initial reactions, and how I felt it connected to what we were learning in class. I put everything back in my backpack and wandered around the rest of the museum. Going down one hallway and then another. Getting lost and finding myself in the second wing of the museum, which was the original house of the Crocker's. I briefly paused at the baby grand piano, gently stroking the keys, and then continued up the large marble staircase to the second floor. I loved looking at all the pieces that were specific to California, as if I could learn a little bit more about myself by looking at the world through these artists' eyes.

I stayed until closing, until the usher had to remind me to exit the building, and then I biked home filled with thoughts of my dad and wondering where I had hidden that soccer ball.

It was the smell of ginger roasting in a pan that woke me up, but it was the music that made me believe it wasn't just a dream. My mom was prepping Thanksgiving dinner. I almost stayed hidden on the staircase, just to listen and watch her without being seen. But I was drawn to her and kept moving forward.

She was dancing to some Santana on the record player as she cooked. She placed a casserole dish in the oven, something delicious simmered on the stove, and the kitchen counter was full of ingredients in different stages of preparation. I tried to play it cool, taking a seat at the counter. I watched her with quiet joy, relishing this moment when she was happy, thankful this was the one social event she never skipped. It was like all year she stayed in the shadows, but then this fateful Thursday arrived and my mom was back.

"Good morning, darling. You're in for a treat. Here, taste this." She stuck a fork in the pan of green beans and then handed it to me. It was her famous recipe: green beans tossed lightly in olive oil, fresh ginger, and chili flakes.

"Yum!" I munched away and looked around. "Danny upstairs?"

My mom nodded. "Upstairs making all kinds of noise. I thought for sure he was what woke you up. It's good, right? Yeah, I think I outdid myself this year. Mac and cheese is in the oven. I'm just glad Fran's got the turkey because that is not my forte." She looked like she was about to mention that it was my dad who always cooked the turkey, but she turned back to pushing her green beans around in the pan.

"Everything smells delicious." I grabbed a cup of coffee from the half-full pot and poured a bowl of Honey Bunches of Oats. "I've still got to make my cake."

"Oh, that's right! I'll be out of the kitchen by ten." She checked her watch. "I have a phone call I need to take." Before I could protest, she continued, shaking her head. "This arbitration I'm in the middle of is nasty and this lawyer will not let me be, even on a holiday!"

I took a sip of my coffee. *So, it's not just my mom who works too much.*

The lawyer ended up calling a bit early, so I cleaned up after my mom and put everything away to have a clean kitchen for my baking. The plan was to make a devil's food cake with cookies and cream ice cream layers, coffee buttercream ganache, and a border of white chocolate Kit Kat bars, all piled high with brownie M&M's. My Thanksgiving cakes were a ridiculous venture, becoming more and more extravagant each year.

I started with the cake since that would take the longest. Once it was in the oven, I left the ice cream out on the counter to soften while I made the buttercream. My secret was to add freshly brewed coffee rather than instant and use vanilla beans rather than vanilla extract. I spooned a generous scoop of frosting into my mouth to taste test and decided it was glorious. I spread the softened ice cream into two cake pans and put them in the freezer to harden.

I worked diligently, aware of the time only to ensure the ice cream didn't melt and the cake didn't burn.

My mom reemerged from her call several hours later. "Woof, that man can talk!" She kissed me and refilled her glass of water. "And I know, now I'm late!" She called over her shoulder as she ran up the stairs to shower. I watched her go with a smile, feeling all warm inside from her kiss.

I had just placed the Kit Kats around the sides of the cake and spiraled the M&M's around the top when my mom came back down the stairs. It was my turn to get ready. I placed the whole cake in the freezer to chill until we needed to leave.

A half-hour later, we walked over to Scott's house laden with our dishes: me holding my cake in my trusty carrier, my mom handling the macaroni and cheese casserole dish, and Danny carrying the green beans in a plastic bowl. We entered the front door of Scott's house without knocking.

"Hello!" my mom called out.

"Hello! Oh, how cute is that bob? Did you just get it cut?" Fran called from the kitchen, already pouring my mom a glass of wine.

I made some room in their freezer for the cake and went to find Scott. I lost my breath a little bit when I saw him. He had just stepped out of the shower, so his hair was still wet. I barely had time to process how good he looked before he ran over and pounced on my back.

"Take down, Scottie!" Danny cried, jumping up to hook his arms around Scott's legs. We wrestled for several minutes laughing, but the fun ended when Scott stopped to take a phone call.

"Hey, Steph, baby, how are you? How's Hawaii?" Scott climbed the stairs two at a time and disappeared into his room. Instead of being frustrated, the idea that there was already a new girl made me laugh.

I ruffled Danny's hair and told him to join the parents. Danny turned away from me and ran into Fran's arms. She laughed and scooped him up like a baby.

I stayed where I was and watched my mom talk with Fran. My mom looked unreservedly happy and normal. She knew Fran back in college when Fran was a professor and my mom a student. Maybe since they knew each other before my mom met my dad, their friendship wasn't tainted by his death. I drank it in and tried to savor everything about their exchange.

Scott caught me on the stairs and we joined our family in the kitchen. We talked for another hour, until Danny exclaimed, "I can smell the turkey!" and we knew it was almost ready. I helped my mom set up our food on the counter and helped Danny fill up his plate: white meat for him, dark meat for me, and finished it off with Fran's famous thick gravy. The gravy recipe was a family secret, handed down to her by her southern grandma who had learned it from her mom. Then, we all sat down at the table.

We were all quiet as everyone dug in and enjoyed their meal. I closed my eyes and let that first bite of turkey and gravy overwhelm my senses.

As we went back for seconds and thirds, I reminded everyone to save room for the cake.

"Oh, I couldn't forget about that." Fran smiled at me. "Your cakes are the best I've ever had."

Even though that's what grandmas always say, I still blushed.

As I passed out the slices of cake, my mom said, "And you made up this recipe?"

I nodded.

She beamed at Fran. "Isn't she amazing?"

I stopped, knife halfway through slicing the next piece of cake, and looked at her. I could hardly believe she was talking about me. Part of me was grateful for the compliment, but a louder part of me wondered why it was so rare that she gave me one. I smiled and nodded my thanks, trying to still the resentment that was simmering within me.

Fran smiled in agreement and gave me a wink. "She sure is. Scott, why haven't you scooped her up yet?"

Scott choked on the bite of cake in his mouth and grabbed some water to wash it down. I glanced in horror from grandma to grandson.

"Oh, they still have time. I mean, if Charlie's not at home, she's here," my mom said.

I tried to give my mom the lockedown and end this conversation like two minutes ago. She averted her gaze from mine.

Scott's cheeks continued to redden.

"Okay, can we stop talking like we're not here?" I demanded, getting increasingly embarrassed at how upset Scott was getting.

"Yeah, we're not five," Scott said.

"Oreo's five!" Danny said. The whole table turned to look at him. "I'm five and three-quarters, but since Oreo is five, I told him I'd help him."

Fran was the first to laugh. "Well, Oreo is lucky to have you, Danny!"

Danny smiled proudly and took a triumphant bite of his cake. My mom gave me a quizzical look, but I just shrugged. *Oh, she could avoid the lockedown, but now there's suddenly time to look my way?* I went back to my cake and became inordinately interested in the crumbs on my plate.

Dessert came to an end, and as the adults were washing the dishes, Scott and I slipped out the front door. We sat on his front stoop in silence.

I tried to act like I had forgotten the whole conversation, but I would never forget the way he seemed to say that being with me was the worst idea. *I don't want to hate myself, but if Scott can't see me that way, then who can? I'm not my dad's perfect little girl anymore.*

Scott ran his fingers through his hair and leaned back on his arms. "If I could kill my grandma, I would. That was so embarrassing."

I looked down at the ground and scuffed my shoe against the step. "Yeah, I wasn't expecting that."

"I mean c'mon, just because we've known each other since forever doesn't mean we're going to date. This isn't the 1800s."

I tried to pretend it was funny, thinking of Scott and me as royalty brought together to unite our lands.

"Yeah, it's like," I put on a British accent, "come, Prince Scott, you must be betrothed to the princess. It is your duty."

Scott sat up and walked down the steps to take a few drags from his vape. He always thought he was sly, but he was terrible at it. This must be something else Fran didn't trip about. But I was too embarrassed by what had just happened to be mad.

He turned back to face me. "You'd tell me if you were dating someone, right? I feel like you know my girlfriends, but I never get to meet yours. You do like dudes, right?"

"Insert 'many' between 'my' and 'girlfriends.'"

Scott pretended to be angry. "Oh c'mon, that was a low blow!"

I rolled my eyes. "Yes, I'm into guys, but so what if I wasn't?"

He shrugged. "But you never answered my question. Do you like someone? Let's be real, Charlie, are you hiding him from me because you know I'd kick his ass?"

I chuckled picturing Scott trying to fight himself. "No, I'm not hiding him."

"So that means you do like someone!"

Scott briefly faded from my mind and was replaced by my Underground Poet. *Was I hiding him?*

When I didn't answer, he sat back down and started poking me in the arm. "Tell me. Tell me. Tell me. Tell me."

I could always just tell him about my Underground Poet. But even as I thought it, I knew I never would. This was my secret and I wasn't ready to share. I shook my head, and suddenly I was reeling with another thought. *Is this my moment to tell Scott how I feel? But what if he doesn't like me back?*

But what if he does?

He took my silence as needing more prodding. "If I guess right, will you tell me?"

He seemed so genuinely excited that I wanted to play his game. I shrugged, trying to be casual. "Fine, but you won't get it right."

His eyes lit up and he gave me a good long look. "Let's see, someone good enough for our Charlie is someone who doesn't get the lockedown too often, but also someone she wouldn't have told me about."

I rolled my eyes again, trying to play off how loudly my heart was beating. "How do you know? Maybe he's as annoying as you are."

Scott laughed and asked his first question. "Do I know him?"

Fear gripped me. "I can neither confirm nor deny it."

"So that's a yes. Huh, so it must be someone we knew back in middle school. Was I friends with him back then? No, that's too easy. Would we be friends now?"

I pretended to consider the options. "Yeah, sure."

Scott nodded like that gave him a lot of information. "Oh, okay, I know. Does he drink Red Bull or Rockstar?"

I didn't occur to me to lie. "Bang."

I waited for the next question by looking for dirt underneath my nails. When I finally looked over to see why he was taking so long, he was standing up and walking away from me.

I stood and followed him in total confusion. He abruptly turned back around and fixed his eyes on me. I watched that scar dip above his eyebrow, but this time it felt like a harpoon through my heart and I realized he had figured it out. Even as I tried to hang on to something rational, I could feel myself slipping.

He took a long drag from his vape and let it out through his nose.

"The thing is," he said, letting the rest of the vapor out through his mouth as he talked, "it doesn't matter. This guy, he's far away, right? He's not in your league. You need to find a guy who pays attention and gives you what you want."

He walked past me. As he swept by, the sweetness of his vapor settled around me. He dashed through the door just as my mom and Danny were exiting.

I ran home on my own, the vapor feeling like a shove, feeling too embarrassed for my mom to see my tears.

"Charlie?" Danny's sweet voice called after me, but I couldn't face him either.

When I got to my room, I sat down on my bed and thought about our conversation in gut-wrenching disbelief. It was over. I hadn't even told him, and he was already telling me he didn't want me.

I heard my mom on the stairs and held my breath. I didn't want her to come in; I couldn't have her see me like this. Her shadow skimmed across the floor and then I heard her door close with a resounding click. I climbed into bed, pulled the covers over my head, and cried myself to sleep, broken and exhausted.

Dear Diary,

Have you ever been broken up with before? I haven't, well not really. To be honest, I've only ever had two boyfriends and I don't know if you could even call them that. One was in seventh grade for one week and I ended things before summer, but neither of us were really that upset. The other was in ninth grade for two months. I liked him, but something just never felt right. I think I was more interested in being liked than I liked the guys I was with. But tonight I got broken up with by Scott and we weren't even together. That has to be a new kind of record. We didn't get to have a first kiss. No trivial high school fights or drama. He wanted to know who I liked and before I even had the chance to say it out loud, he told me he wasn't interested. I'm just not good enough. And now I don't know what to do.

Charlie

ASSEMBLE

The weird, not-really breakup with Scott had me walking under a dark cloud for weeks. I did what I was supposed to do at home listlessly and without question. The only reprieve was dance. Malcolm would give me a light punch on the arm or Lela would rub my back, but no words were spoken outside of "Let's repeat that sequence" or "Instead of moving left, let's cross right." I think they knew I was going through something that words couldn't help. I couldn't even bring myself to respond to my Underground Poet. The words had forsaken me.

By the time of the Winter Showcase, I had worked myself so far beyond mental and physical exhaustion that I didn't even notice the shadow that hung over my world. The only comfort was that being onstage was going to be a welcome release.

I counted down the days, not by the calendar, but by each event: get through this dance choreography, get through this Chemistry final, get through reading to Danny before bed, get through this last rehearsal. As I got ready for bed the night before the Winter Showcase, I didn't even have my usual pre-performance jitters. I said a silent goodnight to my dad and fell asleep with my thoughts on the stage.

I tiptoed onstage in brisk, graceful steps and struck my first pose. After a quick intake of breath, I was awash in lights, music flooded the auditorium, and the dance began. Leg kick towards the audience. Deep breath as I leaned away and into a back flip. Light on my toes as I flew across the stage. My confidence shone through each of my marks with strength and pizzazz. I let the music fill my mind until all I knew were the subtle rhythms of the song and the way my body felt moving to them. I danced from song to song, not even knowing where I was or whom I was performing for.

As the last song came to its close and my twelve minutes of fame were complete, I bowed and accepted my applause. I blew a kiss to the sky in honor of my dad and ran off the stage feeling completely alive for the first time since Thanksgiving.

I went to my dressing room but didn't want to be contained. I took off the snapback I had been wearing onstage and pulled my hair up into a messy bun. With a final smile at myself in the mirror, I pulled on the plaid jacket that had been tied around my waist, and bounded out of the dressing room to find Lela and Malcolm. They had gone before me so now we could all hug and high-five and talk giddily about our performances.

We had grown so much as dancers, and I felt one-hundred percent confident that we were amazing. We stayed together as the lobby filled with family members and one by one we were pulled away. We promised to celebrate over winter break, and with that, I looked for my mom and brother.

When they finally made it through the crowd and to me, I gave my mom a huge hug before I could second-guess it and then scooped up Danny in my arms.

"You were incredible!" my mom called over the din.

The flush hadn't left my cheeks. "Thank you! I feel incredible."

"My sister is a rock star!" Danny gave me a tight hug and then wriggled out of my arms.

My mom and I stood there looking at each other. Even though there was so much to say, it was okay. She pulled me into another hug before disappearing to talk to my principal who was an old friend.

I scanned the crowd and my eyes fell on Scott and Fran. I felt like a hot air balloon: my showcase had brought me on top of the world and now I was losing altitude. *I didn't invite Scott. The last time we spoke I was rejected. And dejected. And heart broken.*

Fran gave me a hug and talked about how great my performance was. Scott handed me a bouquet of flowers, saying, "From the family."

I was suddenly overwhelmed and too hot in this stuffy lobby full of families. Without a word, I pushed through the crowd and broke out into the fresh air and was almost surprised that Scott followed me.

We walked to the parking lot and sat down on a curb. I didn't know what to say and I didn't feel like asking. Then it hit me—he hadn't come here for me; he had come here for Lina.

"So what's with these?" I held up the bouquet.

Scott blushed and rubbed the back of his neck. "My grandma thought you would like them."

He probably bought them for Lina. I did my best not to roll my eyes. I brought the flowers to my nose and inhaled deeply. They didn't smell like anything.

"How does it feel to finally be done?" he eventually asked.

I looked at him questioningly.

"You know, with the showcase? If I know anything about my best friend, you've been working like crazy these last few weeks to make it perfect."

My face involuntarily fell into the lockdown. *Best friend, huh? Why did he suddenly care?* I took a deep breath and let it out slowly, relaxing my face in the process.

"I don't know. Maybe once the adrenaline stops, it'll catch up to me, but right now, I'm still kind of in a daze." *About us,* I wanted to say. I fingered the petals of a rose, wanting to rip the flower apart.

Scott smiled and looked out into the night.

"What's up?" I asked, not even caring to hide my sigh.

"I thought I would be okay seeing Lina here, but it's hard since we broke up. Don't get me wrong, Steph is great, but Lina was different, you know? I mean, I thought I meant something to her. But then she freaks out about a hickey and thinks I'm unfaithful or whatever."

I nodded like I knew what he was talking about. I guess I should by now, considering how many girlfriends he'd had throughout our friendship.

"I mean, if I don't even remember, it obviously didn't mean anything. But she got it into her head that I was looking for something different. Whatever. If she didn't know what she had, then it's her loss, right?"

He looked at me expectantly, but I couldn't give him what he wanted.

His eyes narrowed, and then he stood up and left me without a backward glance.

His callousness shocked me. My anger towards him was unsettling. *This was my night. He didn't even compliment my performance.* I wiped the tears from my eyes with an angry hand and followed him back into the lobby.

On the way home, my mom surprised us by stopping by Gunther's for a congratulatory ice cream cone. I got cookies and cream, Danny got lemon custard, my mom got peach, and the three of us shared a pistachio cone for my dad. We couldn't talk about him, but we could eat his favorite ice cream flavor. It was infuriating.

"Taste good, Danny?" I asked. We were seated at one of the little tables facing the street, eating our cones.

Danny nodded energetically. I smiled and tried to match my brother's energy. This ice cream was delicious and that's all I wanted to think about.

"You were great tonight, darling." My mom looked at me with a smile.

"Thanks..." *Aimee.* I knew I should be happy. It had been a great showcase and this ice cream was delicious. Instead, I felt the lockedown on my face and the ice cream turn bitter on my tongue. I tried to talk myself through it. *She's being nice and that's nice. If I can focus on all the nice small moments and not the rest of it, I can get through this.* But it wasn't working. I felt the need to poke her, prod her, make her uncomfortable.

When it was my turn with my dad's ice cream cone, I took a bite with a chunk of pistachio and played with the napkin. "It was nice that you made it to this showcase." I looked up at my mom and tried to invoke some compassion, but the tone of my voice couldn't hide the sneak attack.

My mom's eyes grew big and then narrowed. "So am I."

Ever the adult. I sighed and took another bite of the ice cream cone. I handed it to her. "Do you even remember the last one you went to?"

She was reaching for the cone but her hand stopped halfway and looked at me with shock and hurt. "Of course I do, Charlie. Why would you ask such a thing?" She took the cone.

I dodged her question and avoided the sinking feeling in my stomach that I was being a brat and making things worse. I steeled myself against her and went back to eating my own ice cream. "I'd just be surprised if you remembered is all."

"Charlie, why are you being like this?" She tried to search my eyes, but I glanced away. She sighed and rubbed her forehead. "Enough." She stood up. "C'mon, Danny, time to go." She pulled him up by the arm, tossing my dad's cone in the garbage.

I had to admit, I was shocked. I didn't think she'd break that easily. I gave her the lockdown and ran after her.

"Mom! Mom! Aimee!" Calling her by her first name got the desired response.

She turned around.

"Just admit you don't remember. I'm not saying you're a bad mom. Just tell me the truth. You only went to my dances because of dad, and since he died you haven't been back."

Her weariness quickly turned to humiliation. "I do remember!" She yelled at me. I took a step back. My mom making a scene was quite the scene. Her face was red, her voice pitched in anger. "Don't you dare tell me what I have and haven't done. Get in the car now! Not another word."

My heart hammered and I followed her orders. Danny looked at me with fearful, wide eyes. I gave his cheek a soft stroke as I clipped him into his car seat and tried to whisper that everything would be okay. I sat in the backseat with a melting ice cream cone dripping down my hands. My lip trembled and by the time I made it to my room, I was sobbing.

The first morning of winter break, I woke up with a smile on my face that faded as I remembered how much my life sucked. Gunther's ice cream was such a tease. Everything would be different if Aimee would just say his name.

Didn't she know that by not talking about it, she made his death unreal? That when she didn't grieve, I couldn't either? That it's probably confusing to Danny, who never met his dad, to never hear about him?

I was too tired to think. From anger at my mom, I dove straight into misery about Scott. I looked at my clock. 1:07 in the afternoon. I hadn't even been up five minutes and already my day was shot. I got up and put on some comfortable clothes. If I was lucky, I could dance for the next several hours and try to move out some of this energy.

My body was still tired from the showcase the night before, but as I stepped out on my patio, I woke up with the sunshine. Suddenly inspired, I headed back inside and grabbed my CD player and a stack of old CDs, ones that I had burned myself.

I laughed out loud in surprise hearing the first track, a song I hadn't listened to since I started dancing a decade ago. I sat there mesmerized, listening to song after song, forgetting I was supposed to be dancing until a song began playing where the choreography was still in my body.

I got up, shook out my limbs, and started taking those steps that my six-year-old self remembered. I skipped the track back and started from the beginning, building a few more steps of the choreography until I had solid choreography for the first half of the song. When I couldn't remember the rest, I added new moves, moves that my younger self could only have dreamed of doing. In a way, I was bringing a piece of my past into the present. In a way, I was finally learning to accept the change.

Only when my mom poked her head through the open sliding glass door and asked me if I had plans for dinner did I realize how much time had passed.

"Is it that late already?" *Oh, are we talking now?*

My mom checked the clock in the kitchen. "It's 5:27. Was that from Sacramento Dance Academy Youth?"

I was surprised out of my anger that she remembered, even given our fight of the previous evening. "Yeah, it was. I haven't listened to these songs in ages, but I still remember some of the steps."

"Oh, of course you can. I swear you loved dancing more than life itself."

No, I didn't. Why would she say that? I thought back to dancing as a kid and could feel some of that love again. *Yeah, I guess I kind of did.* But it felt distant now. *Is that just because my dad had been the one to take me to watch my first professional dance production? Because now that he's gone, there's no one cheering as loudly?*

I didn't have the energy for another fight and if she was pretending that everything was fine, then so be it. "I don't have plans for dinner."

"Okay, then I'm going to make a big ol' salad."

I nodded my assent.

I sat down on the patio and stretched out my tired limbs, listening to the noises of the world—the crickets coming awake, the cars passing by on the freeway, people's voices from a few houses down. Maybe winter break would be all right.

After finishing my choreography, I joined my mom and Danny for a superficially pleasant dinner.

I took a quick shower and then went to my bookshelf to figure out the book referenced in the last text from the Underground Poet. I had been thinking about him a lot but still hadn't figured out his other book. I read the text again to try and jog my memory.

> "Such silence exists because we bury it away and pretend it's just a missing piece, a lacuna. So I'll sing this song until you find me, 'How sweet to be a cloud floating in the blue!'"

I grabbed *Will Grayson, Will Grayson* from the shelf and began flipping through it. John Green got high school emotions exactly right, while still adding that little bit of magic that made me hope for something better. *Something better...*

The text back to my Underground Poet started building in my mind, but I hadn't figured out the other book he was quoting. I read the part about being a cloud. Who would want to be a cloud?

Suddenly, it hit me. *Winnie-the-Pooh!* I went downstairs and looked at Danny's shelf of books. *There it is. When Pooh's on his adventure for honey and hopes it won't rain.*

I got out my phone and texted him.

> "Every little cloud always sings aloud. Not like they who walk up and down and wonder if it looks like rain, looking up at life thinking, 'Wow, I look much happier—I think this is the life I need to get!'"

If he was a Winnie-the-Pooh *character, who would he be? I'd obviously be Pooh; maybe he'd be Piglet? No...Eeyore? He's mentioned the sadness and the silence, as well as wanting to sing to banish the clouds.* But life wasn't that simple. It wasn't as glorious as Pooh finding a pot full of honey.

After I hit send, I scrolled on my phone for a while, my body on alert for the ding that meant I had a new text from the Underground Poet. Even though I knew it was silly to expect anything from him immediately, I craved it. I needed the validation that I was worth a response. And he seemed to think that I was.

When I got the familiar sense of self-loathing from watching people's Snapchat stories too long, I locked my phone and reached for my dad's book instead, flipping through the pages until I figured out which scenes I could adapt into a five-minute film.

I grabbed my laptop and began furiously writing a rough draft for my French project. I wrote until I had four pages of script. I smiled at my handiwork and wiped my sleepy eyes. I set my computer to the side and reached for my phone to text Rebecca my idea. Her ears must have been burning because I found an audio message waiting for me. She said:

> *"Hey...so sorry if this is awkward, but my parents are drunk and fighting and my grandmother decided to bring up my mom's green card yet again, so I'm working on my project...I feel like I've been researching for ages and I've got some good stuff, but I've got nothing to go on for the storyline. I'm so sorry. Here, I'll just send you an email with what I have. Tell me what you think or if we need anything else."*

I looked at the time, 2:32. I played the message again, unable to believe how normal it all sounded. And vulnerable, filling me in on her family drama. I checked my email and true to her word, she had sent the info. It was a lot. The girl had done her homework.

Full of new energy, I started plugging in the research I had with Rebecca's info and began crafting the scenes we would need. At four in the morning, I smiled to myself, satisfied, and fell asleep.

Danny let me sleep a glorious six hours before he was bouncing on my bed asking to make Wiffles. It was my dad's old recipe; a quick misspelling of waffles that we ended up using for all kinds of meals. Today was pigs-in-a-blanket.

He was my great little helper, grabbing all the ingredients, turning the stove on to medium heat, whisking the pancake batter. While Danny puttered, I poured myself some coffee and sat at the counter daydreaming.

I was back in the bookstore. The only lighting was from the streetlights outside. My Underground Poet was waiting for me. He took my hand, and we began to dance.

"Charlie!"

I snapped my eyes open. The pancake Danny had tried to flip had somehow ended up over the side of the pan and was sparking flames, sending wafts of smoke up from the burner. I helped my brother scrape the bad pancake away and then showed him how to get the spatula all the way under the pancake. I kissed his head and offered to do the next one.

"You know Dad had a trick where he didn't even use a spatula. You want to see?"

"Yes!" Danny laughed with a look of disbelief.

I poured some more batter into the pan and waited until it started to bubble. Then I lifted up the edge of the pancake with the spatula and started swishing the pan back and forth to get the pancake to slide. When it slid easily, I used a fierce sideways and upward motion to flip the pancake. After a few swishes, the pancake ended up on the floor and Danny and I dissolved into laughter.

Several lopsided pancakes and poorly executed rolls later, Danny and I tore into some pigs-in-a-blanket. I loved the flavor combination of pancake, sausage, and coffee. I smiled and clinked a pig-in-a-blanket with my brother's in "cheers."

Before I knew it, it was Christmas Eve and Danny was pulling me up to his loft bed to listen for Santa's reindeer.

"Shh, you have to be quiet or they'll hear you!"

Danny giggled with his pal, Oreo, but couldn't follow orders. "Oreo hears them. I want to hear them!"

"You will! Animals have better hearing, but if you listen hard, you'll be able to tell which reindeer is which. The sound of their hooves hitting the roof makes a different sound for each one."

Danny strained against the silence to try to hear.

"Maybe if we sing 'Rudolph the Red-Nosed Reindeer,' they'll let us know they're here?" I asked him.

Danny agreed and we began a very off-key rendition. When the song was over, I hugged him and said goodnight. "Remember, Santa can't deliver presents unless you're asleep."

Danny shut his eyes, then opened them again and told Oreo to go to sleep.

I left Danny's room and headed down to the kitchen. Our mom had stealthily pulled out the cookies Danny and I had made earlier that day and was taking huge bites out of them.

"Want to help?" she said around a mouthful. She offered me the plate of cookies.

"Cheers." I clinked cookies with her and ate one. After cookies, we moved onto the carrots. We took "reindeer-sized" bites and tossed them in the grass outside, sprinkling glitter around the patio for the reindeer magic. We headed back inside, took the rest of the plate of cookies, and moved to the couch in the living room to sit in front of the twinkling lights of the Christmas tree.

I tried to relax. *Come on, Charlie, this is normal, this is great. Mom and daughter hanging out enjoying the Christmas tree.* But I couldn't help side-eyeing my mom to see if she was feeling the same way. She was in the La-Z-Boy recliner, her feet resting on the footrest, her hands clasped lightly on her stomach. She seemed to be lost in a daydream, the twinkling lights of the tree lulling her to sleep. Maybe she was thinking of dad too.

"Hey, mom," I said softly.

She fluttered her eyes open. "I'm awake. Just enjoying the time with my daughter. We never get to do this."

I laughed involuntarily.

My mom's eyes opened up all the way. "You don't have to stay."

"No! Of course I want to be here. It's such a rare opportunity."

"You don't have to rub it in, Charlie. I know I work a lot. But I'm here now. Can't you just let it be for once?"

Heart hammering in my chest, I tried to relax, but the moment was ruined. I was too anxious. I crept quietly outside to the patio and started to dance.

It was strangely exhilarating to be dancing in the dark, in a way dancing for my mom even though she could barely see me. I must have danced that way for hours—no music, barely a sound, just the soft steps of my feet on the wood, my arms floating through the air, my head lost in the moment of what could be. The moment became a bridge uniting me on one side with my parents on the other.

I heard a noise behind me. My mom had gotten up from the chair and walked into the kitchen. I brought my arms down to my sides and stepped to the sliding glass door. I watched her go about her night routine—checking her phone for last minute messages, grabbing some water from the fridge. I watched in disbelief as she shut off the light and headed upstairs to bed. She never once looked in my direction. I was invisible.

I placed my hand on the sliding glass door, mentally reaching for her and the Christmas magic we used to have. I took a few steps back and saw the light flick on in her room upstairs. I was so close, yet I felt like we had never been further apart. I opened the sliding glass door and went back to the couch, heart in pieces.

Growing up, decorating the tree with my dad was my favorite part of Christmas. Sure, presents were great. But looking back on the memories, Christmas was more about the way the tree and the decorations brought the magic alive. The way the tree could sit alone in the dark, just a lighter shade of grey in the darkness. Then, with a flick of a button, the whole room came alive in brilliant colors.

The first weekend of December, my dad and I would spend the whole day together getting ready for Christmas. First, we would go to a tree lot to pick out the best, most beautiful tree. Then we would pull out all the decorations and deliberate where the best spot was for each ornament—the fire-glazed snowflake I painted when I was three or the book ornament, and so on. All the while, my mom would be stringing popcorn and cranberries along a thread, laughing at the crazy zeal with which her family enjoyed Christmas.

Danny's cries of "MERRY CHRISTMAS!" startled me awake. I wasn't sure when I'd fallen asleep or what time it was, but my mom brought me a cup of coffee and together we watched Danny organize all our presents. I blew a kiss to the sky for my dad and wished him a silent "Merry Christmas."

After presents, my mom disappeared upstairs and Danny and I made Christmas French toast. Danny dumped way too much cinnamon on his, but we laughed and drowned it in maple syrup and fresh whipped cream.

Shirking responsibility, I left the kitchen a mess and headed out caroling with our neighbors. Supposedly, my parents started this neighborhood caroling group when they first moved here. But of course my mom hadn't been out since my dad's death and I don't think my dad was ever much of a singer.

We met up with a few others from houses further down, including Violet, the owner of Underground Books, and Mr. DeVault and his husband. If I could adopt someone as family, I would have Violet be my other grandma. She had a mastermind for all things book-related and always gave me the inside scoop on what local authors were debuting. I hadn't had a chance with finals and my Winter Showcase to hang out in the library much this semester, so I enjoyed seeing Mr. DeVault again and being introduced to Jon. As we headed to the first house, we talked about the list of books I wanted to read over winter break, and he told me about his recent $200 book purchase (to which Jon playfully rolled his eyes) which included twelve books, two pairs of book-themed socks, a set of high-quality pencils, and a fox bookmark.

The first house we stopped at was that of Ms. Laney, a bed-bound senior who had lived in this neighborhood since she and her husband, now deceased, had moved in sixty-five years ago. As we began singing, we saw the blinds open, the window lift, and then the smile of her nurse and the slow wave of Ms. Laney. We sang her favorites: "Chestnuts Roasting on an Open Fire," "Silent Night," and "Carol of the Bells." We waved to the nurse and continued onward with some hope in our hearts.

We sang "Jingle Bell Rock" and "Deck the Halls" to the houses on the left and right. We stopped and sang for a group of neighbors sitting in lawn chairs on their porch. We stopped for cups of hot cocoa at the next house, grateful for something to warm our hands.

And that's when the fun ended. Danny decided he didn't want me anywhere near him and kept pulling out of my hand. To make matters worse, he spilled his hot cocoa on one of the carolers. Then, he ran across the street without looking. Luckily, no cars were coming, but he did not respond to my calling his name, so I just got more and more embarrassed and had to run after him.

By the time I caught him and grabbed his hand, I was out of breath and sweaty in my now-too-many layers.

"No!" Danny yelled. He tried to yank his hand away, but I held on firmly for the rest of the walk home. When we got inside, he dumped his coat and hat on the floor and ran upstairs, slamming the door. I picked up his things and hung them on the rack, suddenly bone weary and wanting nothing more than to just fall apart.

I headed up to my room, deciding on the way up that I would treat myself to a bubble bath. I started the water, stripped down to nothing, and slumped into the tub, breathing in the steam to calm the misery. I probably added too much bubble bath, but when the bath was full, the bubbles felt like shedding an old skin.

I stayed in happy bubble bliss until a ding from my phone brought me back. I dried my fingertips with quick dabs on my towel and groped the counter above me until I found my phone. I was relieved to see it was my Underground Poet. I considered what he would think of my reading his text while in the tub. Instead of feeling uncomfortable, I felt warm and giddy and gave in to the feeling. *I like how I feel when I am with him. Well, talking to him.*

> "Popping in and out of chalk pictures takes a lot of practice, so I've learned to be patient, learned to give less of a fuck. But even that has stopped working for me with you. By saying

you don't care if the world falls apart, in some small way you're saying you want it to stay together on your terms."

I read his quote several times to figure out his meaning. *He isn't saying that he wants to give less of a fuck about me, right? No, he's saying that he wants to define life by his own terms…and I think that includes being with me.* I snuggled down deeper in the bubbles and smiled to myself.

Popping in and out of chalk pictures has to be Mary Poppins, *and then those last two lines must be from* Will Grayson, Will Grayson.

I set my phone down and slunk farther into the bubbles, not sure what to do with this boy from the bookstore or if I even trusted myself to believe that maybe I was worth it after all.

He seemed to like me. He was continually showing interest and the lapse in time between texts made sense because we each had to figure out the books we were referencing. But it wasn't a real conversation. *But isn't it?* Even though we were using books to chat, I really felt like I was getting to know him. And I liked what I saw.

I replayed those fleeting moments where I had caught him in-between classes or saw him across the quad during lunch. *He's so cute, but it's more than that.* With him I didn't feel like I had to prove that I was cool or funny or pretty. He had stayed interested, at least interested enough to text me back, with every response I had sent his way.

And no matter what was going on in my life with Scott or even my brief interactions with Jared, my Underground Poet was always tugging my heart back to him. *And I think it's because in some small way he's saying it's okay to be me.*

PIVOT TURN

The rest of winter break, I thought about my Underground Poet's last message. More specifically, I tried to act like someone who knew what she was worth. I danced just for the pleasure of dancing. I played with Danny and Oreo, deciding to enjoy when he wasn't being a brat and not bring up when he was. One morning, I went for a run just to be out experiencing my neighborhood.

I left my watch behind so I wouldn't care about my pace. I was going to let my feet go where they wanted, and when I grew tired, I would let myself slow without shame. I really liked this particular loop around my neighborhood. It was just under three miles, so I knew it would be a push, but it was the kind of push I needed.

I stepped out under the marvelous trees and a shiver of excitement ran down my spine as I danced through the shadows their leaves painted on the sidewalk.

As I ran and marveled at the beauty all around me, I allowed my thoughts to drift back to the message from my Underground Poet. His first line was about jumping in and out of chalk pictures. As I jogged down the street, I jumped into that dream, building my dream house with the walkway full of lights from the house on the corner and with the front door from the house the next street over and with that big oak tree standing proudly in the front lawn next door.

His second line was about how you can't stop caring about others no matter the pain. You have to give a damn and that affords you some clarity about who you want in your life. I came to a full stop at a construction site of a new house, breathing deeply. I peered at the fence adorned with cornflowers and watched as a bee drifted from flower to flower. I was in love with this plant that was striving for life against all odds, and this bee who didn't care where the pollen came from. I could be that bee living in sunshine, passing in and out of the shadows of the flowers. I could be that plant willing to keep growing despite the obstacles around me.

I jogged away in a daze, positive that I now had an image for my relationship with the Underground Poet and ready to accept all he was offering.

I ran down the hill and into William Land Park. I took a few deep inhales and let them out in counts of three to slow my breathing and release the stitch in my side.

Down the path, I passed a tree with multiple low-hanging, almost-as-thick-as-a-trunk tree branches stretching in different directions, spreading big, green leaves over the sidewalk. It quickly became my own Secret Garden.

I made a loop around the park, watching all the families with their dogs, passing by lily pads sitting quietly on the water. I braced myself for the hill up to the light and headed home. As I turned on my street, I spent the rest of my energy in an all-out sprint to my house. I opened the door with my heart pounding, drenched in sweat and feeling something close to happiness.

I plopped on the floor of my living room and did some slow stretches. From my spot on the floor, I could just make out the time in the kitchen. 10:11. Perfect: I had an hour to finish stretching, shower, and bike to Tower Café where I was meeting Rebecca to work on our project. I had the house to myself since my mom took Danny on a playdate. I took a quick two-minute nap after my stretches and then blinked open my eyes and headed to the shower. All clean, I headed out the door.

Tower Café was a two-mile bike ride from my house, which meant that the ride was easy enough to propel me to bike rather than drive, but not easy enough that my poor quads didn't feel the burn from the run. I tried to enjoy the beauty of the trees as I biked and ignore how heavily I was breathing. I pulled to a stop at the bike racks outside the restaurant and headed inside to get us a table. By the time the waitress brought waters, Rebecca had walked in the front gate.

"I'm so sorry I'm late." Rebecca sat down, hanging her purse on the seat, and placing her laptop to the side of the table. She took a swig of water. "We were supposed to do a quick run-through, but then Clarabella twisted her ankle, and it was this whole big thing." She paused to take another sip of water and roll her eyes. "So anyway, sorry. I was able to do my research on emigration out of France." She set the water aside and reached for her laptop.

"Hey," I said gently. I placed my fingers on her laptop. Rebecca looked up at me, startled. "Are you hungry?"

She smiled, embarrassed. "Yes. I haven't eaten anything today."

"I haven't either. Let's maybe get an appetizer and then we can talk?"

"Tell me why I want mozzarella sticks."

I laughed. "Because they're delicious." I perused the menu. "I don't think they have them though. We'd probably have to go to Sampino's next door."

"Damn, I've never had one."

I slammed my menu closed. "Excuse me, what?" I laughed. "How have you never had a mozzarella stick?"

"You remember my mom. None of that was allowed for a ballet dancer."

I almost started. It was so strange for her to acknowledge our past so nonchalantly. "Okay, we need to change that." I opened back up the menu. "But maybe a Caesar salad for now?"

"That sounds perfect."

We fell silent as we decided on our entrées. I didn't know if Rebecca felt as nervous as I did. If she had been the Queen Bee, then at least I'd know where we stood. But it seemed like my old friend was sitting in front of me and that made me excited, but uncomfortable.

We awkwardly stared at each other for a few moments before the waitress came back to take our orders. Then we were truly alone, with no interruptions until our food arrived.

"So, um," Rebecca started, "how's dance going?"

I raised my eyebrows in surprise but decided to answer honestly. "It's been good. We just finished our Winter Showcase and now we're looking at summer. I still dance with Malcolm and Lela and we're building all our choreography around 'A Change Is Gonna Come.'" I reminded myself that I didn't need to explain more because Rebecca knew most of these things from way back when.

"Yeah, we're coming up on our Spring Recital." She started speaking in an uppity British tone. "The goal of dance is to transcend the dance, to transform the beauty of the art from dancer to audience, to feel the grace and ephemerality of life." She relaxed her voice back to normal, then paused while the waitress delivered our salads. "I'm just so over it."

I nodded and started eating. I didn't realize how hungry I was until I still hadn't said anything in response, my salad was gone, and Rebecca had made no visible dent in hers. I dabbed my mouth with my napkin, took a sip of water, and took a deep breath.

"If you could make the dance whatever you wanted for the recital, what would you do?"

Rebecca's eyes widened, and I thought at first that she might blow me off. Instead, she dabbed her mouth with her napkin and sat back in her seat. She crossed her arms. "I just want to shove all the ugly in my parent's faces. I want them to wake up and see the mess that they've made of their lives and what that's done to me."

"Me too." *Me too?*

"I buried all that stuff a long time ago, so I highly doubt it's worth it." She gave me a pointed look that made me think maybe she wasn't talking about her parents anymore.

Once she was finished, the waitress pulled away our salad plates and replaced them with our entrées. We let the silence settle between us as we ate. Then we left the vulnerability on the table and moved on to our project.

"So, I have an idea for our script."

Rebecca motioned for me to continue, and I told her about Jesus and Jean.

As a prolific author, my dad wrote stories set all over the world, but the series that gained him the most notoriety and won him the Pulitzer was the one set in Mexico about his friends, Jesus and Jean. He had spent many afternoons playing soccer with them while he lived there from the ages of seven to fourteen. He and Jesus would get a ragtag group of kids together for a game of soccer—kids on vacation, transplants like my dad, Mexican kids, whatever kind of kids; the park was a neutral zone.

One day, they were in the middle of a game when a beautiful, expensive, new Mercedes rolled by and parked at a house down the street. The players paused their game and glared at the car and its passengers. That was the first time they laid eyes on Jean, and they didn't like the French kid one bit.

The following weeks at school were hard for Jean. He was made fun of for being fancy, stuck-up, and having a funny accent. As much as my dad disliked him, he didn't like to see someone bullied. So, at one of the next soccer games, my dad brought Jean along. Jesus was adamant about not playing and got all the other players riled up and refusing to play. But my dad finally convinced him and once the game got started, no one cared where Jean was from; he was just the kid on the other team that shouldn't be left unguarded.

"Well, anyway, that was how the story went." I trailed off, acutely aware of how long I had been talking. I braced myself.

But instead of derision, Rebecca had this huge smile on her face. She nodded. "Keep going. What happened next?"

"Oh," I blushed and tucked a piece of hair behind my ear. "Well, after that Jean became best friends with Jesus and my dad. My dad would help them with English, Jesus would help them with Spanish, and Jean taught them French. Of course, since they were little boys, he taught them all the swear words so that when they were playing soccer they could roast each other in French and the other kids wouldn't know what they were saying."

Rebecca and I laughed together.

"That probably shouldn't go in our script though."

"No, definitely not," Rebecca snickered.

"So yeah, my entire time growing up, my dad always talked about those guys and how much he learned from them. He always wanted me to travel because he said it teaches you about the world and how much we have in common with each other, even though we may look different, speak different languages, or come from different backgrounds. I know they came to my parent's wedding, but my dad was really hoping to see them again…" *before he died.*

My eyes had slid down to the table and I started fidgeting with my napkin. I cleared my throat and tried to banish the tears from my eyes with a smile. "So, anyway, that's the idea for the script."

"Charlie, I think it's perfect."

All of a sudden, I was looking at my friend. It was the soft tone of her voice that held no trace of hostility and the way she used my name.

"Thank you." I looked down at the table, embarrassed, and flitted my eyes back to meet hers. Feeling a burst of spontaneity, I said, "I don't think you've called me by my name since elementary school."

In horror, I watched the spell break. Something cold and hard entered her eyes.

"Whatever, locket." She grabbed her phone and started immediately texting.

But I wasn't ready to give up yet. "Rebecca, hey."

She finished her text and took her time raising her eyes back to mine.

"What happened to us?"

"You mean, why did you replace me with Malcolm and Lela?" She set her phone down on the table with a clunk.

"Wait, what are you talking about?"

"I thought we were best friends, but then you stabbed me in the back by ditching me for them. It was always 'Malcolm this' and 'Lela that.'" She sat back in her chair and sighed. "And even when I tried to, like, join your new group, you shut me out."

A thousand thoughts rushed through my head. I felt sick, a deep gnawing pit in my stomach; I was so confused. "That's not how I remember it."

"Of course not."

I tried to go back in time and piece it together. *I lost my dad in sixth grade, so in middle school I was probably a mess and not a very good friend. But why would I push out my best friend and how come I can't remember?*

"So that's where Casey and Emily came in?"

Rebecca nodded. "They are awful, but at least they were there."

I felt like crying. "I'm so sorry. I didn't know. I wish you had told me."

Rebecca sniffed and sat up straighter, the Queen Bee replacing what had been my friend. "It's whatever at this point." She opened up her laptop.

"Well, I'm sorry," I said to the back of her screen. It felt like we had collapsed into a kaleidoscope and she was spinning away from me.

I grabbed my computer and opened it in silence. We worked for the next couple of hours, speaking occasionally and only as it pertained to our project.

I rode home with panting breaths. When I got home, I tried to dance the feelings away, but I was too physically exhausted for more exercise. So I grabbed *Will Grayson, Will Grayson* instead and read on the couch until I was hungry again.

I walked wearily upstairs and stuck my head in Danny's room.

"No girls allowed!" Danny yelled at me, poking his head over the railing of his loft bed.

I stopped at the doorway. "Well, why not?"

"Oreo doesn't like you."

That hit me harder than the news from Rebecca. *What's going on and why is it all my fault?* "Well, can you ask him why?"

"You ask him."

I shrank back a little at the tone in my brother's voice. I was too tired for this. I almost considered walking away. But instead, I took a deep breath.

"Oreo, I don't know what happened, but I'm sorry. Please forgive me." I looked back at Danny for some kind of acknowledgment, but he kept giving me that hard stare. I left an imaginary kiss for him on the beam of his bed. "I love you, bud."

I headed to my room, deciding I didn't care about dinner and that I wasn't going to bed tonight. I flipped open *Ishmael*.

I was finishing the final pages when I heard the front door open and heard Danny run down the stairs to meet my mom. *Good, she can tuck him in then.* Nothing on my shelf was calling my attention, but I had really enjoyed *The Golden Compass* and so decided to look up its sequel online.

At 11, my stomach became more pressing than the story, so I hauled myself out of bed. I poked my head out of my room and listened. Danny's light was off, as was my mom's, and the house was quiet.

I walked carefully to the kitchen, popped in some Pop-Tarts, heated up some hot cocoa, and rinsed a handful of grapes. Dinner of champions.

I snuck back upstairs and settled back into my book online, munching contentedly.

An hour later, I jumped out of bed when something thumped against my window. I stared hard, willing my heart to slow down. The thump came again, but this time followed by a low, "Charlie!"

Scott? What does he want from me now?

I climbed onto my bed again and opened the blinds. Scott was standing in the street, waving at me and sucking on his vape. I opened the window. "What are you doing?" I stage whispered.

"Come down with me!" he stage whispered back.

"Why?"

"Just come down with me, please."

There was something in the tone of his voice that tugged at my heart. My best friend was sad and he needed help. It was the only thing that would have worked tonight, given how we last ended things at my showcase.

But I wasn't ready to give in. "Put that shit away!" I whisper-yelled, pointing at his vape.

"Will you get over it?" He held his palms open like I was the one being ridiculous.

"Why are you so over it?"

He ran his fingers through his hair. "Charlie, the expulsion was last year, why are you so weird about this? Besides it happened to me not you, and I only got caught with the weed not with the selling."

"Yeah, that's why you're not in juvie!"

He took another drag and then put up his hands in defeat and tucked it in his pocket. "Don't worry, I brought something better!" He lifted up two Bangs and walked into the middle of the street and lay down.

I didn't think about what I was doing so I couldn't talk myself out of it. I pulled on a sweater, stuffed my feet in slippers, and tiptoed downstairs. I unlocked the door and closed it as quietly as I could, then half jogged to Scott and stared down at him. He leaned up a little to sip his Bang and motioned to the ground. I looked up and down the street again.

"We're going to die."

"No, we're not. Come down here."

After another few glances and hearing no cars, I acquiesced and sat down next to him. He handed me a Bang.

"Charlie, it's fine. Relax." He took another sip.

I took a big swig, a big breath, and lay down next to him. After a few minutes, I started to relax. Scott had that effect on me. I could never stay mad at him for long. "The stars are gorgeous."

"Mhm, I told you."

I leaned up awkwardly, took another sip, looked up and down the street again, and lay back down.

"Will you relax? We'll hear a car from a mile away. Besides, we live on a quiet street."

I sat up to take another quick look and then lay back down. *This certainly looks romantic.* I gave a quick glance in Scott's direction and was glad the night covered up these thoughts.

We lay there in silence for a long time. It wasn't like Scott to not have something to say. "So you brought me out in the middle of the night so we could stare at some stars?"

Scott shoved me playfully. "It's an adventure, Charlie. Stop pretending you hate it."

I don't hate it and that's the problem. I turned to look at him, but he continued staring straight up, his eyes scanning the stars. I envisioned myself kissing him, but quickly pushed away that thought. *C'mon Charlie, now's not the time.*

"Don't you ever just feel like you need to do something? Like not something big, just something different?" he said, almost to himself.

I looked back at the stars and tried to find the answers he was searching for.

"I guess I just dance when I get that feeling."

Scott took a deep breath and drummed his fingers on his chest. He didn't say anything else. I opened my mouth to offer some encouragement or ask a question, but nothing came to mind.

I was sleepy. I was hopped up on hormones. I laid my head on his shoulder. To my surprise, he grabbed my hand and entwined his fingers in mine. Of course, we'd held hands before but mostly when we were wrestling as kids or fighting for the remote. There was that moment at Jared's and there was this. This was different. They were rougher than I recalled. And bigger. My hand was dwarfed by his.

We saw the lights before we heard the engine and suddenly, we were scrambling out of the road to the loud horn of a car. We ran to the grass in front of my house and collapsed in laughter. We laughed until my sides hurt and Scott stopped snorting. Then we fell silent with the laughter lingering on our lips. We stared at each other for a few seconds, long enough for me to wonder what this meant and if it was my move.

He stood up. "Goodnight, Charlie. Thanks for the adventure." I waved back and watched him walk back to his house. I stayed there for minutes, wanting to run after him and kiss him but desperately afraid to do so. *Wasn't it just a few weeks ago that he didn't want me? So what was this?*

I emptied the rest of our Bangs in the grass and walked back inside. I put the cans carefully in the recycling so as not to make a sound and crept up the stairs trying to be as quiet as when I had left.

I stripped back down to my pajamas, and climbed in bed to continue my book. I looked at the page I was on, and I thought about Scott. I reread the line and my mind slipped back to Scott. I slammed my book shut, closed my eyes, and then opened the book, determined to keep fantasies inside the book I was reading.

Somewhere around 2:45 in the morning, my eyes started to dip, and I found I was no longer tracking the sentences on the page. My body was telling me to sleep, but my brain was screaming at me to avoid revisiting the events of the evening.

I grabbed my phone, dismissed the notifications for who liked my post on Facebook and who was live on Instagram, and reopened my conversation with my Underground Poet. He had written,

> "Popping in and out of chalk pictures takes a lot of practice, so I've learned to be patient, learned to give less of a fuck. But even that has stopped working for me with you. By saying you don't care if the world falls apart, in some small way you're saying you want it to stay together on your terms."

That's right, his lines were from Will Grayson, Will Grayson, *but I came up empty when I searched in* Mary Poppins. I scanned my bookshelf but didn't think it was there. I thought about going back downstairs, but nixed that idea. I scrolled the young adult section on the Barnes & Noble website, but it was all a blur. So I cheated and looked up his quote.

For the first time in my life, the internet didn't immediately reward me with the answer. I had to try a bunch of different searches to find it. And then when I did, I wanted to read the surrounding passage. It was an adorable young adult novel called *My Most Excellent Year*. Amazon had the first two chapters available, which made me want to read this book in one sitting. I purchased the e-book and read into the morning, pausing only for a break to pee and to grab a cup of coffee. The book was pure gold. It should have had a halo and been called an angel. As soon as I was finished, I wanted to reread it. It was the perfect complement to my Underground Poet's *Will Grayson, Will Grayson* quote.

I didn't wait to savor the story or wake up or anything. I took all the feelings I had for Scott and pummeled them into my Underground Poet. *My Most Excellent Year* made me believe love and magic were possible.

I grabbed the next book I wanted to use, *The Art of Racing in the Rain*, and typed. I hoped he'd know how into him I was. That I wasn't trying to second guess myself or wait for the other shoe to drop. That I was jumping in with both feet.

> "One trick I learned is to begin by closing my eyes and imagining candy apples and steam calliopes and when I open my eyes, the chalk picture is waiting for me. That way I don't panic when something unpredictable happens. That way I don't make the mistake of reacting at speed."

RUNNING MAN

What was it about Mondays that made time move faster when it wasn't supposed to but not fast enough with the boring stuff? School was so slow, but then in the rush of dancing at the Academy to picking up Danny from his afterschool program to making dinner to getting ready for bed, I forgot to prepare for my French project check-in the next morning.

I ended up dilly-dallying too long in the shower thinking about what my Underground Poet was thinking, which made me late getting Danny to the bus. I had to run to make it by the second bell, which had me way more anxious than usual. I was wholly unprepared, therefore, for Rebecca to be absent in French class, leaving me to answer how we were doing on our project.

"I...we..." I stammered, trying to get my brain to find something coherent to say.

The door swung open, to my great relief, and Rebecca walked into class.

She didn't look in my direction and sat down with her perfect, Queen Bee airs.

"Perfect timing, Rebecca. Charlie was just giving us an update on your project," Madame Allemand said in French.

"Pardon, Madame," she said, bowing her head submissively. Then she looked up unafraid and replied for us in French. "As you know, we're doing French immigration into Mexico. We're feeling good on the research and the script. All that's left is to film."

"I look forward to hearing more in the coming weeks. Who's next?"

I tried to catch her eye and say thank you, but she didn't look my way.

For the rest of class, we worked on past participle conjugation. I was too tired to focus and despite my best efforts, I kept thinking about Scott. I kicked myself for missing my chance. I trembled at the forbidden thought: *He wants you*. No, I wouldn't think of it. It couldn't possibly be true. But the Underground Poet might want me. I shook my head away from the daydream and began diligently copying the French verb conjugations from the board.

If I thought I could escape from my thoughts in English class later in the morning, I was wrong—we were dissecting Hemingway, and every line seemed to be prescribing relationship advice.

By the time I made it to lunch, I sat down on the brick wall with a sigh. Snuggled up between my two giant friends made me feel a little bit better. That is, until they started talking about Valentine's Day.

"Ugh, can we not?" I laughed, forking and eating a grape from my fruit salad.

"Please do not start on your soapbox about the horrors of Valentine's Day!" Lela bumped me with her arm.

It was true: I hated Valentine's Day. *We should tell people we love them every day. Why is it always teddy bears and chocolate? Why not late-night talks with friends? Or secret texts encoded with the lines from my favorite books?* I could think of so many other things more romantic.

I realized Lela was still going on a rant against my supposed rant. "It's fun to get gifts! Since you're not dating anyone, get me a Valentine's gram."

"Well, maybe I will."

"It's not only about romantic love. Unless you love me." She gave me a deadpan stare before we dissolved into giggles.

"Not gonna lie, that would be pretty hot," Malcolm laughed, taking a bite of a chicken nugget.

"True, but you can't say that," I laughed, pushing him with my elbow.

"Hey, I have gotten way better," he put his hand over his mouth as he finished his bite.

"So?" I arched my eyebrows at him.

Lela shook her head at Malcolm. "While I do agree that seeing two ladies in love is a beautiful thing, Malcolm, you have got a long way to go. I still haven't forgotten, you know."

Malcolm hung his head, playfully embarrassed. "I know, I know. I'm not gonna mess up again and say bi isn't real."

I looked to Lela. "How is your girl by the way?"

She had lined up all her peas in a circle around her mashed potatoes. "She's good. It's hard not seeing her that often, but we're making it work. She is kidnapping me tonight. Won't tell me where we're going."

"That's so cute." I finished my fruit salad and opened up a protein bar.

A few minutes elapsed as we ate our food and people-watched.

Lela turned to Malcolm. "Do y'all have plans?"

Malcolm shrugged. "I mean, we've talked about it, but we don't have anything yet."

Lela shook her head teasingly. "I still don't know how your girl's put up with you for all these years."

"You've both got your girlfriends and I'm over here like," I swayed back and forth and sang Eric Carmen's refrain, "All by myself!" We all started laughing, but I stopped singing when it felt too real. The conversation rolled into other topics, but I sat there quietly until the bell rang, no longer hungry.

In my afternoon classes, a thought started percolating in my head that I just couldn't shake. Every Valentine's Day, our local bowling alley held an eighteen and under event. Scott and I had been going every year since we were kids, but now my silly brain was trying to convince me I should ask him as my date.

It was stupid. It was crazy. But maybe this was one of the times he didn't have a girlfriend.

It was possible.

I wanted to puke, but I couldn't get the thought out of my head. All through Algebra II and Chemistry, it kept whispering into my mind. I would momentarily forget about it, caught up in some equation, and then it would enter suddenly, leaning on my lungs and making it hard to breathe.

I left it at the door when we got to the Academy. It was our turn to perform a piece of our Summer Showcase and I needed to be one hundred percent focused. We had decided to go with the routine that was the most complete—the change as you grow older and loss of innocence. Malcolm pulled up some good ol' Lauryn Hill on his phone and we held our pose for the opening four-count.

As the beat faded out at the end of our set, the class gave respectful applause before Jules opened up the floor for feedback.

Lina started us off, "Yeah, so I love what you guys are doing. I think you are portraying the acceptance aspect of change well, but I also feel like there's some, like, oomph missing. I've seen you guys dance separately, so I know that if you keep working it's gonna be great."

I did my best not to give her the lockdown.

Jules nodded and called on someone else.

"I gotta agree," Nikki said. "The moves are good, but everything just falls a little flat. Like Malcolm, you're the king of flips and we only got one from you. I think you guys can push it a little bit and take it to that next level."

"I'll hop in," Jules said. "I think you've got a good foundation for where you want to go, but you aren't there yet. You guys are good enough to make that happen. Charlie, you need to relax! Loosen up those joints. This is supposed to be fun. Malcolm, it's not all about flips, but you do seem a little hesitant. Lela, I want to see you use the space, really make us feel this change. Overall, well done. Continue working out the kinks and you guys will be solid at the showcase."

As we climbed into my car, Malcolm, Lela, and I shared a look.

"Well, that was different," Lela said.

Malcolm snorted. "I think that's the closest Jules can come to telling us we ain't shit. We're really going to have to step it up."

"Ten out of ten, would not recommend." *That was so embarrassing. I really thought we were doing well.*

My friends let go of their anxiety and started texting their ladies, planning the rest of their night, leaving me alone with the dreaded thought of Scott. I tried turning on the music to drown it out, but to no avail. It was either think about that awful critique or think about what I was going to do about Scott tonight.

So, it made it all the crazier when I got home and saw Scott sitting on my front porch. *Man, he looks good.* His hair was still wet and kinky from the shower, my favorite. He was leaning back on the steps in a sprawled, nonchalant way that was so suave. I swallowed nervously and tried to play it off with a smile.

"Hey, Scott, what's up?"

He got up from the steps and pulled me into a hug. I relaxed into his arms with a smile. *Are we finally on the same page? Can we continue from the other night?*

He pushed me gently away and looked into my eyes. "You've got to help me find a new outfit for my date tonight."

I was so far in the fantasy that at first I actually thought he was still talking about a date with me. I sputtered. *Stupid, Charlie. I haven't asked him yet. He's not talking about me.*

I stepped past him, trying to cover the way my face fell in disappointment, tears brimming. "And what's this one's name?" I forced a laugh, still not looking at him.

"Oh c'mon, I'm not that bad."

I whipped around and gave him the lockedown. He acquiesced. "Her name is Claire. And I need to impress her because this one is gorgeous."

Another new one then. I looked him up and down. "Since when do you have to look good to go bowling?" I continued up the stairs.

"So about that."

I turned back to look at him, halfway up the steps.

"My grandma is not happy with me about my grades, but she couldn't say no to our annual V-day thing."

"So you told her you were going bowling with me but you're actually just going to ditch me?" I crossed my arms, heart racing.

"C'mon. You're not that upset, are you?"

I forced all the icky feelings away and covered it in a smirk. "Well, she'll refuse to go out with you if you show up looking like that." *But I wouldn't.* "Let me change real quick."

I jogged up the front steps to my house and disappeared inside. As I changed, I considered how crazy it was that I could be distraught over Scott and excited about whatever this was with my Underground Poet. But there wasn't time to think, and my Underground Poet wasn't real. Scott was the one standing on my steps.

I rushed back out and directed us to the Arden Fair mall.

We sat in silence for a while before he grabbed his phone and found our song, "Kryptonite" by 3 Doors Down. My heart melted a little bit more as I looked at him and we shared a knowing smile. He turned the volume all the way up and rolled down the windows so we could belt it to the world.

When we got to the mall, it took us about as long to find a parking spot as it did to get there. Then, I had to drag him into stores he'd never go in to get the right outfit. I knew he was being stubborn because he knew I liked it. It was so easy being with him, him being aggravating, me laughing.

"Okay, so what do you think about this?"

I was sitting on a chair outside the dressing room at Abercrombie & Fitch. I looked up at Scott, who had his arms open wide.

"Buy it, buy it!" I took his picture and laughed at the terrible design of the shirt.

"But does it look good, or does it *look good*?" He raised his eyebrows a bunch of times.

I snorted. "It looks amazing."

Scott disappeared back inside the dressing room and put on the next outfit. When he came back out, he posed like Superman. He stepped back in the dressing room and then popped back out, showing me his guns. He disappeared again, quickly returning for me to find him popping his butt out and flicking his wrist in the air. I laughed with tears streaming down my face. He disappeared and put on a new outfit before strutting in front of me, growling at me like a sexy cat. I'm not sure how long we were in there laughing or how many pictures I took.

"Okay, seriously, what about this? No? C'mon, don't give me the lockedown. I thought this looked pretty good! Aye, fine." He grumbled and went back into the fitting room.

He was not going home with another white t-shirt on my watch.

The next time he came out, he wore a long-sleeved navy dress shirt and a pair of dark jeans.

I bit the inside of my lip and tried not to blush. "She's dumb if she doesn't love it."

Even if he wasn't wearing it for me, I'd still be the reason he bought it, and that was kind of the same thing. He flashed me the smile that I loved and closed the door to put back on his clothes.

We dipped into Foot Locker for a new pair of Vans and swung by Macy's for a simple silver men's bracelet, and then he hightailed it to Land Park Lanes so he could get rid of me.

I'm pretty sure he didn't even bring the car to a complete stop. I was shoved out, what's-her-name was invited in, and then I was alone, looking up at the giant bowling pin glowing against the night.

There wasn't even a notification on my phone to distract me. It was just me, myself, and all my anxiety about being alone. Even the thought of my Underground Poet didn't help. I briefly considered texting him and inviting him out tonight, but my confidence wavered. *Nope, I just can't. He hasn't texted me a response back yet, and I can't just be like, "Hey, what's up?" That would ruin everything. He might not be that perfect.*

The thoughts about Scott earlier in the day flushed me with shame. How silly that I thought he would ever choose me.

Am I even worth melting into someone's arms? To have someone sweep me off my feet? I'm probably kidding myself to think the Underground Poet could be that person.

Whoever he was, we'd have a great time, but there would come that inevitable point of the night when I would look at him standing there, my bright light against the darkness, and I'd have to tell him that my life had existed for so long behind a shadow that I had missed the sunrises and sunsets. He'd try to convince me that this could be real, and I would shake my head sadly and walk away.

I ran my fingers through my hair, sighed, and entered the double doors. That amalgamated smell of old shoes, French fries, and floor wax bombarded me and made me smile despite myself.

Most of the lanes were filled with people I didn't recognize, but I caught a glimpse of a girl from my Chemistry class. *Maybe she'd let me join her group?*

I headed for the shoe counter and bopped my head to the music as I waited in line. Looking around, everyone seemed so happy. *It can't be that hard to be like them, right?*

"Seven and a half," I told the cashier when I finally arrived at the front. She slapped the shoes down on the counter and stuck the wristband to my right wrist that declared to the world in neon green that I was a minor.

I pulled the wristband gently away from the hair on my wrist and hooked the shoes in my fingers, trying not to grimace as my fingers slipped in like butter. *Don't think about the thousands of feet who have used these shoes before.* I shivered in disgust. Walking to the closest seat to put my shoes on, I noticed an argument in the arcade room.

It took me a second to realize that I was looking at a fight between Rebecca and Colton. Again. *Why would she have gotten back with him? He really messed up if he took her here instead of something nicer.*

They were alone in the arcade so no one else seemed to notice. They were standing close, speaking with a lot of wild arm movements. But it was different than the usual show. This time it was Colton who seemed angry and jealous and Rebecca who was standing her ground.

I looked around and found the source of contention. It looked like Rebecca had been talking to someone else. I rolled my eyes.

Rebecca had had enough. She ran away, tears streaming down her face.

I gave a final disgusted look to Colton and followed her across the bowling alley, but lost her in the crowd. After a few minutes, I decided that rather than force myself to make new friends, I was using Rebecca as an excuse. *Stop being a coward, Charlie.* But first a drink. So, I turned around and headed to the bar.

My wristband afforded me one free virgin beverage. I chose a Shirley Temple. I'm pretty sure the bartender took out his anger at being alone on Valentine's Day chaperoning a kids' event on the soda. It had more ice cubes than liquid, was filled to the brim so that it was impossible to move without spilling, and it tasted like fizz with a splash of cherry. Sipping my drink and trying not grimace at the taste, I left the snack bar and headed to the lanes. As I sipped my drink, I lost my courage to join a random group and decided instead to pee.

After doing my business, I took a seat on the counter, and hoped without hope that my phone would save me with notifications.

"Ah!" I screamed involuntarily as the stall before me banged open and I came face to face with a tear-stricken, red-eyed Rebecca. Without a word, she disappeared back into the stall.

The only sound that could be heard were the pins crashing in the lanes outside and the generic pop music blaring everywhere. I hopped off the counter, grabbed some toilet paper from another stall, and held it underneath Rebecca's door. She took it.

After a few minutes, the door inched opened. Rebecca was sitting on the top of the toilet, her feet on the toilet seat.

I looked at her in silence while she looked everywhere else but me. I didn't want to take up the space when it was her space to use. But as tears kept falling, I said, "He's not worth it, you know. The tears."

Rebecca cried more but nodded.

"You're worth more than this."

Rebecca made a noise between a hiccup and a laugh and used the tissue to blow her nose. "You know the stupid part is, that guy is my brother's friend. I've known him since I was a baby. But Colton's always been such a jerk that I had to defend myself based on principle."

"That makes sense. But you know what doesn't make sense?" Rebecca shook her head. "Why the bartender doesn't know how to make a Shirley Temple. I swear, that was the worst drink I've ever had in my life."

Rebecca started laughing despite herself.

"Here, I'll go get you one. It's awful."

Rebecca snorted. "Okay."

"Stay here. Don't go anywhere."

In five minutes, I was back with two new Shirley Temples.

She took a sip. "Oh no." She laughed, taking another sip, and squeezing her eyes. "How hard is it to mess up a Shirley Temple?"

"Okay good, it's not just me," I laughed. We sipped our drinks, each taking a sip and bursting out laughing at the other's face. We started making it game, taking sips like our Shirley Temples were the most delicious things in the world. By the end of our cups, we were sitting side by side on the bathroom counter and talking about the graffiti on the walls like it was our life fortune.

"Oh, this one's good." I cocked my head as I tried to read the angled scrawl. "'You are worth the stars.'"

"Yeah, but why only the stars? Why not the moon?"

"Or the whole night sky?" I laughed and tipped an ice cube into my mouth.

"Or how about this one? 'Vegans suck.' And then underneath, 'Not as much as your mom.' Nice and classy, don't you think?"

"Why's everyone so mad at vegans? Let them eat their vegetables."

"I know, right? Carrots are my fave."

I looked at Rebecca in shock. "No way. Like of all the vegetables, carrots are what you go for?"

"Oh yeah. I would die for a good purple carrot. None of those baby orange Cheetos. I want the good stuff."

I burst out laughing. "Baby Cheetos. That's the best thing I've ever heard."

The bathroom door smacked open and a group of three girls walked in laughing. They stopped abruptly when they saw us. Rebecca and I hopped off the counter and walked by them feeling like they caught us doing something wrong.

Outside the bathroom and back in the chaos of the bowling alley, Rebecca and I looked at each other. She smiled at me and then waved and walked away. I didn't know if we were friends again, but maybe we were no longer ex–best friends.

I walked back to the front of the bowling alley and looked at the time on my phone. I'd only been here an hour. Scott would be on his date for a long while still and I couldn't call Fran or my mom without throwing Scott under the bus. But I did consider it.

Instead, I looked up the closest scooter to rent and found one on the corner next to Jack in the Box. I left the alley and walked up the street. It took me a minute to figure out how to put my mom's credit card in the app, but finally I was on my way home.

As soon as I was inside my house, I sighed in relief and plopped on the couch.

My heart skipped a beat when I saw I had a new message from my Underground Poet.

> "Don't panic. Listen. Pretend you are a dog like me and listen to other people rather than steal their stories. Listen for the whisper of red flakes falling from my red heart."

Never tell someone not to panic. My heart shuddered and I started second-guessing everything. *What's he saying? Have I missed something?* That part about "stealing people's stories" felt like a slap in the face.

All the happiness of my time with Rebecca blipped out of existence and I was suddenly confronted with what a fool I had been. *First Scott, now this.*

I went back to the beginning of our conversation and suddenly it all became so clear. I had been reading his messages as sweet and insightful and caring. But he was trying to be a teacher to this poor little girl who needed love and he had gotten fed up.

And because I was suddenly wracked with shame, I looked up where his quote was coming from. *He figured out I was quoting* The Art of Racing in the Rain *and then used...Beloved, of course.* I locked my phone, lip trembling, trying not to cry out of embarrassment and resentment.

I opened my phone and read the text again, thinking maybe I'd gotten something wrong. But no, his message rang loud and clear. *I was cute but just a moment in time for him, nothing more.*

Fine, White Teeth *by Zadie Smith it is.* We had studied a section of it in English class ad nauseum. I felt like Toni Morrison would approve of her work being used in conjunction with Smith. This was no light undertaking. Smith's work was laden with history and the complexity of a people transplanted. If anyone knew what Smith was talking about it, it was Morrison. I texted him back.

> "Beloved. He said it, but she did not go. No talking will change this. Roots will always be tangled. And roots get dug up."

*I never asked him to be the one to save me. I just thought...*I couldn't finish the thought. It hurt too much.

My phone vibrated. *He texted me back already?* I was more annoyed than surprised that he had figured out my quote so fast. *But maybe he cheated too, and looked it up online.*

> "Funny thing when you talk about roots, really we're all just branches without roots. Life is not a line, but a circle. That is why you cannot read fate; you must experience it."

The heat flooded my face. *What have I been doing if not trying to experience something!* "I don't have anything! I just wanted..." *you.* I couldn't say the last word. My stomach curled in knots and I felt my face dip into the lockedown. He was basically telling me to stop living in books and step up to the real world.

I got up and paced the room. I didn't want to look up his quote, but I also didn't want to let him win, so I cheated again.

Four impatient taps on website links later, I found the lines were from Zora Neal Hurston's *Their Eyes Were Watching God*. I couldn't allow myself to soften at having loved this book. Instead, I dove straight into Sylvia Plath.

When my dad died, I was obsessed with Plath. My mom made me talk to a therapist about his death, but I always felt that books better understood what I was feeling. As I texted the Underground Poet back, I felt like the words flowed through me. It wasn't my voice, but the voices of a thousand characters.

> "Funny that you're talking about life when this whole story started with Death. What need has Death for a cover, and what winds can blow against him? Whatever this is has failed. So I feed these pages into the night wind, watch them flutter away, like a loved one's ashes, to settle here, there, exactly where I would never know, in the dark heart of Sacramento."

Can't be anything more final than calling him Death from The Bell Jar. I threw my phone on the couch.

My phone vibrated. *Or not.*

> "With you, a wonderful future beckoned and winked like a great fig tree. I wanted you to choose me but instead I was

left with figs wrinkled and black, plopping to the ground at my feet."

I couldn't do this anymore. His line about wanting me to choose him didn't make sense with the rest of his imagery, couldn't do enough to save him. *Why can't I just have the last word? Why is there always someone there to remind me how much I don't matter?* The tears started falling.

If I'm looking for something final, there it is. We had a nice run, but now I'm just a dead piece of fruit on the ground for him to stomp on. I need to dance.

I didn't know how many hours I spent trying not to feel and simply dance when my mom's bedroom light blinked on and a few seconds later I saw her approaching me through the sliding glass door. I stopped dancing but left the music running. It wasn't loud enough to wake her up, so I wasn't sure why she was here.

She was still fully dressed. She looked at her watch. "Darling, it's past midnight. You okay?"

I looked down and noticed how heavy my breathing was. I was tired, but I was also still angry and needed to keep moving so that I didn't collapse into tears.

"Yeah, I'm just trying to finish these pieces for the showcase."

"Which showcase? Obviously, it can't be Winter, but isn't the Summer Showcase still four months away? I'm sure you still have plenty of time to dance in the daylight." She gave me a nice smile and I wanted to be nice, but I had nothing left in me to give.

So all I said was, "Yeah."

She gave me a look that only made me more annoyed. "I'm just worried about you."

"Well, don't be."

She cocked her head. "As a mom, that will never change. That's one thing you can't know until you have kids of your own."

"I'm not going to have kids. They're just nuisances that drain all your resources."

"Oh, darling! Where is that coming from?" She searched my face.

I gave her a hard stare.

"Charlie," she started to say, but I cut her off.

"I have to finish this song. Please go away." Then, under my breath, "Just like you always do."

I looked from the ground up into her eyes and was shocked to see she was crying. *Wait, did something I say actually get to her? Maybe I went too far.*

She closed the sliding glass door and let me be.

I saw myself running after her and apologizing. Instead, I took a deep breath that came out in a sob, and started the choreography from the top.

FREEZE

March stepped to the fore and brought midterms right along with it. I always felt like midterms were a sneak attack. No matter how hard I worked, I was still behind. My mom and I hadn't talked in weeks, and besides, she was embroiled in a new case that kept her away longer, which only piled more responsibility on me to take care of Danny. And that was on top of all the choreography I still needed to practice for the Summer Showcase. Each morning, I gave myself barely enough time to say goodbye to Danny at the bus stop before I ran to my car.

Today, I made it to English by the second bell, which set up my whole day to fail. I needed to be seated by the first bell, but that's just how it was.

I could barely pay attention in my classes. The whole morning, my brain screamed at me that the information we were going over was important, but I could not focus. I was too stressed about school, thinking too much about my failure with the Underground Poet, and feeling overwhelmed by a general sense of dread. Even running into Rebecca in the halls didn't faze me. I gave her a cursory nod and a small wave—such had become our norm since the bowling alley—and then put my head down and headed to my next class.

By lunch, I was so full of bad energy that I blew off my friends and ditched the rest of my classes, getting a pass from the nurse to go home. I texted my mom that I was cramping so she needed to get Danny from school. I figured she would care more about my physical discomfort than my emotional fatigue, so I lied. *So ditching my friends is suddenly okay? Oh, shit. How are they going to get to the Academy without me? Well, too late now.*

On my way home, the tears came out of nowhere and poured so hard I could barely see the road. By the time I walked through my front door, I was numb and exhausted. I avoided all mirrors because I knew that even the lockedown wouldn't save me from these feelings.

I dumped my things at the base of the stairs, opened up Netflix, and chose the first action flick they recommended: *Jason Bourne*. I was in the mood for some gritty violence playing at the loudest volume.

All three movies had been consumed and I was entrenched in a black hole of TikTok videos when the front door opened and Danny ran into my arms.

"Can we go swimming at Scott's house?" he said, looking up at me.

I sighed and rubbed my eyes. "Bud, you don't know how to swim yet."

"Scott can teach me!"

"I don't think so, bud, it's way too cold."

But Danny was already running over to Scott's house to ask. I looked up at the sky. *Can't I just be in my own misery without adding Scott to it?*

I dragged myself upstairs to grab our bathing suits and followed Danny down the sidewalk, through Scott's open front door, and into his backyard. Danny was hard to say no to, so minutes later, we were all standing in Scott's backyard, lathering on sunscreen. I averted my eyes from staring at a shirtless Scott and paid extra-special attention to making sure all of Danny's exposed skin had a layer of white.

My cheeks burned as Scott watched us. I sighed in relief as Scott turned his back on me and waded into the heated pool.

"All right, Danny, join me in the water," Scott said.

"Charlie, make sure Oreo's okay." Danny pointed at "Oreo," and took hesitant steps into the water towards Scott.

I nodded dutifully and entered the pool after him, trying to pretend like I knew what I was doing. After a couple of minutes I stopped trying to "talk" to Oreo and looked over at Scott and Danny. They seemed fine, so I allowed myself to relax. Tipping my face to the sky, I let my feet float to the surface, and I closed my eyes.

A sweet memory with my dad trickled in. He was teaching me how to swim, supporting my torso with one hand while I kicked and practiced my strokes.

Danny bumping into me broke my concentration. He was in a full blown meltdown and was yelling at Scott. Danny never yelled and he would never yell at Scott. *What the hell happened?*

"Danny!" I was shocked.

But my little brother ignored me and continued grappling with something in the water until he had climbed up the steps. I looked to Scott.

Scott shrugged. "Minor freak out."

"No, it isn't!" Danny yelled, marching out of the pool. "C'mon Oreo." He reached for Oreo's "hand" and stuck his tongue out at us.

"Danny!"

He turned away from me and went to a corner of Scott's yard to be alone.

I whirled on Scott. "Explain!"

"He just freaked out about drowning." He climbed out of the pool and wrapped the bottom half of his body in a towel; I followed suit. We sat down on the grass. "A little more complicated since he kept telling me Oreo was drowning, but it's all the same."

This is so not what I need right now. And how come I can't stop looking at how good Scott looks?

I turned my gaze to Danny. *What is going on with him lately?*

"Charlie, it's not a big deal. This is totally normal." Scott ran his fingers through his hair, fluffing his curls.

"Is it?"

"Yeah, I'm pretty sure I freaked out multiple times with Toby."

Toby...Toby, oh, Toby! "That's right! I totally forgot about her."

"Like I know you're there for Danny as much as you can be, but he still probably feels very alone. I needed someone my age when my parents left for Afghanistan the first time, you know, and he probably does too."

It made sense, but something still didn't feel right. "So that's it? He just started freaking out?"

"Yeah, I don't know. I was supporting his stomach so he could practice the breaststroke, and I glanced at you doing your little twirls in the water over there." I started, looking up at him with red cheeks. He laughed. "And then all of the sudden Danny was flailing and saying Oreo was drowning."

"And I was supposed to be watching Oreo, so this is my fault too," I whined, putting my head in my hands. I was trying to process it all, but I was also suddenly reeling with the fact that Scott had been watching me. *Is he saying I'm cute or is he making fun of me?*

Scott rubbed my back. "It's okay, Charlie. Danny will bounce back. He's gonna be fine." My body came alive with his touch. I stiffened reflexively and then relaxed and let him comfort me.

He stood up, slicking the rest of the water off his body. I looked at Scott and fought the urge to fall for him like always, to see all the sweet and wonderful and forget about the rest. But it was no use. I was a goner. He waved goodbye and headed inside.

I watched him walk away, sighing with yearning, and then left with Danny through the side gate. Danny refused to let me hold his hand and ran down the sidewalk ahead of me despite my calling after him. Instead of going inside, I went and lay down in my backyard. I resisted the urge to do anything but look at the sky. I lay there until the sun dipped below the horizon and all I could see were stars. I lay there until goosebumps appeared on my arms and I was shivering.

When the sliding glass door opened, I figured it was my mom coming out to yell at me about something.

But instead it was Lela.

There was no hiding from anything today.

Lela grabbed one of the outdoor chairs and sat down without a word. I looked back up at the night sky and we stayed like that for a while. She asked no questions; there were no pointed accusations. She looked at me, sipped her water, and waited.

I thought about trying to blow her off again, but the anger and the pity that had gotten me this far had dissipated. Now I was tired and hurting. And my history with Lela, not just as friends, but as dancers, made it impossible to tell her anything but the truth.

Thoughts streamed through my head like a movie reel, too fast to understand the full picture. There was so much I needed to say, so much I still didn't understand.

I sat up. "I'm angry." Lela nodded like she understood. I kept going. "Since my dad died, it's just been me. All me. All me to take care of Danny. And who's taking care of me? Nobody." I was embarrassed that last part came out more like a wail, but I pressed on. The words tumbling out like dancers in a studio.

"And this whole time, I've been trying to be the good daughter that I'm supposed to be, and that means trying to forget he's dead. Be like my mom and move on. But that's messed up, right? Like, my dad died. I'm supposed to feel that. But it's too much. I don't want to feel it. I can't feel it alone."

My throat got tight, and I couldn't keep talking. I felt like I wasn't making sense, and I knew I sounded pathetic, but I couldn't stop. All the worries and anxiety of my life were now at Lela's feet.

"I'm so mad," I continued. "Why don't people love me? Why isn't my mom home? What does Scott want? Why is Danny mad at me? Why can't I do this stupid routine about my dad?" *What did I do to push the Underground Poet away?*

I cried hard, and then I cried harder. I tried to stop crying, but that only resulted in me hiccupping and not being able to breathe. Lela came over and sat down, rubbing my back until my throat stopped burning and I found my way back to almost-normal breathing.

But I still had more to say. "I can't change my mom or Danny or Scott or anybody, but I can't do this routine on my dad, either. It feels stale and awkward. Because I'm mad at him too. Because he left me. But how messed up is that?"

Lela pulled me into a hug. I resisted and broke away. She let me go.

After a moment she said, "You should be angry. Your dad was stolen from you and your mom left you alone." Her words made it hard to breathe. "And that's awful, but you didn't have to do it alone. You still don't."

I looked at her sharply, suddenly defensive and not interested in anything she had to say.

"We missed you today. I'm not saying that to make you feel bad, although we do need to have some words about how you made us get to the Academy on our own. I bring that up because Malcolm and I have always had your back. But you never let yourself use us. It's like you choose to be alone rather than let us help you face the pain."

She was right. *Why do I feel like I have to do everything myself? I was mad at my mom but then here I was doing the exact same thing.*

Lela held my gaze. "Honestly, Charlie, if you had been using dance as a release, you would have realized how hard it's been for Malcolm and me too. You think it's easy for Malcolm as a young black man, or for me who's from a tribe that is barely recognized by the government? It's really fucking hard, but we're doing it. We promised each other that we'd face the trauma, and we're using dance to figure out how to do that."

I swallowed my tears, wanting nothing more than to disappear. It was hard facing her words. I didn't like the version of myself she was presenting. I thought of myself as a good friend. But look how much I had missed.

Lela wasn't done. "Dance is this incredible tool to feel, but instead you've used it to numb. I see you when you step into the studio. Your back gets a little straighter, your mouth a little more resolute. You're like a soldier entering battle."

Line after line rained down on me and I was swept away in shame.

"I know you; you can work for hours on a routine and never tire. If you're doing this right, the emotional and physical fatigue should meet somewhere in the middle."

I felt so small and insignificant. *Why is she still sitting here? I don't deserve her friendship.* I looked everywhere but her eyes until I couldn't resist any longer and met her gaze. I was surprised to find nothing but tenderness.

My lip quivered. "I'm sorry." *For everything.* I sniffled and cleared my throat. "I promise to be better."

She opened her arms for a hug, and this time, I let her hold me. She felt so strong and safe. I buried my face in the crook of her collarbone and cried. I cried out the shame of being a bad friend. I cried out the fear of pushing her away and losing her too.

She didn't let me go. She just held me until I was ready to hold myself up and I made a promise to myself that I would do the same for her and Malcolm.

Then, she took my hand in hers. "This routine about your dad is going to be hard, but this time, you've got us. Because Charlie, we're hip-hop dancers. It's never easy, but it's always real."

I let those words roll around in my head long after she left. *We're hip-hop dancers. It's never easy, but it's always real. It's never easy, but it's always real.* Even when Danny ignored me at dinner. Even when I said goodnight to my mom and noticed how she gave me a sad smile in response. Even when I felt more shame at remembering that Malcolm and Lela's routines on identity weren't just hard in the past tense; that this was shit they were still dealing with in the present. Through all that, those words rippled through me. *It's always real. It's always real.*

The next day, Lela and Malcolm came over to my place after school to help me with the routine. Malcolm didn't give me any grief, meaning Lela had briefed him. Regardless, I knew I owed him a real apology.

"Hey."

"What's up, locket." He said it more like a statement than a question.

"I need to tell you that I'm sorry. Lela had a talk with me yesterday and set me straight on a couple things. And um, I need to do way better.

I'm sorry I haven't been there for you as an ally, but I'm going to show up, okay? I promise."

Malcolm looked me up and down solemnly. "I'd appreciate that, to be honest."

"I know and I'm sorry." *Now I need to prove it.*

I nodded to myself and then we got down to business. We collaborated on ideas for moves and figured out how to integrate this piece into our entire set on acceptance.

When we were ready for the music, I looked to my friends for encouragement, faced my fear, and pressed play. The piano chords began and Holly Near's voice rang out strong and powerful. When the rain sprinkled across the track and she started hammering out the piano chords, I wanted to puke. Instead, I fell into her words and gained strength.

I thought the song I had chosen was softer, diminutive, but this song had power. The repetitive notes of the piano rang through me, spilled out of me, threw me across the patio. Every corner of my body felt the rage I felt towards my dad for leaving me. Every corner of my soul expanded and compressed to fit the notes of the music. I moved my body in new ways to express his story and to understand my loss.

Normally, I kept the songs I choreographed on repeat, so I wouldn't be interrupted during the creative process. But this time, we paused after each replay of the song to check in on where we were at. We weren't trying to perfect the piece; we were making sure we were being true to my dad's story. And that wasn't perfect. It was messy and broken.

We danced for hours as I let those rhythmic nails close his coffin. As the silence consumed me once again, I realized I wasn't in pain anymore. I wiped the tears from my face and took a deep breath. I hugged them both as a thank-you. And this time when they left, I didn't feel so alone.

Dear Diary,

It feels weird to even write it down, but I'm mad at my dad. How is that even possible? He's DEAD. You can't be mad at a dead person, can you?

Well, I guess I was. Am. I don't know. I didn't know until Lela knew. I guess that makes sense. Your best friends are supposed to help you when you're being dumb about things. I've always thought the only person I should be mad at is my mom. Isn't that why I refuse to call her "mom"?

The truth is, I'm not mad at my mom because she makes me take care of Danny or any of that other stuff. I just want a parent. I don't want to be the parent. I want to be taken care of. So when you think about it like that, then it kind of makes sense that I'd be mad at dad too. But it still feels weird in my soul.

The good thing is Lela finally made me dance about it. Like I thought I'd been dancing about it my whole life but I guess I've still been running. But tonight, Malcolm and Lela helped me dance about it and there's something different in my heart. Like maybe I could forgive him. Like maybe even I could be okay with my mom...eventually.

Part of me doesn't even know if I deserve friends like Malcolm and Lela. Forgiving me for being ignorant even when I'm not sure

I've ever been there for them the way I need to be. The only way to change that is to be better, right? Stop hiding from the pain of what's it like for them. Next time we're in the Academy, I'm actually going to open my eyes and be there for Malcolm and Lela about their pieces on culture clash in America. I won't hide from the pain. I'll be there no matter what it takes.

Love,
Charlie

STEP TOUCH

The smell of coffee and pancakes woke me up the next morning. *That's different.* And mom was singing. I tiptoed downstairs as quietly as possible and sat at the bottom, just listening and watching her sway around the kitchen.

My curiosity got the better of me and I headed towards her. "What's all this?" I said good-naturedly.

Mom continued to sway side to side as she finished up breakfast and set the food on the table. "Good morning, darling. Take a seat."

I did, gratefully accepting a cup of steaming coffee, breathing in the wafts of cinnamon and oak escaping from the brew. I set down the coffee and pulled a pancake to my plate, breaking it apart with my fingers and eating a piece at a time.

She sat across from me with her own cup of coffee, and I started to feel the weight of the silence.

She dragged her finger around the rim of her coffee cup and took a hesitant sip.

I looked at her with squinting eyes, questioning. I opened my mouth and then closed it.

"Is it okay if we talk about your dad?" She said it almost in a whisper.

The last bite of pancake scratched against my throat and fell heavily into my stomach. I felt a thousand things all at once. *Finally! I've always wanted to talk about him. What kind of question is that? Why is she bringing this up now? Yes, please, please, please!*

I nodded.

She sighed. "It goes without saying that I have been unable to face living life without your dad, Devin…my husband." She acknowledged each of his titles, like she wanted to hear how they sounded out loud again.

I held my breath, unsure if acknowledging this statement would encourage more vulnerability or stop her from speaking. She continued without my prodding, not yet meeting my gaze.

"That I have had no idea how to be a mom without him by my side. At first, I thought if I could just push the hurt away—" she broke off in tears.

She really has missed him. All this time I thought she had turned against him.

"I know it doesn't make sense, Charlie, why I did the things I did. Why I disappeared into work. That's the exact opposite of what you and Danny needed. But," she took a deep breath, "but accepting help meant accepting he was gone, and even now, even now the pain is so close."

I sat there stunned, unable to move, barely able to process what I was hearing.

She hastily brushed her tears away and forced a sad smile. "Darling, what do you remember about your dad?"

I started to answer, but realized I didn't have anything to offer. I'd been waiting for this moment for the last five years, but when it came time to talk, I blanked. I took a sip of coffee and tried to call something forth, wading through my memories as if searching for koi in silty waters. "He used to tell me stories before bed."

Mom nodded. "You loved those stories."

Another memory popped into my head like a magic trick. "We used to go to the park! He would push me on the swings." I paused, approaching the memory on tiptoe and peering around the corner as it all came back to me.

There was seven-year-old Charlie, giggling on the swings, soaring higher and higher into the air. Suddenly, dad grabbed my seat and ran with it from the back of the swing set to the front, pushing me to the sky. I laughed in fear, gripping the chains of the swing with all my might. My hair whipped around me. The sun warmed my face and shoulders while the wind sang coolly by me.

"Okay, Girl Wonder, jump!" Dad called.

"I can't! I'm too scared," I yelled.

"You can do it! I'll catch you." He extended his arms, giving me that famous dad smile.

At first, I shook my little head, refusing to make such a colossal mistake as jumping from a swinging chair. But my dad's outstretched arms looked so safe and inviting that I swallowed my fear and jumped. And for a brief moment, I flew.

He caught me in his arms. "That was fantastic!" He hugged me tight.

"Did you see me? I was flying!" I wriggled away and jumped down, excited.

"Yes, I did, my Girl Wonder. And I couldn't be prouder of you." He crouched down to look at me, holding my arms in his hands. "There will be times in life when we're too afraid to jump, but we must. Always remember how that felt flying through the air untethered by restraints. Will you do that for me?"

I came out of the memory with blurry eyes. *What if I had remembered how it felt to be untethered by restraints? What if I had taken his advice, let myself fly?*

I wiped the tears from my face, embarrassed. I cleared my throat. "He used to call me 'Girl Wonder.'"

"Oh, he was so proud of you! He loved you so much." Mom paused. "And I love you, you know that?"

I felt my throat catch. I tensed my jaw to keep from crying harder. I looked at my hands in my lap and tried a bit of courage. I took one of her hands in mine. "I was always here for you."

She held my hand with both of hers. "But you were eleven! And not only was I facing losing a husband, but I was also going through a pregnancy alone. And we had just bought this house and I wasn't sure how to pay the mortgage by myself." At my worried look regarding our finances, she waved it away. "We're fine. I figured it out, but it was a lot all at once. That's what I'm trying to say. I felt so lost and so I pushed everyone away. And I'm sorry, I'm so sorry, Charlie. In trying to do it alone, I left you alone. And that is unforgivable."

Mom took back her hands and covered her face.

I let my hands fall to my lap, unsure how to respond. "Mom, it's okay."

From behind her hands she said, "The best I can do to explain is that I felt like I'm the one who caused the accident."

"Mom, how?" My heart was a flurry in my chest.

She uncovered her face. "He went out in the rain to get me food from the store. I didn't need it. I just wanted it. Typical pregnant cravings. And you know your dad: no weather bothered him. He refused to take the car. He loved to ride that motorcycle. But it was too dark, and the car didn't see him. He died on impact. And it was all my fault."

She started hiccupping as she tried to stop the tears. I got up from the table and grabbed her some tissue. When I handed it to her, I gave her shoulder a squeeze.

When she could speak again, she said, "I'm still working on that one in therapy. I understand if you can't accept my faults, but I can promise to be better. Will you at least accept that?"

I looked at her and tried to process what she was sharing with me. It was like I could almost see the pain sitting on her shoulders. My dad's death had affected her and it was just as painful to her as it was to me. Maybe she saw dad as some kind of phantom or shadow being too. A shade like mine.

Dad was a shade for both of us. While my shade is warm and loving, I'd been holding all kinds of resentment towards him anyway. Mom's shade brought fear and self-loathing. Of course, she would have a hard time dealing with a shade like that.

Becoming an adult, having responsibilities, having kids—none of that meant she had the answers. Mom was still learning like I was. That also meant she was going to make more mistakes. For whatever reason, realizing the likelihood of mom's future mistakes comforted me. It was as if for the first time I was looking at a parent instead of some woman I was supposed to call "mom."

I gave her one last smile. "Yeah, mom, I think I can accept that."

After our heart-to-heart, I headed upstairs and crawled into bed, burrowing into the cocoon of safety within my covers to think more about my life. All the anguish of the last five years and how my mom and I had been suffering through it alone, apart from each other. I felt the anger coming back, so I took a deep breath and let it out in a big sigh. *Time to let it go.* I knew it would take time to truly be done with that resentment, but I wanted this moment to be the first step forward.

I let myself fall asleep dreaming about memories of my mom and how we might rebuild our relationship. An hour later, I woke feeling refreshed and with the energy to figure out how to let this thing between Danny and me go too.

I got out of bed and went to his room, knocking softly on his open door. I pushed it open and found him playing Legos on the floor. The way the Legos were spread out, it was clear where Oreo was sitting, so I took a spot across from them and started adding to his set.

After a few minutes, I said, "Hey, bud, can I talk to Oreo for a second?"

Danny looked to his left to confer with Oreo and then looked at me and nodded.

"Oreo, I love Danny and I'd do anything to be closer to him, so I'd like you to tell me why you're mad at me."

Danny's mouth moved as he whispered to Oreo before returning to his Legos. "He's angry you don't pay attention to him anymore."

I nodded at the empty space next to Danny and placed a yellow Lego onto his blue base. "Oreo, please know that I would love to spend more time together."

Danny nodded, deliberating with his friend again, and then said, "He also doesn't like your room."

I paused with my Legos. "Oh no?"

"He hates it."

I looked at my little brother. "Oreo, that's a strong word."

Danny stood firm in his decision, sticking up his chin at me.

"Bud, can I do anything to change that?"

"Get rid of that picture," Danny said instantly.

I thought of the one he threw to the ground a few months ago and tried to understand why. And then I remembered where that picture of me with my dad was taken.

"Danny, when was your 'Bring Your Dad to School Day'?"

"A while ago. Mom couldn't go."

So that's why Danny has been so upset. He's angry that he doesn't have a dad or a mom to show up for him when he needs them most. And Oreo's been a channel for that grief.

I set down my Legos and reached for Danny's hand. He shied away from me.

"Oh, bud. Can I tell you why I like that picture so much?" Danny nodded reluctantly, so I continued. "Well, on 'Bring Your Dad to School Day,' dad came to my class to talk about being an author. The kids thought he was okay, but not as cool as another kid's dad who was a clown. At the end of the day, that dad painted all our faces and I even persuaded dad to get his face painted with me. We got matching butterflies."

I fell silent and looked at my baby brother. I began again, softly, "Danny, if dad were still alive, you know he would have gotten his face painted with you and Oreo, right?"

This time, instead of consulting with Oreo, Danny started to cry. For a minute, silent tears streamed down his face and Danny let me hold his hand. Then he stepped around the Legos and curled up in my arms. I rocked him back and forth, rubbing his forehead. He looked up at me through big, wet eyelashes.

"Why did dad have to die?"

I stiffened, not knowing what to say. I looked down the stairs and wondered if my mom could hear us and what she would say.

I hugged him a little tighter. I felt the full weight of my baby brother never meeting his father, and I felt a sinking feeling that I was getting further and further away from my memories of my dad. "I don't know, bud."

"Can I tell you something?"

"Yes, bud, anything."

"The kids at school say that I'm not a real boy because I don't have a dad."

I sat up and accidentally let Danny fall from my lap. "They said that?"

"Yeah! That's why I pushed Kyle. They were all laughing at me and calling me names."

I was suddenly so embarrassed and angry that I had missed that. That I had assumed it was a little boy thing. That I hadn't been there to protect him. That his teacher let this happen.

"Danny, I'm so sorry." I pulled him into a hug again. "You are absolutely a real boy and will continue growing up to be a big kid, okay? Nothing can take that away from you."

Danny nodded. "It's okay."

I hugged him for a little while in silence.

"Do you know what death looks like?" he asked me.

I shook my head and sighed. "I don't, but if I had to guess, I would say death looks like all the colors of the rainbow, but impossibly bright so you can't see."

We sat quietly for a moment. Then I said, "Did you know I still talk to dad?"

He looked at me in disbelief.

"You know that picture on the piano? I sit on the bench and talk to him about my day. I haven't talked to him in a long time, but I know he'd love to hear about my showcase, and I think he'd want to hear about school or karate or whatever you want to tell him."

Danny sat up thinking. "Can we go talk to him now?"

"I think that's a great idea." We held hands and headed down the stairs. Once we were seated on the bench and staring at our dad's picture, Danny got shy.

"Why don't you tell him about Oreo?" I nudged him with my elbow.

Danny smiled and burst into a long story about meeting Oreo and all the games they played together. After telling him about Oreo, he told our dad's picture about school and all his gold stars. He moved on to karate and showed him the new moves he had learned that week.

Then it was my turn.

I told him about dance and figuring out the choreography about his accident. I refrained from telling my dad how angry I had been with him—I wasn't sure he or Danny needed to know that. I talked about Lela and Malcolm and how I was lucky to have such good friends. I told him about midterms and how I thought I did well.

I heard a noise behind me and turned to find mom watching us. I reached out a hand for her to join us.

We scooted over on the piano bench. She kissed our heads and sat down. She stared at her husband's photograph, searching his face for answers he didn't have. She wiped the tears from her eyes, then looked at Danny and me. She turned back to the photo and said, "Our kids are so beautiful. You would be so proud."

I was also moved to tears. Danny looked up at us and asked why we were crying, which only made us dissolve into a silly tickle fight, chasing him around the house, laughter from all three of us filling the house for the first time in years.

That night, mom helped me put Danny to bed with tickles and bedtime stories. He sat in her lap while leaning against my arm and we finished our latest *Magic Tree House* book together. Sometimes she would do funny voices that made Danny giggle. He made it through all five chapters this time without falling asleep, so she and I tucked him in and kissed him goodnight.

When we headed down the hallway, we both stopped at my room. Mom cupped my face, tucked a piece of my hair behind my ear, and kissed my forehead. "Why don't you do something fun tonight? Go out with your friends?"

I looked at her in surprise. "Yeah, maybe I will."

"Goodnight, darling."

I headed to my room and sat on the edge of the bed thinking about my night. *What a day it's been.* But mom was right. I wanted it to continue. I had the energy to keep going. I didn't want it to end.

I scrolled through social media and saw an Open Mic Night happening at Broadway Coffee in twenty minutes. I barely had time to change and no time to ask if anyone wanted to go with me. But I wanted to capture the moment, so I pulled on a pair of jeans, grabbed my hoodie and high-top sneakers, and rushed out the door.

I was one of the last people entering the room and slid into the first seat I saw near the door. The lights flashed three times and then dimmed. I breathed in with exhilaration and eased into my seat. The MC's voice entered the room before he did.

"All right, all right, all right!" The stage lights came up with him. "Y'all ready for a show tonight?" The crowd erupted in claps and cheers.

"The beats come slick, so listen up quick, and catch these riffs. A rollercoaster of emotion, watch out and don't get sick! It's all part of the thrill, we're all counting on you to enjoy it, so without further ado. Andy's their name, spitting poetry is their game, but stop before you think they're tame, their words will make you feel no longer the same in the world they create."

He left the words hanging in the air as he exited stage right.

The poet entered stage left and walked softly to the middle of the stage. They gripped the mic. "This one's called 'The Space Between Breaths.'" They took a deep breath and let it out.

> *"I inhale dusk, wander with wraiths,*
> *stay in this dark as long as it takes,*
> *tapping unheard notes,*
> *reprising memory of a memory*
> *of you—wisps of the end that came*
> *too soon. Dissect, reflect.*

*Conversational volta
of tacit meant-to-says
and should-have-saids,
crescent of my spine
as I curl inward. You—
I waltz, dizzying
myself with shades and intonations.
Voices echo of cruel imagination,
laughter rehearsed in front of mirror,
script I write for whispers I can't make out.
But a palm, bare, reaching for me.
a palm, my own,
yet with finespun flesh
promising to take me with her,
bitten down nails and all, part of her.
Finger twitches.
Heart trammels in chest.
I can't get enough air.
Wobbling to these broken chords until
in the space between breaths
hand steadies, stillness finds me.
Relief in the hush, only the sound of an exhale.
Shadows wax across my face,
mottle with pansy and thistle, waning
into amaranth, peach, and cornflower.
A smile, air gilded and saccharine,
take first breath worth breathing,
body tingling in the warmth
of the beginning after the end.
Let light dust gold across flesh.
Perhaps I will meet you there
with outstretched hand."*

    I was so stunned, I forgot to clap. Even as the audience broke into applause around me, I sat there lost in their words. I saw myself in the dark, pretending the shadows and leftover pain were enough. I replayed meeting my Underground Poet; the way he seemed to shine. I took a deep breath and felt the air fill me up like a balloon. *Is this what it feels like to take a full breath?* I watched the shadows shift into day, the sunset exploding into beautiful truth.

No more heartache but the space to find my truth. And then above it all. *I need to go back to those texts.* But before I could, my thoughts and attention were swept up by the next artist.

At the end of the two-hour show, I sat there in a daze as people filed out around me. I felt like all the creatives on the Open Mic Stage were speaking only to me. I felt like somehow my Underground Poet had been there, giving me one last push. I pulled out my phone and looked at our texts. He had said,

> "Don't panic. Listen. Pretend you are a dog like me and listen to other people rather than steal their stories. Listen for the whisper of red flakes falling from my red heart."

He wasn't calling me out. He wasn't trying to put me down for being caught up in my stories. He was commiserating, encouraging me to trust myself rather than listening to the fear, the way he was trying to do as he fell for me.

He had said,

> "Funny thing when you talk about roots, really we're all just branches without roots. Life is not a line, but a circle. That is why you cannot read fate; you must experience it."

That was his way of trying to apologize when he could tell I had missed something. That when reacting out of defensiveness, we were reacting out of the hurt we've had in the past. That he was asking me to stay. That he had found me and wanted to experience this relationship in full.

He had said,

"With you, a wonderful future beckoned and winked like a green fig tree. I wanted you to choose me but instead I was left with figs wrinkled and black, plopping to the ground at my feet."

When I started running away faster, he tried again and again to chase me, to keep me, to not let me go. Because he saw what our future might hold. Something beautiful to continue to blossom. And the strangest part of all was he knew me, so he knew I would push him away. It was his final attempt to get me to understand.

I sat there overwhelmed, saddened, and embarrassed. *How could he know me like that? Am I even worth knowing anymore, after I have ignored him for so long?*

He was being real, right in front of me, and I had left him alone. I had no words, only shame. I drove back home wracking my brain with what to do.

Finally, it came to me. I'd start with *Snow Flower and the Secret Fan*. The pages would have the answer, the lines would be there to tell me what to do, to answer for the full weight of the heartbreak and misunderstanding.

After skimming the pages of *Snow Flower* for about an hour, I got up and paced my bedroom. Maybe I needed some Mary Shelley too. These weren't books of great hope: they were books of fierce judgement and utter sorrow over wrongdoing. They were books of humanity laid bare.

I texted him back cautiously,

"There is something at work in my soul that I do not understand. You always saw me, knew me, even when I didn't know myself. I hope one day we will soar together."

I took a deep breath, turned off the volume on my phone, and continued reading *Snow Flower* so I would be ready if he decided to accept my apology. It took every bit of my being to not look at my phone every few minutes. Even though it took me months to respond—the last text

I received from him was on Valentine's Day and here we were in the second week of April—I wanted his response *now*.

Snow Flower and the Secret Fan was the Lisa See book that made me feel the deepest and so I had no problem falling into the story. I devoured the story and let myself get lost in the consequences of miscommunication. I shamelessly compared my life to the characters and yearned for my own exoneration. I could only keep my fingers crossed that my Underground Poet would follow through.

GRAPEVINE

School was that breezy time just after midterms but before finals. The days fell into each other like cards from a dealer's hands. Nothing at school fazed me now that what I was coming home to finally felt like home.

My mom was actually home. Not all the time, not every time I came home from the Academy, but most days I came through the door and was welcomed home with a hug. A Real Mom hug, full of love and warmth. Some days, she even picked up Danny straight from school, enabling me to come home to his giggles and her laughter.

That Thursday, I let Malcolm and Lela know I wouldn't join them for lunch and walked around campus looking for Rebecca. I found her sitting on the rock wall overlooking the school garden. It was one of those places that was tucked away but still not off limits, both quiet and peaceful.

"Hey," I called out softly as I walked up, hoping not to startle her.

Rebecca looked over her shoulder, smiling when she saw it was me. "Oh, hi."

"Mind if I join you?"

Rebecca shook her head and scooted over to let me sit. We sat in silence, watching the breeze roll through the grass, flipping over a few leaves with gentle hand.

"I did it, you know."

I turned and met her gaze.

"I changed my recital routine. After we talked that one time at the Tower Café, I couldn't stop thinking about needing to talk to my parents, to do the routine about them. So, last minute, I added some new choreography during class—or as my instructor called it, 'some undignified moves.' It felt awesome."

I bumped my shoulder against hers. "Congrats, Rebecca. I'm happy for you."

Rebecca blushed and clicked her feet together. "Now, we just have to see what my parents think at the recital at the end of the month."

I nodded, and we met each other's gaze for a while, letting everything unspoken sit between us.

We jumped when a kid slammed his locker behind us. I grabbed a notebook from my backpack. "Here are some of the scenes I was thinking we could shoot for our film."

Rebecca took the page. "Charlie, this is fantastic."

"I agree." I smiled. "I think our movie's going to be great. Want to meet at my place this weekend?" With only a few weeks left before the project was due, we needed to get on it. But we had the research, so I figured the filming wouldn't take too much time.

Rebecca nodded. "Yeah. But Spring Formal is this weekend."

"Oh, that's right." *That's a thing. Going to school dances. I just always feel too awkward to go. But Rebecca always has friends and boys to go with.* I realized Rebecca had continued talking and tuned back in.

"...had talked about going with him, which is obviously never going to happen now, and I don't want to go alone so I thought it would be fun if we went together. What do you think, locket?" She looked up at me expectantly.

It took me a second to register her question—and to realize she was using my old nickname, but this time with total tenderness. "Oh, sure! Um, yeah, sure, let's do it."

Rebecca smiled. "Should be fun. And if not, we can just ditch it and eat popcorn in my dad's office."

I started in surprise. *So she does remember.* "I would love that."

"So, Formal this weekend and then our French project on Wednesday?"

I smiled. "Sounds good."

Friday came and went. On Saturday, I raced home after dance, not even telling Malcolm and Lela why I was in a hurry. They didn't seem interested in going to the dance and I couldn't bring myself to admit aloud that I was excited to go.

As soon as I got home, I ran up the stairs, showered, then stepped out with a towel wrapped around my body, hair still dripping. "Help! What do I wear? I never even bought a dress," I called out to my mom.

Mom walked into my room and opened up my closet. "You've got tons of dresses!"

"Not good enough for Spring Formal!"

"Shush and try this on."

And so the next hour went as I tried on different dresses and mix-and-matched shoes. To be honest, I was a little nervous about my outfit, but mostly what I wanted was my mom to help me. I wanted this mother-daughter moment. I'd catch myself watching her and then she'd catch me staring and smile at me, and we'd go back to looking at my clothes and the process would start all over again.

Danny ran in. He joined me on the bed, but got bored and started scavenging through the mounds of shoes.

"I think you should wear these!" He held up a shoe with sparkly silver straps and two-inch heels.

I tried to imagine those shoes with the red dress mom and I had picked out.

"All right, Danny. I'll wear them, but only because you're so cute." I ran through my jewelry box in my mind and picked out some silver earrings and silver bracelet that would go along nicely.

Mom rubbed my back and kissed me on the side of the head. "Are you excited? Did you tell me who you were going with? Lela and Malcolm?"

"Yeah, I am excited. Um, actually, I'm going with Rebecca."

"Oh really? I didn't know you two were still friends."

I put up my hands. "I know, it's been a weird year." I turned away and grabbed all my things—the dress, the jewelry, the shoes, and my purse.

"Well, have a great time tonight. Be safe."

"Thanks, mom, I will." And with final hugs, I was out the door and headed to Rebecca's house to finish getting ready for Spring Formal.

I hadn't been to her house in years, but I thought I would still remember the way. I made one wrong turn and then sat in my car looking at her house. I rode the wave of nostalgia, watching the minutes tick by until I couldn't drag my feet any longer. I grabbed my things and made that long walk up her walkway. At the door, I recognized the seven doorbells, one with a nameplate for each person in her family, one for Business for each of her parents, and one for Government. I pressed the one that said "Becks."

In response to pushing the button, Nick Carter started singing. His voice cut off as the door swung abruptly open.

"Sorry about that." Rebecca laughed, breathing heavily. She motioned for me to come in.

"I can't believe you never changed it!"

She looked at me curiously, her expression softening when she remembered I would know. "Oh, yeah, nope. Now, I just race to the front door to try and kill the sound as soon as possible." She tapped her nameplate wistfully and then looked at me with a sad smile and closed the door behind us. I wanted to say something about the nickname her dad used to call her, ask a question about when he stopped calling her that or if it was taken over by Colton, say something to validate what she was feeling. But there was too much to say, too much unknown. Instead, I smiled back and hoped that was enough.

I followed her up to the bedroom, walking past the gigantic staircase sitting in the middle of the room, down the long, dark hallway, through the kitchen, and up a smaller staircase. We stepped into the light of her room, and I laughed. "It looks exactly like I remember it."

Rebecca leapt onto her bed, grabbing the large purple stuffed unicorn. "It's the one place that makes me happy. I don't care if I'm too old for it."

"Makes total sense," I smiled.

Rebecca sat up and looked at her Apple Watch. "We've got about an hour. I guess we should get dressed? Were you going to wear makeup? I mean not that you have to."

"Doesn't makeup take the longest? I wouldn't know. I have no idea what I'm doing."

"Oh my gosh, let me do your makeup!" Without waiting for an answer, Rebecca ran into her bathroom. I followed hesitantly.

She motioned me forward and pointed to where I was supposed to sit. While her bedroom seemed a space out of time, exactly as I remembered it from when we were eight, her bathroom had grown up with her. She had a legit chair and vanity mirror for makeup and hair. I sat down feeling totally out of place.

Regardless, I closed my eyes and decided to trust she knew what she was doing as she began working on the foundation. She talked as she applied all the layers, though most of it went over my head. All I know is that it did take a long time.

At some point, she said, "Open your eyes and look up." I did as I was told as she applied mascara. I did my best not to blink but my eyes started watering and I was wondering how much longer when she said, "All right, I think we're there."

She finished up with something on my cheeks and then moved away from the mirror so I could see. I had to blink a couple of times to realize that I was looking at myself. I mean, of course it was me, but I just never thought I could look like that. Could look so...magical.

"Do you like it?" Rebecca asked quietly.

I nodded, mesmerized. "I don't know what you did to Charlie, but that is not the same girl," I laughed.

Rebecca put her hands on either side of the chair and hovered down near eye level with me. "Of course it is, Charlie. You couldn't hide it if you tried." We stared at each other for a few seconds smiling. Then, she said, "My turn."

I got up from the chair and went to change. Somehow, in the amount of time it took me to step into my dress and awkwardly zip up the back, Rebecca finished with her makeup.

"Now that is magic," I said. She had amplified her eyes with winged eyeliner and smoky eye shadow.

Rebecca shot me a big smile and walked past me to change. After slipping on her slinky black dress and six-inch black heels, we took some selfies. I tried to take it all in, but I was so happy that I kind of forgot and just lived.

We headed out the door and blasted the tunes as we drove to Haynes High. When we arrived, a line had already formed at the door.

The nerves hit me again as we stepped onto campus. The line seemed to never move, allowing ample stretches of awkward silence between Rebecca and me.

When we finally made it inside, there were cries of "Charlie! How are you? Rebecca! Don't you look gorgeous!" followed by many hugs and side kisses. Rebecca kept her arm tucked through mine and together we weaved through the crowd. We ran into some of Rebecca's old crew and after a slightly awkward "You remember Charlie," we left them and stepped onto the dancefloor.

Dancing was the part of the dance I was most worried about. *What if I didn't know how to dance at school dances? What if I fell from dancing in high heels? What if Rebecca left me for Colton or someone else?* But all that panic died down when Rebecca kept saying what a good dancer

I was and kept laughing at herself. We ended up trying to dance the stupidest to see who could laugh the hardest.

The songs slipped into each other and suddenly it was an hour later. Rebecca grabbed my hand and guided us off the dance floor. We grabbed drinks from one of the chaperones and found an empty spot to sit along the wall.

"Are you having a good time?" Rebecca yelled over the music.

I nodded and finished the rest of my drink. "Who knew dances could be so much fun?" I yelled back.

"Is this your first one?"

I thought about lying but ended up telling her the truth. "Yeah." I paused as I thought about what I wanted to say. "This really isn't Malcolm or Lela's thing."

"Well then, it can be our thing. Promise we'll go to prom together next year?" She held out her pinky finger.

"Deal!" I linked my pinky with hers. We finished our drinks and popped back onto the dance floor. We held hands while we were dancing, doing some of those best friend moves you see in the movies, and laughing as we failed to do them right.

Too soon, the lights were blinking back on, and the teachers were herding us out to go home.

The night felt glorious as we stepped out of the gym. Rebecca grabbed my hand and said suddenly, "Let's not go home yet."

"I agree. Let's...go get ice cream! Gunther's?"

"Yes!" She reached for her keys.

"No, let's walk."

"Walk? But isn't it far?"

I shook my head. "It's like around the corner."

"But we're in heels."

I looked at our feet and shrugged. "I'll carry you if you get too tired."

Rebecca giggled. "Okay, locket, I see you." She linked her arm through mine again and we set off down 35th Street.

As we walked, we talked about life and we talked about nothing. We laughed about the night, and we dreamed about the future.

I stopped when I saw the dark lights of an obviously closed Gunther's.

"Who closes an ice cream shop before eleven?" I whined.

"C'mon," Rebecca grabbed my hand and marched me several feet until I laughed begrudgingly and followed her to the McDonald's up the street. But their dining room also turned out to be closed and they wouldn't serve us in the drive-thru without a car.

"How hard is it to get ice cream around here?" Rebecca demanded.

"Wait! I have an idea! Let's go to Mel's Diner."

"But now we have to walk back," Rebecca whined.

"I promised," I said, kicking off my heels and kneeling down on one knee so Rebecca could hop on my back. Rebecca giggled but hopped on. I stood up too fast, nearly knocking us to the ground and prompting Rebecca to squeal.

"Shush, I got you," I laughed.

Rebecca was so tiny that I barely felt her weight on our walk back.

In no time, we were back at Rebecca's car and zooming to the diner. "Now this is what I'm talking about!" she exclaimed as we stepped into the light, warmth, and safety of the '50's restaurant. "I am totally getting mozzarella sticks."

"And French fries!"

We both agreed on Oreo milkshakes.

We kicked off our heels underneath the table and swung our legs up onto the booth to sit cross-legged. While we waited for our food, we argued over the best Leonardo DiCaprio movie and how many Oscars he should have won. We shared our appetizers as we reminisced on our favorite parts of being friends as kids and made plans about what we should do as friends now.

While she was away in the bathroom, I looked through my phone notifications for the first time that night. Even though I told myself not to, I clicked on Scott's Instagram post. He was at a party, swinging some new girl around in the air, and then landing a large kiss on her cheek. I crumpled. The tears were falling before I could think about stopping them. I tried to wipe them up before Rebecca could see, but she sat back down and took my phone from my hands. She surveyed the picture and handed the phone back to me.

"As a wise person once told me, 'He's not worth the tears.' And to be honest, locket, Scott's never been worth you."

"I know. And it makes it worse that I know."

"Believe me when I tell you, I know exactly how you're feeling."

I asked quietly. "So, how'd you get over him?"

Rebecca sighed. "You don't. You just get more distance from the heartache until someone new catches your attention." She paused for a moment. "I'm working on that someone being me," she finished quietly.

We finished our food in silence. By the time I was done, I felt better, finally solidifying some truth I always held about Scott.

Later, as I was driving home from Rebecca's house, something clicked in my heart, something I didn't know I was missing fell back into place. I thought back to my adventures of the night and smiled. I thought back to Scott and for the first time felt nothing. I kept poking and prodding the thought of him, but where red hot had always been, neutral beige had pooled in.

When I got home, I kicked my heels off at the door. My mom was eating Oreos in the kitchen. Even though I had just had a milkshake, I sat at the counter with her and grabbed an Oreo.

"You know, you're just like your dad." She took a bite of one of the cookies. "He used to dunk them just like that. It used to be one of our arguments. This," she split the cookie in half, "is the only way to eat an Oreo." She licked up the filling and then ate the crunchy cookie halves one at a time.

I laughed and shook my head. "No way! That's sacrilegious. It's like this." I took another Oreo and dunked the whole thing in the milk, waiting an extra second to prove my point. But instead, the cookie turned to mush and I lost my grip. My mom and I burst out laughing.

When I finally made it to my bed, I fell asleep bone-tired with a smile on my face, something I hoped to hold on to in the future.

JAZZ SQUARE

And just like that, it was the week before finals. Rebecca and I worked feverishly on the final touches of our French film. I thought we didn't have that much to do, but filming took way longer than either of us thought it would. As the day stretched longer into the night, we found ourselves cutting corners and rationalizing that this was the best we could do. I crossed my fingers that it would be enough to maintain my A.

The fateful French class arrived. We were given the third slot for presenting our film, so we didn't have to hold our breaths for long. I was a bit relieved when the first video looked like it was made the day before but became increasingly anxious as the second video rocked it. I shared a knowing look of dread with Rebecca. *It was so good!*

When our names were called, Rebecca and I stood in front of the class and introduced our film, *Saved by the Ball*, on French immigration to Mexico. Madame Allemand pressed play and the film began. We stood off to the side, fidgeting and hoping it would all turn out okay. The class clapped politely at the film's end and we returned to our seats. I breathed a sigh of relief. The hardest part was over and I could turn my attention to my other finals and my showcase.

Malcolm, Lela, and I had all our choreography completed, but I still felt like we were missing something. I thought maybe it was my too-tired-from-studying-for-finals brain, but the thought kept tickling the back of my mind as I fell asleep that night. I thought about texting my Underground Poet, but I still didn't know if he wanted to hear from me and thought that might be pushing it.

What I did know was that words were always the right answer. Though I mostly looked in books, sometimes songs held the truth too.

The next day after my Chemistry final, I ducked into the library and settled into my favorite armchair. Then, I pulled out my phone and pulled up the information from the Open Mic Night I had attended. I scanned the list of artists and found the one who opened the show. I followed the supplied links to their Instagram and scrolled through their content. One post caught my eye. It was the artist singing a song called "Don Quixote," accompanying themselves on an acoustic guitar.

I put in my headphones and began to listen.

> "Don Quixote rides his sunken sullen mare
> waiting for the day that he can say, 'Now I am whole,'
> for I have found a friend I need no other goal.
> And each day brings a journey to some well-forgotten land
> with obstacles to overcome and strategies to plan,
> but is the flag I'm fighting for worth the price I'll pay?
> Or have I just convinced myself it really is that way?
> Don Quixote rides his sunken sullen mare
> waiting for the day that he can say, 'Now I am home,'
> for I have found myself, I need no other goal.
> So I'll live tomorrow as I've lived each day before
> waiting for the day that I will chase the wind no more.
> Though it isn't easy to go through the things I do,
> I'll keep on chasing windmills just as long as I have you.
> Don Quixote rides his sunken sullen mare,
> he's waiting for the day that he can say, 'Now I am home.'
> For I found you, girl, I need no other goal,

for I have found myself I need no other goal."

I felt like Harry Potter when he was given his first wand. I knew this song held the secret I had been looking for. It wouldn't have occurred to me before, but listening to it again I realized the tragic hero chasing windmills was exactly the image my group needed.

Malcolm, Lela, and I all had a final at eight the next morning and were dismissed from school as we finished. We celebrated the end of the year by walking to Fixins and grabbing lunch. Malcolm could never resist the chicken and waffles, Lela loved her some gumbo, but for me there was nothing more satisfying than oxtails. We all agreed on the blue Kool-Aid. After we finished, we walked over to McClatchy Park to rest in the shade, fully committed to our food comas.

Or so we thought. Malcolm heard the sound first. We followed the lilting notes and rhythmic bass until we found the instrumentalist on the other side of the amphitheater. He played the violin while accompanying himself with a trap backbeat that he seemed to have mixed himself. We stood watching him, bopping our heads and swaying to the beat. He finished his song and started playing one of Gucci Mane's older songs.

"Ey!" Malcolm hopped forward and started dancing. Lela and I laughed and joined him.

No one called the shots—the violinist's harmonies seem to come alive and create the space with us. I lost myself in the dance. A murmur of emotion passed through me. I swear I felt a physical connection to Malcolm and Lela and our accompanist. Instead of feeling uncomfortable by the emotion, I felt exhilarated. Instead of wanting to hide my vulnerability, I stepped further into the spotlight, the music and the growing crowd guiding this new emerging sense of self.

The violin's vibrations ended with elegant subtlety as the beat faded out. When we reawakened to the world, we noticed the large crowd amassed in a half-circle around us and the loud claps of their appreciation. We pointed to the violinist and began clapping for him. The crowd dispersed, dropping folded bills and coins into his open case. Though he tried to share, we let him keep the earnings and walked away with smiles on our faces.

As we wandered through the park, I thought about my dad, but this time with happiness. He would have loved to hear about this moment. I could almost sense him there with us.

"So that was pretty cool, right?" Malcolm turned to us. "Like, there was something there, right, locket?"

"I..." I began, then stopped, not knowing what I wanted to say.

"I know what you mean." Lela picked up his thread. "I could feel something when he started playing. Something between the music and our dancing."

And suddenly it came to me. "It's a shade. A shadow. A phantom. Don Quixote's windmills."

Lela and Malcolm looked at me not entirely getting what I meant, so I kept going.

"Okay, not the actual Don Quixote but check this out." I pulled out my phone and showed them the song with the same name. I could see their eyes widen and their understanding grow as they nodded along to the song.

I continued, "We all have shades. We're alive, but there's something in shadow, something reaching out to catch us."

Lela's eyes lit up. "We all experience trauma and have shades of what's been left behind. We can build that into our choreography."

Malcolm nodded as he started seeing it. "Each routine can have an individual shade, but our set should have a universal shade. And for the first time, we can catch it. We can bring it to light."

I closed us out. "For what is a shade but a desire too vulnerable to be exposed?"

We looked at each other in amazement and then laughed in awe. We found a bench to sit on so we could plan how to add shades to each of our routines.

The hours slipped by as we brainstormed and created. Adding shades to our routines strengthened and deepened the feelings we were trying to portray. By adding a shade to our break-up routine, we were able to show the ache that remains as the relationship fades. For Lela's identity routine, we were going to have an inception of shades where Malcolm and I would dance as shades around Lela as she found her place in society. We entered that beautiful space of flow where we weren't aware of anything outside our dance and the story we were trying to tell. I didn't know what it would feel like to witness our showcase, but I felt that by adding the shadows we tried to ignore, the audience would be invited to step into the world we created.

At the end of our brainstorming session, we sat back on the bench and smiled. The shades were the missing piece. My friends stood up and started putting their notebooks and pens back into their backpacks. Then we all walked back to campus. Malcolm's dad and Lela's mom were already there waiting for them.

"See you at the party tonight, locket?" Malcolm asked. "My cousin's going too, and can drive us."

"Yeah sure, I'll see you tonight." I noticed how quickly I said yes. *Interesting.*

I gave them hugs and we parted ways. I was struck by how many shades existed in our lives. My dad was most definitely a shade. Dead, but still present, the pain of his departure still palpable.

Oreo is Danny's shade. And what about my Underground Poet? He feels more real to me than anyone else, yet we've never spoken a word to each other in real life. I've shared more with him about my life than I have ever shared or received from Scott. So, who's the real shade?

I was reminded of the author that brought us together. I had just finished reading Markus Zusak's *The Book Thief* and so I had picked up *I Am the Messenger*. In the first work, Death's big theory was that our lives were bursting with color, but we don't take the time to see it. *What colors have I stopped observing? What colors within myself have I ceased to recognize?* It was time I changed that.

The universe must have been listening because when I got home, a response from my Underground Poet awaited me.

> "With you, my dear Snow Flower, I became a poet and for one year lived in a paradise of my own creation."

I smiled with happiness and relief. I bit my lip, unsure of this fountain of longing springing forth from me. *A paradise of our making! No, you didn't make it all up! I'm coming home.*

He called me Snow Flower so that I'd know he understood my reference to Lisa See's work. By sticking with a singular line from Mary Shelley's *Frankenstein*, he was perhaps ensuring that his subtext wouldn't be misread this time. It was never about Frankenstein's monster, but recognizing the monster inside of me. Without the courage to look within, I had created the monster I was so afraid of. *But not anymore.*

I grabbed *Mary Poppins* from my bookshelf and skimmed the pages until I found the quote I wanted. I was stepping out from the shadows and presenting myself fully.

> "I stood there wondering and waiting, hoping beyond hope that you might still accept me. The Merry-go-Round had disappeared. Only the still trees and the grass and the unmoving little path of sea remained."

I set my phone down and then jumped in the shower to get ready for the party. As I lathered, I realized that I was stepping off the merry-go-round in *Mary Poppins* and into his waiting arms. That I didn't need to jump into a chalk picture to experience the kind of joy I was looking for. That for the first time in my life, I was ready to accept someone's love, and I was learning to do the same for myself.

Getting out of the shower, I laid the conversation to rest and directed my thoughts to the party. For some reason, I wasn't nervous. I thought back to the first party at the beginning of the year and shook my head laughing at myself. No more pretending. I put on what made me feel cute and confident—a V-neck shirt, jeans, my high-top sneakers, and a necklace with a silver bee my dad had given me for my eleventh birthday. I pulled my hair into a ponytail, pulled some wisps of hair around my ears, and finished off the outfit by applying some mascara. I was dressed up and I still felt "me."

My phone buzzed letting me know Malcolm was outside. I climbed into the backseat with Lela, said hi to Malcolm, got introduced to his cousin, and then we were off to the party over on Land Park Drive. We found parking a couple streets over, and then walked to the house, entering through a side gate into the backyard.

We grabbed some drinks in the kitchen and weaved through the party. Lela got pulled away to catch up with some friends that she hadn't seen in forever, so Malcolm and I found our way to the backyard and sat chatting on the couch through our first drinks. Then he got pulled into a game of flip cup. I graciously bowed out and went to get another drink.

I wandered farther into the backyard, wondering who I'd see. I only recognized a few of my classmates, ones that I waved and said hi to but didn't feel like joining. Until I saw Jared and Carmella.

"Charlie!" Carmella called from the couch where they sat and waved me over. She hopped up from Jared's lap and gave me a big hug and wouldn't let go.

Jared laughed. "Carmella gets very lovey when she's drunk. Hope you don't mind."

Carmella had my face squished against hers. It was a little uncomfortable and I wasn't sure why she was so happy to see me, but it was nice to make someone this excited by my presence. I gave Jared a thumbs-up.

Carmella broke away. "We were about to get the next game of beer pong. You should be my partner! Jared, go find a boy. It'll be girls against guys!"

It was hard to say no to Carmella. She had such a presence about her, you *wanted* to do what she asked. Jared disappeared to find a new partner while Carmella asked me a bunch of questions a mile a minute about how I'd been since I last saw her. Jared returned before I'd answered the first two and we started our game.

Carmella and I were a great team. We came up with this crazy handshake each time we sank a cup and did a little twirl every time we were on fire. When we had the boys down to their last cup, they made a crazy comeback and suddenly we were even. Jared sank his first ball, then his partner sank his. It was time for our rebuttal.

"You go first. You got this," Carmella said.

I took a deep breath, closed my eyes, opened them, tested the wind, and tossed the ball. Perfect shot, straight into the cup, no rim.

"Ey!" I screamed. Carmella pounced on me, and we jumped up and down with ecstatic cries. "Okay, your turn. It's all you. You got this," I cheered her on.

She let out a mighty bellow and threw her ball. It hit the rim of the cup, circled around twice, and bounced out.

"No!" she said, crumpling into my arms in a dramatic show of losing the game. The boys high-fived and did a victory lap around us. Jared gave us handshakes for a good game and tried to scoop Carmella up in a romantic gesture. She pushed him away playfully and ran away giggling with Jared chasing her.

I placed my hand on the table to steady myself. *Oops, I may be a little drunk.*

I glanced around and noticed Rebecca leaning against the banister by herself. I liked how confident she seemed, like she was enjoying her solitary contemplation. I walked up next to her and placed my arms on the banister. "Hey." I bumped my shoulder against hers.

She gave me a dazzling smile. "Hey!" She reached over for a hug. I hugged her back. "How beautiful is this view?" Situated in a darker corner of Oak Park, the house had a gorgeous view of the night sky, unaffected by the normal presence of streetlights. I nodded.

"I beg to differ," a male voice said behind us.

We spun around to find ourselves looking at quite possibly the best-looking guy I'd ever seen. Standing tall over us, he had a beautiful smile, cute eyes, dimples in his flushed cheeks; he was a big, teddy bear of a man. I had to remember to breathe.

Rebecca still looked in her element. She fluttered her eyelashes up at him. "And why's that?"

"See, it's my humble opinion that I'm standing in front of the prettiest view right now, no need for the stars. I'm Pierre." He stuck out his hand to Rebecca.

That was so smooth! I stayed long enough to see Pierre hit it off famously with Rebecca and then made my exit. It was about time she found someone new. I hoped he was worth her.

I weaved my way back through the party, needing to pee. The first bathroom I opened was occupied by a girl throwing up. There didn't seem to be any other bathrooms downstairs. I briefly debated whether to pee outside or go upstairs and awkwardly knock on a bunch of bedrooms, hoping not to stumble on anyone hooking up. I went back and forth until I headed upstairs.

The first room was unfortunately taken, so I backed up quickly and smacked right into Scott. "Oh," I faltered. I didn't know why, but I wasn't expecting him here and that threw me off. We hadn't seen each other in weeks, and in that time, I had started to move on.

He was crying and standing there with his head down.

Instinctively, I wiped the tears from his eyes. "Scott, what happened?"

"Charlie," he whispered, before taking my hand in his.

Before my brain had time to process, Scott was kissing me, and I was kissing him back. He tasted like sunshine and earth and the wind in the trees.

His hunger took my breath away. He walked me back against the wall, pressing his body comfortably against mine, hands entwining above my head. My body flooded with heat, tingling at every place he kissed; goosebumps rose to his touch as he caressed my arm and scooped his arm behind my back.

The few kisses I had with other boys didn't feel like this. It was both scary and exhilarating.

I wanted all of him and could think of nothing else but how badly I had always wanted this to happen. How many stolen looks, how many yearning daydreams, how many lost nights thinking about him and if he would ever think I was good enough.

Good enough. Is he good enough? A faint voice began to build in my head. The voice was doing a better job of resisting his sweet kisses. They were like little air bubbles escaping from his well of emotion.

I gained enough control to take my lips from his and whisper in his ear. "Scott, what are we doing?"

His hand snaked around to cradle the back of my head. He looked down into my eyes. "Nothing, Charlie, I just want you. You can't tell me you don't want me too."

He moved in on me again and swallowed me up. For a fraction of a second, my brain tried to connect thoughts to answer his question, but I was soon consumed. My skin came alive, shivers ran down my spine, and suddenly the warm sensation between my legs wanted desperately to be connected with what Scott was offering. His fingers moved down my neck and scratched gently at my breasts. He nuzzled his nose into my neck and with kisses brought his lips back to mine. "Come with me."

I started following him into an adjacent bedroom. At the entryway, I stopped, coming alive to the picture before me—my hand in Scott's, outstretched into the darkness. *Was I ready for this next step? Did I want this to happen right now like this?*

I balanced precariously, teetering on the edge of the world that was about to come crashing down.

"Scott."

The tears bubbled over. "Mary broke up with me." He angrily wiped the tears from his eyes before rushing up on me for another kiss.

This time, though, I shoved him back, trying to get a grip on reality. I was crumpling as my dream of being with Scott fell away, but I was also surprised to find resolve and brazenness entering that space instead. It was like I was truly seeing Scott for the first time in my life.

He looked at me in surprise.

"What the hell, Scott?"

"What?" He started to get angry. "I know you love me. Why are you fighting me? I'm just giving you what you want."

I shook my head and looked at the ground. "You only want me when no one else will have you." I said it quietly, almost a whisper. Then something deep within me snapped. It felt like the lightbulb that had always been on for Scott had exploded.

"I love you so much, Scott, and I would have done anything to be your girl. But I'm worth more than *this*." I looked up into his eyes and spit the last word at him.

I turned away from him and started walking away, increasing my pace until I was running down the hall. My lips felt raw. I felt dirty. I grabbed my phone to call my mom. I needed to be gone. I needed to be home, curled up in bed and away from the world.

She dropped everything and was pulling up outside the house fifteen minutes later. When I got in the car, she pulled me into a big hug and didn't ask why I was crying.

When we got home, she said, "I think a shower would feel good."

I nodded and took her advice.

An hour later, I was lying in bed in the fetal position when she knocked on my door.

"Would you like your mom, or would you rather be left alone?" She had one hand still on the door, waiting for my answer. She'd probably be able to tell I was drinking, but I needed her right now, so I moved over to let her in. She came and sat down and rubbed my forehead. She then sang me the lullaby she used to sing to me when I was little.

I closed my eyes and listened to her tell me about the dappled and greys of all the horses. Suddenly things didn't seem so bad. The softness of her voice cradled my poor broken heart. She sang the song twice and then let the silence cuddle me like a purring kitten.

"What's wrong, darling?"

I took a deep breath and opened my eyes to look at her. "Scott kissed me tonight. But only because someone dumped him." I started crying again. "I love him, and he always uses me."

Having to relive that moment made me shudder. I didn't know that something I had wanted for so long could feel this violating. I touched my lips, but they felt like they no longer belonged to me.

"That doesn't surprise me about Scott, but I'm so sorry he did that to you. You hope that the kid will turn out differently than the parents, but the trauma usually just continues."

I felt like pouting. I knew what she was saying was true—I knew about Scott's parents—but it also felt like she was justifying his actions.

But it was like she read my mind. "And that's not on you to fix, my love. You've given him more than probably anyone ever has. But that also means you're the one he turns to when he's lost. I'm proud of you."

I looked up at her. *Proud? Why?*

"For being so strong and knowing your worth."

Will she still think I'm so strong when she really knows me?

I started crying uncontrollably, and mom let me curl into her arms and cry out all the worry and stress and anxiety and questions. When I had no more emotion left to vent, I got up and blew my nose. When I came back to the bed, I sat cross-legged in front of her and fidgeted.

"Do you hate me for drinking at these parties?"

"Hate you? Oh, darling, never." She took my hand and gave me a gentle squeeze.

I looked up into her eyes. "Promise?"

Her hand squeezed mine another time. "There is nothing you could do that would make me love you any less or be any less proud of you."

Tears welled up in my eyes and I brushed them away.

"Besides, you think I don't remember what it was like being a teenager?" She gave me a little smirk.

I smiled and looked back at my hands. *I guess that's true.* It made me think of the ways I've been a typical teenager and it made me think of Danny and his little kid antics. I glanced away from my hands and looked around my room. My eyes fell on the picture of my dad and me.

"So, um, I need to ask you a question," I said, turning back to her.

"Shoot."

"Why didn't you go to Danny's 'Bring Your Dad to School Day'?"

"What do you mean? What did I miss? Oh no. No, no, no." She hopped up from my bed and ran out of the room, quickly returning with her phone. She opened up her calendar and scrolled back looking for the day.

"Oh." Her lip quivered. "I missed it. I had it in my calendar, but it didn't alert me, and I missed it, didn't I?" She stared at her phone in disbelief. "Was Danny mad? He never told me."

For a split second, I felt resentment rise up reflexively. But I saw how much she was hurting.

"He's been really upset. At first, I didn't understand why, but then he told me he hated this picture." I pointed at the photo of my dad and me with matching butterflies painted on our cheeks.

Mom wiped the tears from her eyes. "Just when I think I'm getting better, I learn new ways I've messed things up. How to fix this, how to fix this," she muttered.

I didn't have an answer for her, so I brought up the other issue she needed to know. "Did you know that Danny has an imaginary friend?"

She seemed less surprised at this one. "Oh, is that Oreo?"

"Yep," I sighed. "It's a kangaroo named Oreo."

She was silent for a moment and then sighed. "In a way, it makes sense."

"Why?"

Mom looked sadly down at my comforter. "Because your father's death split me apart and I passed that trauma onto my kids." She caressed the side of my cheek. "You stepped in to fill the hole I left behind for Danny, but he needed both of his parents and Oreo is everything I wasn't able to give."

I squinted my eyes at her, unsure if she was being ridiculous or if she had missed her calling as a therapist.

"In any case, I'm glad he had someone. And I'm glad he had you." She gave me a kiss on the forehead. "Do you know how much I love you?"

And for the first time in a long time, I did.

She said goodnight. It didn't take me long to fall asleep.

The next morning, I woke up to a sweet face snuggling up with me under the covers. "Hey, bud." I blinked open my eyes as they adjusted to the light and Danny's face.

"Hi."

We snuggled for a little, then he said, "I miss Scottie." My eyes grew big. I rubbed his head as I thought what to say. Danny continued, "Can we invite him over to play?"

I put my face in his hair and sighed. "Danny...Scott won't be coming over for a while."

"Is it because of me?"

I pulled away so I could look him in the eyes. "Oh, bud, no. No, you did nothing wrong."

Danny nodded and cuddled back into my chest. "Did he do something to make you really sad?"

I realized I had been holding my breath and let it out. "Yeah, bud."

"So he just has to say sorry and then he'll be able to come over?" He popped up into a sitting position to look at me.

I looked at my little brother and thought about his question. "Maybe, if he's really sorry."

"Then you can be happy again!"

I laughed and pulled him back into a hug. "I'm already happy because I get to tickle you!"

"No!" He giggled as he collapsed into laughter. The tickle fight lasted a few minutes before he got away from me and raced downstairs. I chased him around the kitchen until mom shooed us out so she could finish making breakfast. We collapsed in heavy breaths on the carpet, with reverberations of giggles still catching us. Once we caught our breath, we calmed down and came to a table filled with steaming plates of waffles and eggs. I didn't know she knew dad's recipe. Another lovely little surprise.

"Hey, Danny," I said.

"Mhm?" Danny looked at me but kept chewing.

"Want to go to the zoo today?"

Danny bounded up in his seat. "Yes!"

I turned to my mom. "Want to come?"

"Oh, I would love to, but..." She couldn't bring herself to finish the sentence.

I reached out a hand. "It's okay, Mom. I know you'll be there next time."

She took my hand in hers and looked at me gratefully. And the thing was, I believed it.

I headed upstairs to get dressed and buy our tickets online. I saw a new message from my Underground Poet. It just said,

"Dance With Me
5/22 @ 7pm."

I looked at the date. Today was May 22. *What's happening tonight?* My heart hammered in my chest. I would figure it out. Whatever it was, when the time was right, I would know.

Danny and I drove over to the Sacramento Zoo. He pulled me into the zoo with zeal, choosing a route and zooming down it like an excited dog taking in all the scents. As we wound our way to the kangaroo exhibit, I realized something was different. I watched him bouncing toe-to-toe with the joey in front of him. I felt his easy, lightweight excitement about the kangaroos. I saw the way he was talking to the joeys, asking them about their day, and showing off his hopping skills. "Danny, where's Oreo?"

"He had to go home."

"Are you going to miss him?"

"Yeah, but that's okay, right?" He paused and turned to look at me.

I ruffled his hair. "Yeah, bud, that's okay."

Danny was amazing. So full of love and curiosity. Losing his dad did nothing to taint his experience of life. I had so much to learn from him.

When we got home, I headed outside to dance. I scrolled on my phone until I found the song that was playing in my head. Ella Johnson's voice snuck out from the speakers. I danced with my eyes closed and didn't open them until the song was over.

As I gathered up my phone, I noticed four missed calls from Scott. I dismissed the notifications and headed inside. I would forgive him eventually, but he no longer got to dictate when that would be.

As I showered, I thought about seeing my Underground Poet. I had no idea where I was going, only that I needed to be somewhere important tonight and I had an hour to figure it out.

The streets were by no means empty when I started my search, but the chaos that usually consumed city streets wasn't there for me. I felt calm and almost outside myself as I drove through the city looking for a sign. I weaved through Oak Park, up one street and down the next. Lights at Underground Books caught my attention. *Of course.*

I rolled by slowly and noticed that the place was full, one person standing at the mic at the front of the room. I came to a stop in a parking stall down the street.

It was quiet as I walked through the propped-open front doors, standing room only. Violet waved to me, and I squeezed in next to her behind the counter. She pulled me into a tight hug and then winked at me. My heart fluttered as I waited for whatever was about to happen.

The lights dimmed as a person made their way to the stage. "Ladies and gentlemen, please give a warm welcome to a favorite on the Underground Stage, Noah Coleman."

The lights brightened and there he was. My Underground Poet.

He stood at the mic, a woman on a keyboard behind him to his left. He caught my eye, acknowledging my presence with a knowing smile. Like he was expecting me. Like I had answered his final riddle.

Of course, I've been waiting for his song.

His voice came out soft but powerful. The room filled with the rhythm of the piano and the blues of his song.

> *"We've seen so many like us come and go before,*
> *giving so little away and getting nothing more.*
> *Can't you see we're half alive*
> *just waiting for others to take the dive?*
> *Let's drop our camouflage, take our fear of love to task.*
> *I know the faces we wear are better than our masks.*

Let's let the beautiful that's behind our brick wall show.
It's safe and warm inside, but it's time for us to grow.
I'm not asking you to forget the pain you felt before today,
but you'll get no loving back if you're not giving it away.
So open up your heart;
you won't find a better time to start.
I'll drop my camouflage, take my fear of life to task.
Will you love the face I wear better than my mask?
I'll let the tenderness that's behind my brick wall show.
It's safe and warm inside, but it's time for me to grow.
Just like you I built up defenses,
then my walls became my cage,
but I want to let you in
and now I'm standing on the stage.
No matter what your fright,
you can walk with me into the light.
Please drop your camouflage,
take your fear of life to task.
I know the face you wear is better than your mask.
Just let the beautiful that's behind your brick wall show,
I'm sure you're warm inside,
but you've got to let me know.
I'm sure you're warm inside,
but you've got to let me know."

After the set, he found me outside. I took his hand in mine. Together we stepped from the lights and into the darkness. Sometimes life would be joyous and full. Sometimes overcast in shadows and muted darkness. I was ready to experience it all. I had seen my beautiful and no fear held me back from letting it show.

DENOUEMENT

Loud applause was our cue as Lela, Malcolm, and I headed to the stage for our Summer Showcase. I peeked around the curtain and gave a thumbs-up to Noah who was positioned stage right, standing at a microphone. A lonely light shone down upon him, and he began to sing.

"Dance
When there's nothing left to give."

His voice echoed out into the auditorium, his harmonies lilting on each word. The stage brightened with soft golden light. We entered the stage in graceful twirls and paused mid-pose.

"Dance
When the wounds are fresh
Let them go."

We changed our pose, shifting our height. The lights brightened again and faded into a pink hue.

"Dance
When you can no longer fight
Let the darkness reign."

The lights darkened, covering the stage in blue.

"Dance
Let the light flow through you."

We chased the light as it moved downstage.

"Let it rain down, rain down
Dance when you're free

Free."

The light left Noah and circled us. We hit our opening pose and Noah began singing those fateful Sam Cooke lines to tell the audience what kind of change was going to come.

"Accepting Change" closed out the "A Change Is Gonna Come" Showcase as the grand finale. We accepted the change from year to year with abrupt and fierce moves, as awkward and jolting as the loss of innocence feels. The dance built up energy as we accepted the changing dynamics when parents remarry. The dance slowed, creating tension as we moved through first loves and the ache of first breakups. The song faded out to a whisper, giving us pause. We moved to the confrontation of self as we exploded into the dance between cultures, the ebb and flow of sunny skies to thunder and lightning. We continued to dive into the pain as our routines moved into accepting loss of life.

I swallowed the growing lump in my throat, locked eyes with my group, and hit our final beginning pose. The lights brightened, the song started, and we brought the shades out of the darkness and into the light.

Shades had accompanied us through each of our routines—the shade of childhood innocence, of the veil being removed as we move into adulthood, of what remains as relationships fade and grow, of lost identity, and of what is left behind by the death of a loved one. Now it was time for the final shade routine, the routine that would tie all the loose ends together and create a bridge for the audience to enter our world.

Lela cartwheeled upstage, I moved out of the spotlight, and Malcolm did a running slide onto his knees behind her. I reentered the light, jumping over Lela as she kicked out her feet and began breakdancing on the ground. Malcolm did a backflip back up to his feet and then we all danced in unison to bring the shadow alive.

When we hit our final pose, I could feel the audience holding its breath. The moment hung between us, the audience and the dancers creating a shade of our own that would be lost forever if anyone moved. But move it must.

The applause began, and it was thunderous. I had never heard such applause. I beamed and clasped hands with my dance partners. Noah ran out and joined us on stage. We bowed three times, then exited. As we ran offstage, I blew a kiss up to my dad.

We ran into the backrooms, the happy nerves exploding out of us. "We did it!" The compliments poured out all at once.

"Malcolm, that backflip was amazing!"

"Lela, the breakup routine was so sexy!"

"Charlie, that rainstorm was unbelievable!"

"Noah, you have the voice of an angel!"

We burst out into the lobby together. Outside, the crowd was even crazier. Every dancer was complimenting every other dancer, while all the parents and siblings and grandparents and friends were also trying to congratulate their daughters and sons and siblings and grandkids. I was giving hugs left and right, unsure of the faces of my family and friends blurring past me until I saw Noah. My beautiful Noah, with his half-turned smile, high cheek bones, and deep umber skin. Noah took my hand and gave it a kiss. I spun away from him beaming.

I felt alive in a brand-new way. Somehow, I just knew that this moment was going to be one of my favorites for the rest of my life. I wanted to stay here—with Malcolm and Lela, with mom and Danny, with Jules, with all the audience members, and with Noah. I wanted to take it all in so that years later, when I was telling my kids about it, I could remember every detail.

I spun in a slow circle, looked at the laughing faces of the crowd. The sound seemed to disappear, leaving me alone with my thoughts. I left the lobby and headed back to the auditorium.

I dragged my fingertips along the tops of the seats, trying to recapture all the pieces of this moment—the guests who had sat in *these seats*, who had witnessed *this showcase*. I made my way to the stage. *These lights* and *these curtains* had brought me forth and shrouded me in this moment. I stood in the middle of the stage and looked out at the seats, one more time. I knew I'd be here again next year. But there was something special about the quiet after the roar.

I walked back to the dressing room and sat down on my stool. I closed my eyes, letting the moment wash over me. Dad's face came clearly to the front of my mind. Smiling at me, encouraging me, congratulating me on the woman I had become. I hugged myself and let the tears fall. I opened my eyes. They didn't look so tired and there was a glint in them I hadn't noticed before. The sadness had ebbed away and left freedom.

I noticed a cyan cornflower sitting in a cup on the counter before me. I picked it up.

Shadows wax across my face
mottle with pansy and thistle, waning
into amaranth, peach, and cornflower.

I tucked it behind my ear and smiled. Life's perfect moments have nothing memorable in them— no dream outfit, no fireworks, no long-awaited lover's kiss—just the feeling of utter contentment with the gift that is the present.

I clicked off the light as I left the room and smiled at the perfection of this moment.

Dear Reader,

Thanks for listening. I think that's really all that most of us want. To feel heard.

Turns out writing in a diary was the right decision for me. Getting the thoughts out of my head helped me sort through what I thought to be true against what was actually happening in my life. But if it's all in my head, why can't I just sort it out myself? I guess things just don't work out that way.

It wasn't until I wrote about how angry I was with my mom that we actually started talking to each other and figuring out how to be a mother and daughter. It wasn't until I tried to figure out why I was still in love with Scott and why Noah (well, I didn't know he was Noah yet), was interested in me at all, that I realized I was asking the wrong question the whole time. The real question was, "Who is Charlie and what does she want?"

To be honest...I didn't even know that was something I could ask. Since when do teenagers, let alone girls, get asked what they want like it matters?

But if you learn one thing from my story, I hope it's this: you don't have to change a thing to believe yourself worthy of love. You don't have to lose weight to be beautiful, you don't have to do better on tests to be smart, you don't have to be popular to have true friends, you don't have to define yourself based on how people treat you. You are enough and you don't have to accept how the world tries to break you. Have compassion for others, care deeply about making things better for your community, be passionate about the things you love, and be unafraid of making mistakes.

I believe in you.

Love,
Charlie

Appendix

A CONVERSATION

I Am the Messenger, a book recommendation by the Underground Poet

"*Imagine the softest, toughest most beautiful song you know, and you've got it.*"

The Elegance of the Hedgehog

"When I walked into the bookstore and saw you reading, even though you were in my space, I could not disturb you. You seemed like a work of art, like a *still life*, and I wanted to *delight in* your beauty, *a beauty borne away by something we need not want, may cherish something we need not desire.*"

The Elegance of the Hedgehog, **The Giver**

"If this is life, *constantly poised between beauty and death*, then I'll gladly accept a partner in helping me *track down those moments that are dying*. I'll accept the Giver's **warmth**, his offer of **family**, that feeling of being **a little more complete.** I like the light it makes, shining bright on where I'm supposed to go."

The Giver, **Slaughterhouse-Five**

"*We relinquished color when we relinquished sunshine.* I've been **delivering** myself **into rural silences ever more profound.** Help me bring back the sunshine."

Slaughterhouse-Five, **The Lacuna**

"Let me *ask about* this silence: *how wide it* is, *how deep it* is, *how much* is *mine to keep.* I'd like to add some **sunrise** to your **pocket and** some **mercy in** your **shoes.**"

The Lacuna, **Winnie-the-Pooh**

"Such silence exists because we bury it away and pretend it's just *a missing piece, a lacuna.* So I'll sing this song until you find me, '**How sweet to be a cloud floating in the blue!**'"

Winnie-the-Pooh, **Will Grayson, Will Grayson**

"*Every little cloud always sings aloud.* Not like they who *walk up and down* and wonder if *it looks like rain,* looking up at life thinking, '**Wow, I look much happier—I think this is the life I need to get!**'"

Will Grayson, Will Grayson, **My Most Excellent Year**

"**Popping in and out of chalk pictures takes a lot of practice, so** I've learned to **be patient,** learned to give less of a fuck. But even that has stopped working for me with you. *By saying you don't care if the world falls apart, in some small way you're saying you want it to stay together on your terms.*"

My Most Excellent Year, **The Art of Racing in the Rain**

"One trick I learned is to begin by closing my eyes and imagining candy apples and steam calliopes and when I open my eyes, the chalk picture is waiting for me. That way I don't panic **when something unpredictable happens.** That way I don't make the mistake of **reacting at speed.**"

The Art of Racing in the Rain, **Beloved**

"Don't panic. Listen. *Pretend you are a dog like me and listen to other people rather than steal their stories.* Listen for the **whisper that the flakes of rust made** falling from my **red heart.**"

Beloved, **White Teeth**

"*Beloved. He said it, but she did not go.* **No talking will change this. Roots will always be tangled. And roots get dug up.**"

White Teeth, **Their Eyes Were Watching God**

"Funny thing when you talk about roots, really we're all just **branches without roots.** *Life is not a line,* but *a circle. That is why you cannot read fate; you must experience it.*"

Their Eyes Were Watching God, **The Bell Jar**

"Funny that you're talking about life when this whole story started with Death. *What need has Death for a cover, and what winds can blow against him?* Whatever this is has failed. So I *feed* these words into *the night wind,* watch them flutter away, **like a loved one's ashes, to settle here, there, exactly where I would never know, in the dark heart of** Sacramento."

The Bell Jar

"With you, *a wonderful future beckoned and winked like* a *green fig tree. I wanted* you to *choose* me but instead I was left with *figs wrinkled and black, plopping to the ground at my feet.*"

Frankenstein, **Snow Flower and the Secret Fan**

"*There is something at work in my soul that I do not understand.* You always saw me, knew me, even when I didn't know myself. **I hope one day we will soar together.**"

Frankenstein

"With you, my dear Snow Flower, *I became a poet and for one year lived in a paradise of my own creation.*"

Mary Poppins

"I stood there wondering and waiting, hoping beyond hope that you might still accept me. *The Merry-go-Round had disappeared. Only the still trees and the grass and the unmoving little path of sea remained.*"

"*Camouflage*"

"We've seen so many like us come and go before,
giving so little away and getting nothing more.
Can't you see we're half alive
just waiting for others to take the dive?
Let's drop our camouflage, take our fear of love to task.
I know the faces we wear are better than our masks.
Let's let the beautiful that's behind our brick wall show,

it's safe and warm inside, but it's time for us to grow.
I'm not asking you to forget the pain you felt before today,
but you'll get no loving back if you're not giving it away.
So open up your heart,
you won't find a better time to start.
I'll drop my camouflage, take my fear of life to task.
Will you love the face I wear better than my mask?
I'll let the tenderness that's behind my brick wall show,
it's safe and warm inside, but it's time for me to grow.
Just like you I built up defenses then my walls became my cage,
but I want to let you in and now I'm standing on the stage.
No matter what your fright,
you can walk with me into the light.
Please drop your camouflage, take your fear of life to task.
I know the face you wear is better than your mask.
Just let the beautiful that's behind your brick wall show,
I'm sure you're warm inside, but you've got to let me know.
I'm sure you're warm inside, but you've got to let me know."

THE READING LIST

Arranged by order of appearance by author, asterisks note books alluded to

Markus Zusak: *The Book Thief, I Am the Messenger*
*Jane Austen: *Pride and Prejudice*
*F. Scott Fitzgerald: *The Great Gatsby*
Philip K. Dick: *Do Androids Dream of Electric Sheep?*
Anthony Doerr: *All the Light We Cannot See*
*Carolyn Keene: *Nancy Drew*
*Lewis Carroll: *Alice's Adventures in Wonderland*
Philip Pullman: *The Golden Compass, The Subtle Knife*
*Gregory Maguire: *Wicked: The Life and Times of the Wicked Witch of the West*
Mary Pope Osborne: *The Mystery of the Magic Tree House*
Muriel Barbery: *The Elegance of the Hedgehog*
Daniel Quinn: *Ishmael*
Lois Lowry: *The Giver*
Kurt Vonnegut, Jr.: *Slaughterhouse-Five*
Barbara Kingsolver: *The Lacuna*
*N. K. Jemisin: *The Fifth Season*
A. A. Milne: *Winnie-the-Pooh*
John Green and David Levithan: *Will Grayson, Will Grayson*
Steve Kluger: *My Most Excellent Year*
Garth Stein: *The Art of Racing in the Rain*
Toni Morrison: *Beloved*
Zadie Smith: *White Teeth*

Zora Neale Hurston: *Their Eyes Were Watching God*
Sylvia Plath: *The Bell Jar*
Mary Shelley: *Frankenstein*
Lisa See: *Snow Flower and the Secret Fan*
*J. K. Rowling: *Harry Potter and the Sorcerer's Stone*
P.L. Travers: *Mary Poppins*
*Miguel de Cervantes, translated by James H. Montgomery: *Don Quixote*
Rumi: "Dance"

BIBLIOGRAPHY

I treasure books. To hold the world in the palm of my hands. To feel the possibility in a mere handful of words. That a carefully crafted phrase can crumble my reality to dust, making room for a thousand new realities that validate the way I suffer, grieve, and love. That pages become bridges connecting me to my community.

It is my intention with *Dance With Me* to honor the incredible authors who shaped my world by sharing them with you.

Please find below a complete list of the authors mentioned in Charlie and Noah's conversation; the italicized portions of each quote highlight the words that were quoted directly.

Barbery, Muriel. *The Elegance of the Hedgehog.* Translated by Alison Anderson. (Paris: Europa, 2006): 204, 273, 325.

> "But when we gaze at a *still life*, when—even though we did not pursue it—we *delight in* its *beauty, a beauty borne away* by the magnified and immobile figuration of things, we find pleasure in the fact that there was no need for longing, we may contemplate *something we need not want, may cherish something we need not desire*" (Barbery 2006).
>
> "*Constantly poised between beauty and death*, between movement and its disappearance? Maybe that's what being alive is all about; so we can *track down those moments that are dying*" (Barbery 2006).

Green, John, and David Levithan. *Will Grayson, Will Grayson.* (New York: Penguin Group, 2010): 65, 182-183.

"See it in its shiny box and look inside the plastic window and catch a glimpse of yourself in a new life and say, '*Wow, I look much happier—I think this is the life I need to get!*' take it to the counter, ring it up, put it on your credit card" (Green and Levithan 2010).

"*By saying you don't care if the world falls apart, in some small way you're saying you want it to stay together on your terms*" (Green and Levithan 2010).

Hardy, Breanna. *The Space Between Breaths.* (California: Elegance Press, 2022).

"*I inhale dusk, wander with wraiths,
stay in this dark as long as it takes,
tapping unheard notes,
reprising memory of a memory
of you—wisps of the end that came
too soon. Dissect, reflect.
Conversational volta
of tacit meant-to-says
and should-have-saids,
crescent of my spine
as I curl inward. You—
I waltz, dizzying
myself with shades and intonations.
Voices echo of cruel imagination,
laughter rehearsed in front of mirror,
script I write for whispers I can't make out.
But a palm, bare, reaching for me.
a palm, my own,*

yet with finespun flesh
promising to take me with her,
bitten down nails and all, part of her.
Finger twitches.
Heart trammels in chest.
I can't get enough air.
Wobbling to these broken chords until
in the space between breaths
hand steadies, stillness finds me.
Relief in the hush, only the sound of an exhale.
Shadows wax across my face,
mottle with pansy and thistle, waning
into amaranth, peach, and cornflower.
A smile, air gilded and saccharine,
take first breath worth breathing,
body tingling in the warmth
of the beginning after the end.
Let light dust gold across flesh.
Perhaps I will meet you there
with outstretched hand."

Hurston, Zora Neale. *Their Eyes Were Watching God.* (New York: HarperCollins, 2006): 16, 84.

"You know, honey, us colored folks is *branches without roots* and that makes things come round in queer ways" (Hurston 2006).

"What need has Death for a cover, and what winds can blow against him?" (Hurston 2006).

Kingsolver, Barbara. *The Lacuna*. (New York: HarperCollins, 2009): 27–28.

> "People who make a study of old documents have a name for this very kind of thing, *a missing piece. A lacuna*, it's called" (Kingsolver 2009).
>
> "Then he must have *sunrise in his pocket. And mercy in his shoes*" (Kingsolver 2009).

Kluger, Steve. *My Most Excellent Year: A Novel of Love, Mary Poppins, and Fenway Park*. (New York: Penguin, 2008): 285.

> "*Popping in and out of chalk pictures takes a lot of practice, so be patient.* You may not be able to master it until you're at least ten. (*One trick I learned is to begin by closing my eyes and imagining candy apples and steam calliopes*. That always helps)" (Kluger 2008).

Lowry, Lois. *The Giver*. (New York: Random House, 1993): 94–95, 123–126.

> "*We relinquished color when we relinquished sunshine* and did away with differences" (Lowry 1993).
>
> "'*Warmth*,' Jonas replied, 'and happiness...*Family*...'*A little more complete*,' The Giver suggested" (Lowry 1993).

Milne, A. A. *Winnie-the-Pooh*. (New York: Penguin Group, 2005): 15, 17.

"I wish you would bring it out here, and *walk up and down* with it, and look up at me every now and then, and say 'Tut-tut, *it looks like rain*'" (Milne 2005).

"*How sweet to be a Cloud Floating in the Blue!*" (Milne 2005).

"*Every little cloud Always sings aloud*" (Milne 2005).

Morrison, Toni. *Beloved*. (New York: Vintage, 2004): 137–138, 205.

"'*Beloved.' He said it,* but she did not go. She moved closer with a footfall he didn't hear and he didn't hear the *whisper that the flakes* of rust made either as they fell away from the seams of his tobacco tin…Softly and then so loud it woke Denver, then Paul D himself. '*Red heart*" (Morrison 2004).

Plath, Sylvia. *The Bell Jar*. (New York: HarperCollins, 1998): 77, 111.

"I saw my life branching out before me *like* the *green fig tree* in the story. From the tip of every branch, like a fat purple fig, *a wonderful future beckoned and winked*...I wanted each and every one of them, but *choosing* meant losing all the rest, and, as I sat there, unable to decide, the *figs* began to *wrinkle* and go *black*, and, one by one, the *plopped to the ground at my feet*" (Plath 1998).

"Piece by piece, *I fed* my wardrobe to *the night wind*, and *flutteringly, like a loved one's ashes,* the gray scraps were ferried off, *to settle here, there, exactly where I would never know, in the dark heart of* New York" (Plath 1998).

Robinson, Mark. "Camouflage." Arranged by Conor Robinson. *White Collar Crime*, Redding Church of Religious Science, 1985. Vinyl EP.

"We've seen so many like us come and go before,
giving so little away and getting nothing more.
Can't you see we're half alive
just waiting for others to take the dive?
Let's drop our camouflage, take our fear of love to task.
I know the faces we wear are better than our masks.
Let's let the beautiful that's behind our brick wall show,
it's safe and warm inside, but it's time for us to grow.
I'm not asking you to forget the pain you felt before today,
but you'll get no loving back if you're not giving it away.
So open up your heart,
you won't find a better time to start.
I'll drop my camouflage, take my fear of life to task.

Will you love the face I wear better than my mask?
I'll let the tenderness that's behind my brick wall show,
it's safe and warm inside, but it's time for me to grow.
Just like you I built up defenses then my walls became my cage,
but I want to let you in and now I'm standing on the stage.
No matter what your fright,
you can walk with me into the light.
Please drop your camouflage, take your fear of life to task.
I know the face you wear is better than your mask.
Just let the beautiful that's behind your brick wall show,
I'm sure you're warm inside, but you've got to let me know.
I'm sure you're warm inside, but you've got to let me know."

Robinson, Mark. "Don Quixote." *White Collar Crime*, Redding Church of Religious Science, 1985. Vinyl EP.

"Don Quixote rides his sunken sullen mare
waiting for the day that he can say, 'Now I am whole,'
for I have found a friend I need no other goal.
And each day brings a journey to some well-forgotten land
with obstacles to overcome and strategies to plan,
but is the flag I'm fighting for worth the price I'll pay?
Or have I just convinced myself it really is that way?
Don Quixote rides his sunken sullen mare
waiting for the day that he can say, 'Now I am home,'
for I have found myself, I need no other goal.
So I'll live tomorrow as I've lived each day before
waiting for the day that I will chase the wind no more.
Though it isn't easy to go through the things I do,
I'll keep on chasing windmills just as long as I have you.
Don Quixote rides his sunken sullen mare,
he's waiting for the day that he can say, 'Now I am home.'
For I found you, girl, I need no other goal,
for I have found myself I need no other goal."

Rumi, Jala al-Din, and Coleman Barks. "Dance." *The Essential Rumi*. (San Francisco: HarperCollins, 1996).

> "*Dance*, when you're broken open. Dance, if you've torn the bandage off. Dance in the middle of the fighting. Dance in your blood. *Dance when you're perfectly free.*"

See, Lisa. *Snow Flower and the Secret Fan*. (New York: Random House, 2005): 243.

> "*I hope one day we will soar together*" (See 2005).

Shelley, Mary. *Frankenstein*. (New York: Penguin Group, 2013): 10, 12.

> "*There is something at work in my soul that I do not understand*" (Shelley 2013).
>
> "*I* also *became a poet and for one year lived in a paradise of my own creation*; I imagined that I also might obtain a niche in the temple where the names of Homer and Shakespeare are consecrated" (Shelley 2013).

Smith, Zadie. *White Teeth*. (New York: Vintage, 2000): 68, 100.

> "*No talking will change this...*Their *roots will always be tangled. And roots get dug up*" (Smith 2000).
>
> "It's not a line, *life is not a line*—this is not palm-reading—*it's a circle,* and they speak to us. *That is why you cannot read fate; you must experience it*" (Smith 2000).

Stein, Garth. *The Art of Racing in the Rain*. (New York: HarperCollins, 2008): 41, 102.

> "*When something unpredictable happens* you have to react to it; if you're *reacting at speed*, you're reacting too late" (Stein 2008).
>
> "*Pretend you are a dog like me and listen to other people rather than steal their stories*" (Stein 2008).

Travers, P. L. *Mary Poppins*. (New York: Houghton Mifflin Harcourt, 1997): 25.

> "*Even the Merry-go-Round had disappeared. Only the still trees and the grass and the unmoving little path of sea remained*" (Travers 1997).

Vonnegut Jr., Kurt. *Slaughterhouse-Five, or The Children's Crusade: A Duty-dance with Death.* (St Albans: Granada, 1972): 21, 29.

> "Avoiding Germans, they were *delivering* themselves *into rural silences ever more profound*" (Vonnegut Jr. 1972).
>
> And I *asked myself about the present: how wide it was, how deep it was, how much was mine to keep*" (Vonnegut Jr.1972).

Zusak, Markus. *I Am the Messenger.* (New York: Knopf, 2002): 334–335.

> "*Imagine the softest, toughest, most beautiful song you know, and you've got it*" (Zusak 2002).

THE PLAYLIST

TWO STEP
"Rainy Dayz" by Mary J. Blige ft. Ja Rule
"Not Today" by Mary J Blige ft. Eve
"Hey Y'all" by Eve ft. Snoop Dogg, Nate Dogg

LOCK AND POP
"Check" by MC Lyte
"Everybody" by Logic
"Me, Myself, and I" by De La Soul

WINDMILL
"The World is Yours" by Nas
"Mama Who Bore Me" from *Spring Awakening*, sung by Lea Michele
"Mama Who Bore Me (Reprise)" from *Spring Awakening*, sung by Lea Michele, Lilli Cooper, Lauren Pritchard, Phoebe Strole, Remy Zaken
"The Stranger" by Billy Joel
"My Life For Hire" by A Day To Remember

PIROUETTE
"I'm Just a Kid" by Simple Plan
"Suavemente" by Elvis Crespo
"Someday" by Flipsyde

FAÇADE

"What More Can I Say?" by Jay-Z
"Yesterday" by The Beatles
"A Part of That" from *The Last Five Years,* sung by Sherie Rene Scott

JETÉ
"Nuff' of the Ruff Stuff" by Queen Latifah
"We Are The End" by Alexisonfire
"I'll Be Missing You" by Sean Combs and Faith Evans ft. 112

MIME
"The Cave" by Mumford & Sons
"Hotel California" by Eagles
"Back Down" by 50 Cent

ARABESQUE
"I'll Be" by Edwin McCain
"Oye Como Va" by Santana
"Fall" by Something Corporate

ASSEMBLE
"Don't Walk Away" by Jade
"Changes" by Tupac Shakur
"Carol of the Bells" by Peter J. Wihousky and Mykola Dmytrovych Leontovych, arranged by John Williams

PIVOT TURN
"Sweet Baby James" by James Taylor
"Faithful" by Common
"Lost Ones" by Lauryn Hill

RUNNING MAN
"Holdin' It Down For The Underground" by A Day To Remember

"Kryptonite" by 3 Doors Down
"Take It to the Limit" by Eagles

FREEZE
"King Kunta" by Kendrick Lamar
"To Raise the Morning Star" by Holly Near

STEP TOUCH
"Breakaway" by Kelly Clarkson
"Just the Two of Us" by Will Smith
"Moonshadow" by Cat Stevens

GRAPEVINE
"Seasons of Love" from *Rent*, sung by Original Broadway Cast
"Coastin'" by Zion 1, K. Flay

JAZZ SQUARE
"Don Quixote" by Mark Robinson
"Mr. Wop" by Gucci Mane
"The Next Episode" by Dr. Dre ft. Snoop Dogg, Nate Dogg, Kurupt
"Someday" by Nickelback
"Since I Fell for You" by Ella and Buddy Johnson
"Camouflage" by Mark Robinson

DENOUEMENT
"A Change is Gonna Come" by Sam Cooke

PEOPLE AND PLACES

This work of fiction is set in Sacramento, California, focused in and around the neighborhoods of Land Park and Oak Park. I invite you to explore the city through Charlie's eyes, then join me in Sacramento and engage in the community and its surrounding spaces. Get started with a brief introduction below, then find out more about these incredible spaces on my website: www.ElegancePress.com

Check out the interactive Dance With Me Google Maps List by typing this link into your browser: https://goo.gl/maps/cAJKYpCjm-PpAj1VW7

People and Places

Pam Haynes

The U.S. history of renaming cities, institutions, and landmarks with western names is the story of colonialism, erasure, violence, and racism. When naming Charlie's high school, I wanted to flip the narrative and honor someone local to Sacramento who championed education. Haynes Charter High School is named after Pam Haynes who has dedicated her life to serving students in higher education through her work in the California Labor Federation, California State Assembly, Los Rios Community College District Board, and California Community Colleges Board of Governors. She believes passionately in getting students the resources they need to succeed and in the ability for students to be successful in the community college system.

Wilton Rancheria

Sacramento is the dispossessed land and the unceded territory of the Miwok and Nisenan people. This acknowledgement seeks to recognize the peoples who were here long before Sacramento was colonized and developed by westerners, and to address the violence brought against natives and the erasure of their culture. This acknowledgment seeks to recognize that the Miwok and Nisenan communities still exist today, that we must not relegate them to a relic, that this land we live on requires our participation in bringing back their voices, their right to life, and their right to land.

Bookstores

Underground Books

Part literary hub, part library, part non-profit, part independent bookstore, part cultural center, Underground Books is a space to "find your freedom." Enter the double doors and be greeted like family. Come in and investigate black art, black culture, black legacy, and black future. Find a comfy seat and settle in with the book you just have to have. Attend speaking events by local and national authors and workshops, and engage in your community.

Capitol Books

After a decade of running a successful online book review business, Ross and Heidi hoped to expand their love of books into the Sacramento Community by opening Capitol Books in 2018.

Coffee Shops

Old Soul Co.

From the beginning, Tim and Jason were interested in producing locally sourced, quality coffee and baked goods for their community. What started out as a wholesale enterprise quickly turned into four retail stores that serve as food hubs in the Sacramento neighborhoods of Downtown, Midtown, and Oak Park. The goal is simple: be a platform to uplift and celebrate farmer and artisan voices.

Broadway Coffee

A community-first coffee shop that offers friendly service, free Wi-Fi, and sustainably sourced coffee.

Entertainment

AMF Land Park Lanes

A black light, retro bowling alley complete with an arcade, billiards, and full bar.

Grocery Stores

Nugget Markets

A family-owned and -operated grocery store chain local to the Sacramento Valley since 1926.

Parks and Zoos

McClatchy Park

Founded in 1927, McClatchy Park was transformed from an amusement park into a city park that offers jungle gyms, fitness areas, a skate park, and a host of sports areas including baseball fields, basketball courts, tennis courts, a disk golf course, and a jogging path. It is also the site of a weekly farmer's market.

William Land Regional Park

Founded in 1911, William Land Regional Park was one of the first parks in the country with open public access. The park is a gorgeous, sprawling 207 acres and home to two theme parks, a lake, ample picnic spots, and a host of recreational sports areas including a golf course, basketball courts, jogging trails, softball and soccer fields. The neighborhood where the park resides in Sacramento is called "Land Park" to this day.

Sacramento Zoo

Founded in 1927, this Association of Zoos and Aquariums (AZA) accredited non-profit houses roughly 500 animals and 125 different species. The Sacramento Zoo partners with UC Davis to provide residency for their zoological veterinarians.

Restaurants and Bakeries

Faria Bakery

A local Oak Park bakery since 2019, Faria Bakery and founders Chris and Grace have been serving their community for more than ten years from their cottage bakery at home! They see bread and pastry as vehicles to build a healthy, sustainable community. Sacramento is a great place for a bread revolution thanks to the abundance of farmers and millers in this farm-to-fork capital.

Fixins Soul Kitchen

A local Oak Park restaurant since 2019, Fixins Soul Kitchen aims to highlight black excellence through its delicious soul food sourced from local family recipes, by providing jobs for disadvantaged youth and those formerly incarcerated, by ensuring their unsold food gets to community members in need, and with its zero-waste facility.

Florez Bar & Grill

A local Land Park restaurant since 1981 that serves fresh, delicious, homemade Mexican cooking using locally sourced produce.

Gunther's Ice Cream

A Sacramento Historical Landmark and treasured ice cream shop since 1940. Visit for the generous portions, the creamy taste, and to see Jugglin' Joe in action.

The Original Mel's

Originally founded in San Francisco in 1947 as a drive-in, this 24/7 restaurant brings you a dash of the 1950s and all the late-night comfort food you could want.

Tower Café

The neon lights of the iconic Tower Theater stand high above US 50 and are impossible to miss, but it's the café tucked away in its own secret garden beneath the neon lights that you won't want to overlook. The restaurant feels like a journey around the world with art from a myriad of countries and a menu that is just as eclectic.

Additional Landmarks

Arden Fair Mall
Sacramento's local mall since 1957 with more than 150 shops and restaurants.

Crocker Art Museum
Though the original house was built for residential use in 1908, Crocker Art Museum has been a Sacramento staple in the art community since 1978. Its mission is to enrich the lives of the Sacramento community by using art in unexpected ways to connect people to the world around them.

The Old Sacramento Waterfront
The original birthplace of the City of Sacramento, the Old Sacramento Waterfront was launched as a part of a Mexican Land Grant, and expanded during the 1848 Gold Rush as miners came to outfit themselves before heading off to find their riches. Four floods in the early 1800s prompted the city to take dramatic action and raise the city above flood level. Visiting the Old Sacramento Waterfront is like stepping into the past, as the city has kept the raised sidewalks for stepping off your horse-and-buggy, the old cobblestone streets, and with fifty-three Historical Buildings to visit. Access it via the Tower Bridge that crosses the Sacramento River from West Sacramento into Downtown Sacramento. Today, the Old Sacramento Waterfront offers six museums, unique shopping for candy and socks, the famous Evangeline's costume store, restaurants and bars, and even a Ferris wheel and carousel.

Sutter Health Park
Created in 2000 to be used as the home ballpark for the Sacramento River Cats Minor League Baseball team, Sutter Health Park changed its name from Raley's Field after the twenty-year term ended for the naming rights of the facility.

Looking for more from Shea Robinson?

FIND DETAILS ON HER NEXT BOOK, SEE WHAT SHE'S GOT ON HER BOOKSHELF, AND MORE BY VISITING:

www.ElegancePress.com

Shea Robinson was reading before she started walking. She started writing shortly thereafter. Her biggest frustration is that she can't read and write at the same time. When she's not lost in a good book, she is dancing with her three-year-old niece, listening to her husband nerd rant about superheroes for his movie review channel, and dreaming about the last time she had French Silk ice cream in the fifth grade. She currently lives in Sacramento.

CPSIA information can be obtained
at www.ICGtesting.com
Printed in the USA
BVHW051805120622
639612BV00004B/115